The Twin

ALSO BY STEENA HOLMES

**BERVIE SPRINGS SERIES**
Book 1: ENGAGED TO A SERIAL KILLER
Book 2: THE TWIN

**STANDALONES**
THE SISTER UNDER THE STAIRS

# THE TWIN

## STEENA HOLMES

*Bervie Springs Book 2*

Joffe Books, London
www.joffebooks.com

First published in Great Britain in 2024

Cover art by Nick Castle

ISBN: 978-1-83526-684-7

## AUTHOR'S NOTE

Dear reader,

How is your #tbr pile doing?

From one book addict to another, it's probably doing just fine, with new books being added all the time. I'm excited you picked this one to be your next read!

If you love to chat about what you're reading and you happen to post about this book, be sure to tag me! You can find me in these awesome reader groups on Facebook: Readers Coffeehouse and Psychological Thriller Readers, plus the Instagram. I love chatting about books.

A special thank you to Carol Ann Starr and Kelly Erickson. For those in my own reading group, Steena's Secret Society, thank you for your help in answering research questions, for your encouragement to write another book for you to read, and for always being there just when I need you!

Happy reading,

Steena

PS: Calling all travelholics — did you know I host 'reader tours'? Head on over to my website to find out where we're headed next!

# CHAPTER ONE

*Present Day*

Death is a permanent fixture in my life, but I'm not ready to shake hands with that Angel and be welcomed into its embrace.

Sometimes, those decisions aren't ours to make.

I feel death drawing close. I feel its breath on my skin, feel its touch brand my bones, and it smothers me with its constricting suffocation as fear blooms within my cells.

I don't know where I am. I don't know what's happened to me. I don't understand why I can't see or even move.

The only thing I do know is this: I'm scared.

A weight covers my face, its heaviness pressing against my cheeks and nose. The tight band of pressure increases and grows in strength until I'm about to drown in whatever hell hole I've been left to die in.

An intense, piercing pain spirals through my body, starting the moment I try lifting my head. I whimper, the sound filling the heavy space around me.

A tingling sensation, starting at my fingertips, creeps upward, one painful inch at a time, eliciting a torturous moan.

I tear away whatever is on my face, the fabric coarse against my fingertips, until I touch something wet, slick, sticky. I probe the area; each touches a sharp blade, inducing pain. I bring my fingers to my nose and inhale a sickly, sweet, metallic scent.

Blood.

My blood. Why? What happened to me? Why can't I remember?

I mentally catalog my body, starting with my head, down my cheeks, chin, neck, and shoulders, across my chest, hips, and legs, taking inventory of what hurts and what doesn't.

My chest feels like a massive pile of bricks uses me as a shelf, with the growing weight pushing down until my ribs are going to be crushed into tiny pieces.

I'm bruised. Broken. Breathing is a struggle.

My hips ache as if I've been kicked multiple times. They're probably covered in bruises, at the very least.

Terror grabs hold, vice grips around my chest, squeezing, twisting, taunting me with oblivion, but I fight back against the panic attack, determined not to let it overwhelm me.

I need to stay calm. I'm alive. If I want to remain that way, I need to figure out what happened and where I am.

My instinct is to call out for help, the need to find safety, but something stops me. Why?

The unknown is a black hole of terror, and right now, what I know is I'm lying on something soft and lumpy, I'm not bound, I'm hurt, but I'm not dead.

Breathe. Listen. Focus.

I hear nothing but silence. It's thick. Heavy. Stifling. There's an earthy, moist scent to the air. I reach my hands out and touch a cold wall with indents reminding me of a cold room bricked in my grandmother's basement, where she kept all her jars of canned vegetables.

I know I can't remain here, so I struggle to raise myself into a seated position, pushing past the pain that shoots through my body. My fingers grip the thin mattress as sweeping waves of dizziness attempt to bury me.

With my head bowed, I push past the pain, past the fatigue and everything that pulls at me to lie back down and sleep, and instead, work at easing the dressing around my head enough so I can, at least, see.

I need to see. I need to figure out where I am.

I need to get free, free from wherever it is I am.

I need to stand and move. I need to find a way out, but at the very moment I believe I've found the energy to push myself to my feet, I hear a click. It rings out like clanging bells, breaking the silence. I freeze all movement and listen.

The click of a lock, a rustle of keys, wood scraping along the ground as it was pushed open, and a clearing of a throat.

I flinch. Still.

A sliver of light repels the darkness in the room, highlighting enough features for me to see I was right, that I'm indeed in a cold storage room, with empty shelves lining one wall and a single bed on the other. There's a haze over my eyes, like I'm looking through slits between swollen folds of skin.

"Oh good, you're awake."

The voice is familiar. From a memory. From a nightmare.

# CHAPTER TWO

*Six Months Ago*
*Brynn*

I stared at the casket in front of me, and I felt nothing. No guilt, remorse, not even a semblance of sadness, and that was definitely the one emotion I probably should have felt, if nothing else.

That was my father in the casket, after all.

Every seat in the room behind me was full of people wanting to honor my father. It was so full, there was standing room only now by the doors. It was like everyone plus their cousin had come today. Tears flowed, noses ran, babies cried . . . and all in my father's name.

If only people knew.

Well, Anthony Kern knew. He knew exactly what his funeral would look like, and he'd even planned it down to every detail.

He wanted his daughter to give his eulogy. Why? Of all the things he'd done, requested, demanded, that was the most confusing. Me, of all people.

I refused to get up there, in front of everyone, and fake an emotion he never deserved.

I wasn't sad about his death. How could I be? He wouldn't have expected it, either.

What he would have expected, however, was for me to put on a show, to be distraught that I'd lost my remaining parental figure.

Considering I'd always been a disappointment to him, why change things now?

In my hand was a script Anthony wrote out. He'd master-planned every single detail of this memorial — including the words he wanted uttered over his cold, lifeless body.

I couldn't do it. Actually, I refused to do it. So, instead, I stood at his casket, my back to the crowd. My slumped shoulders might have portrayed the visual that I was emotionally distraught, but the reality was I wrestled with myself in showing any emotion at all.

Eventually, there was a presence beside me, and for the first time that day, my chest wasn't as tight. A hand grabbed mine and held fast. I didn't need to look to know it was my brother.

We stood there, side by side. The sniffling intensified the longer we remained. Eventually, Bryce whispered the words I wanted to ask, but wouldn't.

"You don't have to do this. I've got you."

I knew how we looked, standing together. Twins. One with long white hair, the other cut short. One had ocean-blue eyes so clear you could see through them, and the other held a vampiric pink tinge that everyone looked away from.

We were freaks. Why sugarcoat it?

What else would twins like us be called? Albinism is genetic, even if neither of our parents had to live with the condition.

With all eyes on us, Bryce spoke the words our father wanted said. My brother was calm, sympathetic and even heartfelt. He never glanced down at the paper he held in his hands, as if he'd memorized every single word, but he couldn't have. I'd only been given the letter today, sealed in an envelope with my name written across the front.

Unless . . . unless Anthony had given the same letter to him, knowing I wouldn't utter a single word he'd written.

It wouldn't surprise me.

Our father loved to play mind games. He was the master, after all.

The one he loved to play the most was *he loves me, he loves me not*. Instead of pulling petals off a daisy, he would take the things I loved the most and give them to someone else. All to teach me a lesson, or so he claimed.

His aim was never to win Father of the Year, at least not with me.

Bryce stayed by my side the rest of the day; he was my guardian, protector, and, most importantly, my deflector. Every time someone directed a *'you must miss your father'* or *'I'm not sure what our town will do without Anthony,'* Bryce swept in and said the words everyone expected to hear, the words I would never utter.

"Bryce, is it true? Both you and Brynn will continue to run the Kern Funeral Home? I couldn't imagine what Bervie Springs would be like without this place as a refuge for families when they go through loss." Mrs. Ciaccone, a local and president of the Ladies Auxiliary in Bervie Springs, stood in front of us, a plate of canapés in one hand and a cup of coffee in the other.

"Mrs. Ciaccone, you don't need to worry. The Kern Funeral Home won't be closing its doors. Thank you for coming tonight; I know my father held your family in high regard." Bryce's voice was silky smooth, with a touch of patience and deference — the complete opposite of how I would have answered, if Bryce hadn't nudged me with his elbow just as I was about to open my mouth.

"Well, of course he did. Your father and my husband served on the town council for many years together. It's a shame what's happening to our town right now, how Donald Dixon managed to smear our good name." She tsked, her lips pulling together to resemble a clothesline.

I shuddered at the name of Donald Dixon. I couldn't help it. Last year, bodies had been uncovered in various

6

gardens Dixon's company had created. It turned out that Donald Dixon was a serial killer, and he buried the bodies of transients and prostitutes he'd picked up from out of town.

One of those gardens had been ours. After the police finished their investigation, we tore up that garden and installed a memorial patio in its place.

Bryce reached out and lightly touched Mrs. Ciaccone's arm. "Carolina, we are more than what Dixon has done to our town. We'll survive."

Wow, he actually had the nerve to call Mrs. Ciaccone by her first name. Mrs. Ciaccone was one of the founding families and made sure everyone knew it. To her familiars, she was Carolina, and to her close friends, she was CiCi.

Anthony always called her CiCi. Our mother, she called her Mrs. Ciaccone or Carolina. Bryce too, apparently.

"Of course we are. It's still a shame. That man was a monster."

"The man is a monster. He's still alive."

The pause, as Mrs. Ciaccone took in Bryce's words, stretched thin to the point where if it broke, I'd expect her to slap Bryce's face. Slap it so hard that the whole room would have heard it.

I think he expected that to happen, too, but her lips gave way to something that didn't quite resemble a frown.

"Everyone would be better off if he just died, and nothing you say will change my mind." She crossed her arms across her ample chest and waited for Bryce to do just that — attempt to change her mind.

He wouldn't, though. Bryce wasn't that kind of person. There was nothing in him that felt the need to argue, and he was more than happy to agree to disagree as long as there was acceptance of each other's views.

My brother could be exasperating at the best of times.

"I know you used to be close, so the betrayal must hurt. I know it did our father, who once considered Mr. Dixon a close friend. The ramifications of his actions will be felt for a very long time."

Mrs. Ciaccone harrumphed before patting Bryce's hand. She then turned toward me, giving me her full attention. Lovely.

"How are you, dear? Your eyes are paler than normal, I see, and a little redder than I'm used to seeing," she tsked. "Well, that must be from all the tears. You know, eyes are the window to our souls. I can't even imagine what you are feeling right now. Why, losing a man like your father must feel like you've been dropped in a cavern with no way out. First, you lost your mother, now him . . . you poor girl. I'm here if you need a motherly shoulder."

It took every inch of self-control for me to maintain a smile on my face that didn't waver, falter or fade. A smile that said *thank you for coming* and didn't scream *leave me alone*. Everyone assumed I was a doormat, a spineless creature who would never say an unkind word about anyone or anything. Of course, it was how Anthony portrayed me, and I let him because any other option would have made my life a living hell. But the suggestion that I would go to Mrs. Ciaccone for anything remotely motherly had me wanting to lash out.

The words were there, on the tip of my tongue, but Bryce stepped in.

"That's very kind of you, Carolina. But she's not alone." Bryce pulled me tight to his side and gave me a sharp pinch. I wanted to pinch him back, but instead, I played into the expectations of those around us and rested my head on his shoulder.

Inside, I cussed him out. Outside, the smile remained permanently fixed on my face.

"You've always been close, haven't you," Mrs. Ciaccone said, buying into my act. "Well, I'm glad you have each other."

The moment the woman walked away was the moment I was able to exhale finally.

I couldn't wait to leave, to be alone, away from the crowd, but that wouldn't be fair to Bryce. Everything tonight had been too much — too suffocating, too over-the-top, too exhausting. It may have been what Anthony wanted, but it wasn't what he deserved.

It didn't take long for another person to take Mrs. Ciaccone's place. They expressed their consolation, stated Anthony was in a better place, and reminded Bryce that he needed to look after me now.

As if Bryce needed that reminder. That was all he'd done our whole lives — looked after me, protected me, stood up for me when Anthony was too harsh.

Anthony Kern was not a paragon. He wasn't a saint either, which is what endeared him to most people in Bervie Springs. To Bryce, he was the best father in the world. To me, he was my worst nightmare.

Who would understand that? Who would sympathize? No one.

Anthony Kern was a monster in disguise, and I was the only one who ever dared to peek beneath the mask.

# CHAPTER THREE

With the late afternoon sun behind heavy clouds, sitting outside in the garden was safe, a place I always considered my refuge.

Bryce was inside still, playing host to those who lingered, but I couldn't be bothered. While he catered to the crowd that adored Anthony, I escaped to the one place that held strong ties to our mother.

The dichotomy of our family always mystified me. Anthony was passionate about dealing with the dead, while Mom surrounded herself with living things, creating gorgeous gardens from simple tiny seeds.

"We're accountable for what we do with our life," she once said. "Our purpose is to bring blessing, to share the joy seeded deep in our souls. What better way than through nature? Do you think it's a mistake that life comes from death? That the fragrant flowers are birthed from something so dormant, they are almost dead?" Her fingers were knuckled deep in the dirt and encouraged me to bury my own, as she had. "We need to be like the soil, Brynn, the trigger for the renewal process where the seed awakens and brings forth something beautiful."

I missed her. The ache in my heart never decreased in size or agony, even after all these years. A daughter needed a mother; that was a steadfast truth since the beginning of time. A part of me was glad that my brother could now understand my loss, because who our mother was to me, Anthony was to him.

I pushed my feet against the ground and closed my eyes, taking in the peace as my swing glided back and forth.

"I had a feeling I'd find you out here."

I wiggled over enough on the bench swing to make room for Lexi Kaarns, a good friend.

"It's been a while." I leaned against her for a brief moment. "Thanks for coming. I know you never liked Anthony, so you didn't have to."

"I came to support you, not him," she said. "Like he'd care if I warmed up a seat or not."

"You're my angel, you know that, right?"

Anthony and Lexi never hit it off, and that mess with Donald Dixon only made it worse, since she'd worked the case. Donald and my deceased father had been friends.

"He'd care. It would have bothered him if there'd been seats available, you know that."

"True. Anthony did have a thing about appearances, didn't he?"

The one thing I appreciated most about Lexi was that she always called him Anthony, never using the familial tie between us, unlike most people. Something inside me always bristled when anyone would call him 'my father.'

"Here," Lexi said as she handed me some gloves. "Your brother thought you might need these. Your hands are a little red."

I glanced down, and sure enough, even with the sun setting, a slight burn covered my delicate skin. Living with albinism was more of a curse than anything else. Because of a genetic mutation, I lived my life weary of the sun. Long-sleeved clothing, sun hats, gloves, sunglasses and scarves, special body creams, and lotions were my life.

"Oh, thank you." I pulled on the gloves. His thoughtful gesture warmed my heart. He always looked out for me, shielded me, and sheltered me. I couldn't imagine my life without him in it.

"That was a . . . nice service." I couldn't tell if Lexi was being sarcastic or kind. The tone of her voice could go either way.

"It was Anthony's service. Everything he wanted and more. I couldn't believe how many people came." While he might have been proud to know the room had been packed, it surprised me. I always knew Anthony was connected, but considering the amount of floral deliveries and donations we'd received once word of his death got out, I honestly thought the service might have been more low-key.

I should have known better.

"There were a lot of people there I didn't recognize," Lexi pointed out.

I half turned in the seat so I could look her directly in the eyes. "Did you come as a friend, or are you on a case?" Being a detective was so much a part of Lexi that the lines often blurred.

She at least blushed. "Fair enough."

I let that sit between us for a few minutes before I answered the question I knew she reined in. "A few were business associates, but a lot are part of that group of his. But then, you figured that out already, didn't you?"

One lift of a shoulder was all the answer I needed.

"What do they call themselves again?"

"The Final Family." What a stupid name. Her question was innocent enough, even though she knew the answer before even asking it. Just like she knew there was a lot of background behind her words — background she knew I didn't want to get into.

"You know I have nothing to do with his stupid group," I reminded her, "and now that Anthony is dead, there is no reason for any of them to show up at the house anymore. Can we drop it, please?"

The way her lips tightened, I knew nothing was going to get dropped.

"It's a cult, not a group, and you know I wish I could," she said.

"Fine. Cult." I rolled my eyes. "Talk to Bryce, because he has more to do with that stupid cult than me."

I hated discussing the Final Family. I'd tried hard not to with Anthony, and with Bryce, we tended to skirt the subject as much as possible. With Lexi, I needed it to be a hands-off discussion point in our friendship.

I hated everything they stood for, what they believed in, and the devastation they wreaked on my life.

"When something stinks as bad as they do, there tends to be a reason."

"Is that another Spike-ism?" Detective Leon Spikes was Lexi's partner at the Bervie Springs Police Department, and ever since she'd been paired with him, she'd started spouting his weird sayings. Spikes was a newcomer to our small town, having transplanted from the big city. Last I heard, he was looking to retire soon. The Dixon mess had been enough for him.

"What can I say? He's rubbing off on me. You wouldn't happen to have any names for me, would you? Just so I can look into them?" The words were said with a forced casualness.

"I thought this was Spikes' pet project, not yours? Didn't we agree you'd step back and stop with the inquiries? You know how much I hate being used for information." I couldn't have hid the frustration and anger in my voice even if I'd tried.

"I know, I know. Sorry. It just . . . something about them bothers me, you know? But you're right. I promised you I wouldn't hound you, and here I am, at Anthony's funeral, doing just that." The apology in her voice was real.

I nudged her with my elbow and gave her a soft smile that hopefully showed how much I appreciated having her with me. "At least he's gone now, which means no more nightly visits from his sycophants, and I can finally be left in peace."

There would be no more late-night guests, no more being paraded in front of people, being called Sister, and hearing about the fulfillment of a stupid prophecy I didn't believe in. There was nothing inside of me that mourned his loss. Absolutely nothing.

"I don't know how you put up with it all, honestly."

My laughter was full of sarcasm and bewilderment. "I had no choice, you know that." Sure, I was a thirty-year-old woman, but I still lived in the house I grew up in, worked side by side with my brother and, previously, with Anthony. My life revolved around him and our family business. That was it. That was how he'd wanted it.

The Kern Funeral Home was a staple to Bervie Springs, a generational family-owned business. Running it was all I'd wanted to do. I had the business degree and the required certification to have my funeral director's license, not to mention my embalmer license, even though I wouldn't be caught dead down in the dungeon.

Not that Anthony ever noticed or cared that it was my career of choice. He'd wanted Bryce to run the show, not me.

"I hate to ask this, but . . ." her voice trailed off as she gathered her thoughts.

"Then don't." I had a feeling I knew what she was going to say.

"You don't think Bryce would step into Anthony's shoes, do you?"

I sighed. Why couldn't she leave well enough alone? She obviously was not here as a friend, not anymore.

I turned in my seat, all sense of peace gone from my spirit.

"Since this is no longer a friendly chat, let's get into it. But afterward, if you ever bring the subject up again without cause, there will be serious repercussions for our friendship. Do you understand?"

Her nod confirmed this was, in fact, what she had planned all along.

Fine, whatever.

"If Bryce wants to join the group, I can't stop him. They meet regularly, and for all I know, he's already paid the hefty initiation fee and is as entrenched in the stupid cult as Anthony was. I hope he's not, but he was Anthony's shadow, so take what you will from that."

"You mentioned an initiation fee . . . that's something everyone has to pay to join?"

I nodded. "That's what I said."

"What do they get out of it?"

Was she for real? "What does anyone who joins a pyramid scheme get out of it? False promises of protection. Immunity. A place to hide when the world ends."

"Come again?"

I really didn't want to spell it out for her, but it was obvious I had to. It surprised me that between her and Spikes, they hadn't figured it out already. I stood from the swing, my feet planted firmly on the ground, "They're a doomsday cult."

Lexi jumped to her feet. "Say what?"

"Come on, tell me you don't already know all this." Considering she'd told me exposing the Final Family was her partner's pet project, I highly doubted they didn't know any of that already.

She slowly nodded as if piecing the puzzle together, one clue at a time.

"Doomsday cult was not on my bingo card, that's for sure," she said.

"It all goes back to a ridiculous prophecy: *for in the last days, before the rebirth, the twins of white flame will arise and join in. The preparation of the willful blessing will, in one accord, bring about the end of a fallen world, and the anointed ones will be birthed into new life.*"

I glanced off into the distance as raised voices filled the air. My line of sight was blocked, so I took several steps to the left until I had a clearer view. Three men stood together beside a running vehicle. One was my brother. The other two I didn't recognize.

"This is not the time," one of the men said, his hand on the other man's shoulder. My brother only looked on, his hands behind his back, his face a mask of indifference.

What was going on?

"This wasn't what I agreed to. Return my money, and I'll figure out another way that doesn't involve you and that group." The venom spewing from that man's voice surprised me. I watched to see how my brother reacted, but he didn't. Didn't react. Didn't talk. Didn't move, in fact.

"Go back to the hotel and calm down. I'll call you in a few hours, and we'll discuss everything then. You don't want to leave the group. This is all just a misunderstanding."

Within seconds, the angry man was in his vehicle and sped out of our driveway, rocks flung in every direction.

The moment Bryce noticed me, his features softened, and he gave me a small wave.

"Hey, Brynn," Lexi said. "I have a question about that prophecy . . ." she paused. "Is everything okay?" she asked as she realized Bryce watched us. "Does he need you?"

I took the out she provided.

"I should go check in, I guess," I said. "Are you headed out?"

"I'd really like to talk about that prophecy."

"Another time, maybe." I gave her arm a squeeze before I followed the pathway from the garden to the house. Bryce waited for me.

"What was that all about?" I asked him after we waved goodbye to Lexi.

"Nothing to worry about," he said. "Come on, most everyone has left. Why don't we go inside, and I'll put on some tea? Maybe if the rest of the people notice our absence, they'll get the hint and leave." He linked his arm through mine.

"That was nice of Alexius to attend," he said. "Father never trusted her, but I know you consider her a close friend."

After what she just did in the garden, I wasn't sure how close of a friendship we really had. All my life, I'd been used in one way or another, but having a friend do it so blatantly stung.

# CHAPTER FOUR

Three days following the funeral, life returned to normal. Most of the food dropped off had been donated to a local shelter, and things were quiet at home, just how I liked it.

It was crazy how many casseroles, pies, and pasta salads people brought over. I think most forgot Bryce was a chef, and cooking was his way of decompressing.

"Look at this golden brown crust on these chops."

I peered over Bryce's shoulder and inhaled. "That smells delicious. What is it?"

"Orange zest." The grin on his face was infectious. "The caramelization is perfect, if I do say so myself."

My stomach grumbled like a tomcat. "What can I do to help?" None of those casseroles or salads competed with Bryce's cooking.

My brother cooked from not just his heart but his soul. Being a chef had always been his dream and he'd even been listed as one of the top twenty chefs in global dining while working at Rao's in New York City. The only reason he came home and let go of that dream was because Anthony had begged him to after our mother's unexpected death.

I was still angry about that. Never once had Anthony looked toward me as his successor and right-hand person.

I was better equipped, but instead, he forced Bryce to step away from what he was passionate about and to train for his embalmer's certificate.

"How about you cut the bread? There's homemade herbed butter in the fridge."

"Which fridge?" We had two in the kitchen. One was the main household food, and in the other, the men in the family kept their special cuts of meat from the local butcher.

"The main one."

It took me a while to locate the butter. I had to move quite a few things out of the way. "Hey, there's no room left in this fridge for things, and it's so overstuffed. Mind if I move a few of the containers over to yours?"

"No, I'd prefer you didn't. Is there anything in there we can use as a side tonight?"

I sighed. I should have known better than to ask. Bryce had a thing about his fridge, rules he was very specific about. No one touched the meat; it was never to be used for overflow for the main fridge, and in fact, it was best to stay out of it, period.

Everyone was allowed to be a little protective about their things, and considering Bryce did the majority of the cooking, I wasn't about to complain.

I found a baked broccoli casserole and brought it out. "I doubt this will pair well with your dish, but it's this or a pasta salad."

"Can't we donate some of these dishes?"

I laughed. After the tongue-lashing I got from taking the last bit to the shelter, I wasn't about to make that mistake again. "Most of the ladies who made these dishes volunteer their time at any of the places we could give these to, so . . . unless you're ready to piss off one of the town matriarchs, I'd say the answer is no."

While Bryce popped the casserole in the oven to heat up, I grabbed a cutting board and knife for the bread. "If I haven't said this before, let me reiterate: Please don't ever get married.

I can't live on cereal and toast for the rest of my life." It was a sad truth that I had no culinary skills, unlike Bryce or even Anthony. The men in the family always felt more at home in the kitchen than the women, which didn't bother me.

"Like I'd ever leave you. We're a team. Besides, this is your home, too. If I ever found someone to share my life with, they'd have to accept they are coming into our lives, instead of us starting something new." He flashed me one of his *I got this* smiles, and I chuckled. If Bryce ever did get married, he had no idea how much his life would change.

If. That was a big question. I'd never known Bryce to show any interest in any one person, ever. As children, he swore he'd never get married, that he didn't need someone in his life to complete it, that he was perfectly happy just the way he was.

One day, that could change. Who knew?

"I've got one question for you." I leaned close and peered over Bryce's shoulder. "Are you planning on guests I don't know about?" He had six pork chops in the pan.

My stomach growled again.

"I can't tell you how happy it makes me to know you're hungry. Don't think I haven't noticed how you've been picking at your food lately. Maybe I'm hoping you'll eat two of these. The rest we can use for another meal."

"Two?" Sure, I was hungry, but not that hungry. Fine, my appetite hadn't been the same as before, but considering everything we'd gone through, that was more than normal and expected.

"Okay, maybe that's a little too much. Besides, you'll want to save room for dessert. And no," he said before I could interject, "don't bother asking, because it's a surprise. It's something new I've been noodling with."

Noodling? Who said that anymore? My brother, that was who. He was such an old-fashioned soul.

"I can't wait to try it." I brought the bread and butter to the table and waited for him to join me. He always liked to present the main dish with a sense of flair.

The past few days following the funeral had been busy and stressful, and tonight was the first time we'd had time to ourselves. It was nice.

The quiet was even nicer.

Bryce enjoyed the quiet just as much as I did, and for the first time in a long time, there was no background noise — no news, music, or podcast playing in the background. Anthony couldn't handle silence; he said he couldn't think. It was bad enough that elevator music played in the funeral home full-time, but there was no escaping it, even at home.

Until now.

"Do you hear it?" I asked Bryce in between bites.

The upward tilt of his lips confirmed we were on the same wavelength. "I don't hear a thing, and it's blissful."

It was probably one of the best nights I'd had in a long time. Just me, Bryce and the silence, it was golden and came with a feeling that things were finally working out how they were supposed to.

Without Anthony's presence, the possibilities for what our future held were endless. After so many years of living under his hard thumb we were finally free. Bryce could open his own restaurant in town. Maybe he could live the life he'd always wanted to, not the one forced on him. Me, well, I would run the funeral home, something I knew I could do and was good at, regardless of what Anthony had thought.

"Brynn, I've been thinking . . ."

With just a few words, Bryce put a crack into the contentment I finally gave myself permission to enjoy. I was in the middle of cleaning the table when he uttered the words, stopping me mid-swipe.

"We need to talk about the funeral home."

I steeled myself against the heave of anxiety that rolled through me.

"Talk about what?" How my voice managed to remain even was beyond me. "I thought we'd agreed things would continue as they have been. I take care of the guest experience; you handle the deceased?"

He nodded. "Right. That won't change. I was just wondering if we should hire you a helper."

A helper? So, he doubted that I could actually handle things. That hurt more than I wanted to admit.

"What did Anthony say to you?" My words were clipped, masking the hurt, turning it into anger.

Bryce's brows joined together as he frowned. "This has nothing to do with Anthony. I'm just thinking about you. You shouldn't have to take care of everything, that's all."

I stared at my brother, trying to read his face, but it was a mask, completely blank and void of expression. He gave me the face he reserved for our clients. I hated that look, and he knew it.

"Don't do that." There was almost a hint of pleading in my voice. I sounded weak.

Bryce noticed. Of course, he did. He leaned his elbows on the table. "Do what, Brynn? Want to look after you? Want to make sure you're happy? Why not?"

Didn't he hear the way he sounded? Patronizing and archaic?

Swallowing back the bubble of tears that had built up, I grabbed the salt and pepper shakers from the table and returned them to their spot on the stove's top.

I would not cry. I would not cry.

"Brynn?" Concern filled Bryce's voice. Concern for me.

I remained in place, not moving, not trusting myself to say a word yet.

Why did everyone always believe I needed to be taken care of? What about me made me appear soft and weak? It was all I'd heard my whole life from Anthony: that I wasn't enough, that I couldn't handle the real world without there being a buffer, that he'd made the mistake of believing I would ever amount to anything.

Why couldn't someone, just once, have believed in me?

"This has nothing to do with Anthony, I promise." Bryce placed his arms around me and pulled my back toward him. "Brynn, I'm sorry. I'm so sorry. I didn't think . . . I . . . ."
I heard the apology in his voice and relaxed.

I believed him. Of all the people in my life, he was the one I would always believe, always trust. He was my twin. My soul. My compass. I needed him to believe me, too.

"I'm capable, Bryce. I've taken all the required courses to manage this business and even passed at the top of my class. I'm more than qualified to run this place, and you know it. If I need help, that's up to me to determine, not you."

Once again, he wore his public face, appearing to listen to and understand what I was saying.

He listened, but he didn't understand.

He would never understand the tension, the stress, and the frustration of knowing what it was like to be more than capable, but never measuring up.

"You're right," he said. "I'm sorry. I'm an oaf for even opening my mouth and suggesting otherwise." He gave my arm a squeeze and seemed about to say more when the doorbell rang.

"So you *are* expecting company," I said. I gave my head a little shake as a sense of annoyance spread through me. "Nothing actually changes, does it?"

Anthony had guests drop in after dinner at least three times a week, sometimes more. The normal routine was for me to welcome the guests and then hide away in my room or, better yet, go for a walk, depending on the time.

Out of sight, out of mind.

"You don't mind getting that, do you?" Bryce asked. "I'll get your dish ready."

"Am I actually being tossed out of the kitchen? Do you know who else used to do that? Yep, Anthony." I couldn't believe it. "Why did I think you'd be any different?" I headed out, ignoring whatever explanation he was attempting to make.

Like father like son, except Bryce was different. At least, I thought he was.

Opening the door, seeing the face on the other side, hearing the words spoken . . . I realized then and there I'd created a false narrative for myself.

Now that Anthony was gone, Bryce had no choice but to take on his mantle.

Whether I liked it or not.

# CHAPTER FIVE

"I don't know why I let you talk me into this," Mona Darby, my closest friend, grumbled beside me as we completed our savasana, the corpse pose, during our sunrise yoga session.

My arms and legs were spread comfortably, and my eyes were closed, but none of that mattered to Mona, who was already on her feet.

"Life is full of compromise, Mona," I said, keeping my eyes shut. "If you want me to join you, it's either sunrise or sunset, you know that."

Whenever I could, I would attend the sunrise yoga sessions in the town park. I'd leave the house while it was still dark and return home as the sun started its daily rise, feeling refreshed and ready to tackle whatever emergency presented itself — but only after stopping for coffee first.

"Then, for the love of all things holy, can we please do a sunset session next time? This girl likes her sleep, a hot shower, and then two cups of coffee before I'm forced to be around people."

With a long exhale to push any lingering exhaustion from my body outward, I brought my arms and legs in close to my body, opened my eyes, and tried to ignore the sight of Mona standing over me.

"You missed a long curly chin hair," I said, pointing upward. That was a lie. I can't see anything, but Mona suffered from PCOS and was fastidious about eliminating any and all evidence of hair growth on her face.

With her focus off of me and trying to find that non-existent chin hair, I pulled down the sleeves of my shirt, using the thumb hole to keep them secure past my wrists, and climbed to my feet. It was going to be a warm one today, which meant my day would be spent indoors. During the warm summer months, I tended to daydream about moving to the West Coast, where it rained more than not and was overcast more than clear. Unfortunately, ninety percent of UV rays penetrated cloud cover, so as long as the sun was out, my skin needed to be covered and protected — regardless of where I lived.

We said goodbye to the others in the group and headed down the hill toward Main Street.

"Coffee?" I motioned toward Sweet Beans, our favorite coffee shop in town. Mona glanced down at her watch and groaned. "It's too late to climb back into bed, so I guess so. Remember, you said you were buying."

"I had to say that just to get you out of bed. Sunrise yoga is more fun when you drag a friend along."

While she plopped down in the corner booth, I ordered two strong coffees and grabbed freshly baked croissants as well. The place was quiet, which wasn't surprising, given the time.

"Brynn, good to see you," Sharlene Cummings, the owner, said. "Sorry to hear about your father."

I gave her a smile, muttered something that sounded like thanks, and pulled out my bank card.

"I was wondering, have you had a chance to look over my proposal."

"Proposal?"

"I handed it to your brother a few weeks ago. I was going to follow up, but then, with everything that happened . . ."

"Could you send me a copy?" I grabbed a pen, found an odd receipt in my purse, and wrote down my email address.

"I'll chat with Bryce. Things have been a little hectic, so it probably slipped his mind."

A smile of relief appeared on her face. "Wonderful. I should have given it to you directly, but he'd come into the store and said he'd pass it along."

"And knowing him, it's either still in his truck or sitting under a pile of files on his desk." I smiled and kept my tone upbeat, but inside, I was full of questions. Bryce hadn't said a word to me about any new proposals.

"I'll send it over this morning. I know you have a long working relationship with that bakery from the next town over, but I'm hoping my rates are competitive."

I took the offered tray that contained our coffees and croissants and headed to where Mona sat.

Looking over our contracts was something at the top of my to-do list. Anthony had an iron fist when it came to working with vendors and contracts, and no matter how many times I offered to help, showing him time and time again how cost-saving it would be to switch even a few of our vendors, he always shut me out.

Dealing with the vendors wasn't something Bryce had ever shown any interest in, so now was my time to take it over.

"Everything okay?" Mona asked as I slid onto the bench.

"I'm just thinking about how different things will be now, with Anthony gone."

"Is that a good or bad thing?"

I gave her a look.

"I know, I know. The two of you didn't have the best relationship. So, probably a good thing then. Word of advice? Don't make too many changes all at once."

Coffee in hand, I enjoyed my first sip.

"I've got a list of changes that I've been keeping for years," I reminded her.

"I know you do. But take it slow, okay? Not just for your sake but for your brother, your staff, and even your clients. That's my word of advice as a lawyer." She leaned forward and lightly touched my hand. "As your friend, I'm excited about what the future holds for you and that you can finally spread your wings. But do it slowly, please, for all our sakes." Her gentle eye roll was enough to put a smile on my face.

"I hear you," I told her. It shouldn't surprise me she knew me so well, we'd been friends since grade six, when I was the weird girl who never went outside for recess.

"I do feel like I need to prove myself, if that makes sense." I played with my coffee cup, running my finger over the rim.

"Of course it does. But to whom? Yourself? Your brother? Anthony?"

And just like Mona, she hit the issue right on the mark.

"If I'm being honest, probably all of the above."

Her nod said she agreed with me.

"Putting any energy into Anthony isn't worth it, in my opinion. Your brother would probably be more than happy to let you take on the reins, so you've nothing to prove to him. So, if it's a matter of proving to yourself something you've always known, then I say go for it." She grabbed my hand and gave it a hard squeeze. "I believe in you, but do me a favor?"

"Name it."

"Don't lose yourself in this quest, okay?"

I leaned back and studied my friend, and I read the intent behind her words. "Mona," I said, "if I ever get lost within myself, I expect you to save me. Whisk me away to the Amalfi Coast, where we can sip limoncello spritz while gossiping about all the celebrities aboard their superyachts."

Her eyes widened with excitement. "Are you serious? 'Cause, girl, if you are . . . we've always talked about touring Italy, but there's never been time."

I held out my pinkie and waited for her to latch on to it. "Pinkie swear. Sisters in life and . . ."

"Death can go eff itself, 'cause it's not happening for a very long time."

It's a saying we've had since we first met when we pinkie-swore we'd always be friends, no matter what.

"I'm serious, Brynn," Mona said, her face no longer full of excitement. "Anthony overshadowed everything in your life. Don't let his death hold that power, too."

Hearing her say those words meant more than she knew. I've always had people in my corner, people who believed in me, like Bryce, my mother, and my friends . . . but Anthony's presence was dominating, overwhelming, and overshadowed everyone else, especially after Mom's accident.

Before her death, he didn't have much of an impact on my life. Mom was the main parent in our home, the one who made the decisions, who ran all the school runs and who volunteered whenever she could while also spending her days supporting Anthony in the funeral home.

After her death, he didn't waste any time bulldozing the life we'd made for ourselves. Bryce walked away from his dream job, and I became invisible in mine.

To Anthony, I was a glorified secretary who ran the office and did whatever he ordered me to do. The reality was, with my skill set and education, I could efficiently and effectively run the family business if Anthony hadn't blocked me at every step.

Mona said not to rush things, but my list was long, and I had to start at some point.

The first thing I needed to do was chat with my brother to discuss our roles in the family business, how we wanted to run things, and our future.

# CHAPTER SIX

It was clear, from the way my brother hummed, that he felt most comfortable in the kitchen.

He was in the zone, oblivious to anything other than his recipe, his utensils, and his food.

I've always enjoyed watching him cook, everything from how focused he was to the little dance steps of delight he'd take when taste-testing a sauce. My phone was full of videos of him. I never posted any of them online because Anthony was against all things social media.

At the snap of Anthony's fingers, Bryce gave up his dream without a fuss, without even a second thought, and that is something I couldn't forget. Or forgive.

"Are you sure I need to be here?" From the slight jump Bryce gave, he'd totally forgotten I was in the room with him.

"Hmm? Hey, can you pass me the salt?" He pointed to a small white bowl on the counter beside me.

With a small push, I moved it closer to him.

"Thanks, and yes, of course, I want you here. This is a special dinner, with a special guest, one I think you'll like. It's so special, I even used the good cuts." He indicated his fridge.

"Need and want are two different things. I don't want to be here for this dinner, if I'm being honest, but if you need me, then that's different."

"Need, want, tonight, they're the same for me. Please say you'll stay." He flashed a smile while stirring salt into his dish.

The kitchen smelled heavenly with Bryce's braised beef dish.

"Anthony never needed me." Hopefully, he didn't hear the pettiness in my voice.

"Dad was a fool when it came to you. He never saw you the way I do. We're going to do things differently, you and I. Sometimes the old ways aren't always the right ways."

*Do things differently*: heaven to my ears.

"I like the sound of that," I told him.

"You sound surprised. Why? It's always been the two of us," he said, with a look on his face that had me questioning myself. "Why would that change?"

"I still don't get why you are playing host. Why can't someone else from the Family do it instead?" I ignored his question and issued my own.

"Because I offered. This has been in the works for a while, Brynn. Dad's death doesn't change anything."

"It should."

"Not for me." He heaved a sigh. "I wish you'd rethink things."

I didn't bother to ask him to clarify his statement, because I knew exactly what 'things' he was referring to.

"I don't believe in any of that stuff, you know that."

The Final Family was a cult; that was a simple fact. But the last time I said that to Anthony's face, he slapped me hard enough that my ears rang for two solid days. For reasons I never understood, Anthony was like a god within that community, which always sickened me.

They knew the Anthony he wanted them to know.

I knew the real man, and he was no god.

How Bryce believed the nonsense always shocked me. I could never wrap my head around that.

Bryce set his spoon down and turned. How he looked at me, like he was peering into my soul, made me uncomfortable. We had a bond like most twins, but sometimes, it felt like he could read my thoughts.

My gaze dropped.

"And yet, you used to be a part of that life."

"That was our childhood, Bryce, and you know as well as anyone that our memories are skewed as children. What we recall with fondness was actually a nightmare based in reality."

Truth be told, I remember very little from my childhood. Much of that time was blocked, but there were still fragments that appeared out of the blue: arguments between our parents, long drives in the countryside, picnics in wildflower fields, and weird gatherings with the adults in the twilight hours. When I was younger, I'd asked Mom about them, but she'd always change the subject. Over time, I learned to ignore them instead.

Our minds were known to have blocked out parts of our past that could damage our psyche. If that was what happened, then I was fine with it.

"That doesn't make any of it less true. You and I, we're special, Brynn. We're special because of this—" he pointed between us — "and because of what we represent. You can't deny that."

"This is because of genetics," I said, grasping a piece of white hair between my fingers — hair I had always hated. "What we represent is either an anomaly, or our mother had an affair," I said flippantly, because I knew how much it bothered my brother. "Being an albino isn't a gift, any more than it's a curse. It's just DNA, Bryce, that's all."

It took me a long time to come to that understanding. Being brainwashed as a child by Anthony that Bryce and I had a destiny bigger than any one person, did a lot of damage. My mother instilled the art of questioning everything I'd been told at an early age, and I found some solace that death came for everyone and that being albino wasn't destiny. It was purely genetics.

"I don't agree," Bryce said. "I think once you fully understand the scope of things, you'll change your mind." Something of a smile played with his lips, which surprised me, considering the accusation I'd thrown out.

"And our mother didn't have an affair," he continued. "You know I hate it when you suggest that." He picked up the spatula and gave his sauce another stir. "Now, I think I have everything. The table is set, the dessert is chilling, the wine . . . crap, I used what little we had left for the recipe."

"Tell me what you want, and I'll run to the store." I was more than happy to offer anything to move past our current topic of conversation.

Did I believe our mother had an affair? No. The connection between our parents had always been a real one. Despite my feelings for Anthony, I knew he loved our mother — he was always holding her hand, kissing her cheek, forehead, and even the side of her neck in front of us. But either our mother had an affair with someone with albinism in their family history, or it skipped several generations in ours. Having gone over our family history, I doubted this possibility. Bryce and I were the only ones with this genetic disposition, unless I missed something.

In the past, having albinism was thought to be a curse. Babies were drowned. Women burned at the stake. In some cultures, they were supposed to have supernatural powers and were revered to the point of seclusion.

The only difference between us and other people was that we lacked pigment in our skin, hair, and eyes, and we had to be more conscious of the sun. We wore darker sunglasses during the day, hats, and clothing to protect us from sunburn. That was all.

As children, we were called vampires by the bullies at school.

"Hmmm. I think a Bertani would pair well with this. Madison mentioned he had some new stock come in. Tell him to put it on my account, will you? And tell him we want the best for tonight. Our guest is someone who will appreciate it."

When it came to wine, Bryce knew what he liked. Anthony had been the same — he had a taste for the finer things, including expensive wine and liquor. His office was fully stocked with whiskey, gin, and bourbon — only the

31

best of the best, and most of the time, they were all gifts from one person or another.

Anthony knew everybody. From politicians to celebrities, he was in the inner circles of important people, and to this day, I never understood why.

With him being dead, I thought all of that nonsense was behind us, that we could relax into regular life and leave the craziness of Anthony's pursuits in the past.

I guess I was wrong, and I wasn't sure how I felt about that.

# CHAPTER SEVEN

The one nice thing about Bervie Springs was that almost everything was within walking distance, which meant the wine store was only a few blocks down the street. Having been stuck down in the dungeon most of the day doing inventory, it was nice to get out and stretch my legs. Of all the rooms and areas within the funeral home, the dungeon was the one I hated the most.

It was also where Anthony and now Bryce worked. Both his office and the preparation room were down there, and there was always a distinct odor that emanated from that room.

I loved almost everything about working in a funeral home. I loved being there for people — families, parents, and children — and supporting them during the nightmare they found themselves in. I'd always been told I had a comforting presence, and despite my pale features, or maybe because of them, people tended to lean on me for help when they felt most lost.

The only part of working in a funeral home I didn't like was the embalming. With all the chemicals used, the smell was unmaskable. After working down there all day, it became embedded in the pores of my skin and clothes.

Being outside, in the fresh air, during the in-between hours as the sun slowly set, was a good reminder to enjoy being alive.

Crossing the bridge into town was one of my favorite walks. The bridge was always full of flowers and decorated to fit the seasons. Bervie Springs was known as the flower capital of New York State for good reason. Soils and Springs, the local garden center, was still operational despite one of the owners being a convicted serial killer. Dixon's ex-wife somehow walked away with her hands reasonably clean, and after a slight rebranding of the company, she continued to take care of the town gardens.

In fact, a proposal for a new garden area on our property was buried somewhere on my desk.

It didn't take long to reach the wine store. I wasn't paying attention and almost bumped into someone as I opened the door.

"Augh, watch where . . . oh, it's you." Mr. Baxter, a cantankerous older man who was also our neighbor, readjusted the brown bags in his arms.

"Sorry, Mr. Baxter. I wasn't watching where I was going." Of all the people to bump into, he was one of my favorites. I gave him the sweetest smile possible.

"No need to apologize. I ah . . . how are you? I haven't seen you out in the garden much the past little bit."

"Things have been a little . . . busy, I guess. Life goes on, even when your whole world stops."

He snorted. "Don't be telling me what you think I want to hear, girl. You know me better than that." He twitched his nose with his thumb. "Your world didn't stop just because your father died." He grunted a 'harumph.' "This is where your real life starts, without him constantly pushing you down. Grieve because that's what we do as humans, but don't lie. Not to me. Not to yourself."

Having known him since I was little, his frankness was no surprise. Throughout the years, he'd be the one who noticed me sitting in the shade by the garden, knees drawn up tight to my chest, head buried while my tears flowed.

34

He'd often pop over when Mom was in the garden, and they'd have tea and talk about plants and flowers and life in general while I sat there, soaking it all in.

He was the grandfather I never had.

The grandfather Anthony didn't want me to need.

"Is it wrong to say I don't miss him?"

He laughed. A good, solid laugh from the belly that had me smiling. "Child, why would that be wrong? Don't be worrying about other people's expectations, you hear? I watched you, you know, at the funeral. I noticed how quiet you were and how your brother did most of the talking. That was a right shame. At my funeral, I don't want those silly platitudes and people claiming how wonderful and kind I was. You hear me? Say it like it is. I'm a thorn in the butt that won't ever go away, is what I am."

I reached out and hugged him. "To everyone but me, maybe. I'll be sure to remind everyone of all your ugly qualities, don't you worry." We'd already had this talk. Mr. Baxter came in a few years ago and pre-paid for his funeral, giving explicit instructions on what was to be done and not done. He had been very clear that he wanted 'no ridiculous memorial where people sit around eating sandwiches and gossiping like the old women they are.'

"Now listen," he said, his eyes narrowing as he stared at me. "I've been noticing the nightly visitors while letting out Jasper before bed. Everything okay?"

"That late at night? Are you sure?" We had a revolving door of people dropping by since the funeral, but never late at night.

He cocked his head and arched his overly bushy eyebrows. "My eyes are just as good as when I was younger, and I know what I saw. A vehicle enters your driveway, flashes its lights, and then your brother walks out. They chat for a few minutes, and then the vehicle leaves while your brother sneaks back into the house."

That didn't make sense. Sure, I'd been heading to bed before him most nights, but . . .

"Your brother hasn't gone and taken over for your father, has he?"

I wanted to say no, but we both would recognize that lie for what it was.

"Guess it's looking that way," I admitted.

His brow wrinkled as he frowned. "You stay out of all that, you hear? I've heard the rumors, and that's nothing you need to be a part of. I still have that guest house waiting for you, if you ever want it."

His offer was touching. "You're a sweetheart, and I won't let anyone else suggest otherwise."

He harrumphed.

"The offer is there. It's always good to have a backup plan, even when you don't think you'll need it. Now I'd best be getting home. Jasper is waiting for his dinner." He gave me a deep dip of his head before shuffling his way down the street.

Other than Bryce and Mom, Mr. Baxter was the only one who loved me unconditionally, even though he'd never outright said the words. He was always there, never expecting anything in return, and for as long as I could remember, the guest house offer had always been there. A place for me to escape to and hide if needed.

I used to dream of running away and living in a place that was all mine. Now, with Anthony gone, I finally felt safe in my home for the first time in a very long, long time.

# CHAPTER EIGHT

Armed with a rather expensive bottle of Amarone della Valpolicella Classico Bertani wine, all I kept thinking about on the walk home was that the guest had better be important. Not government important; more like movie star important.

When I handed Madison Bryce's message, he didn't look surprised at all, which sent up a few red flags.

Once home, Bryce's whistle of approval confirmed Madison had given me the right bottle.

"This may not impress our guest, but he'll definitely appreciate it. It's the perfect bottle to go with the perfect cut of meat, too." Bryce opened the bottle and poured it into the waiting decanter. "We've just enough time for this to aerate before he arrives."

"I hope the guy is worth it." I still couldn't get over the price. "Please tell me you haven't developed a taste for these types of wines."

"What type? The good type?"

"The expensive type."

Bryce shrugged, which told me much more than I wanted.

"And who is it that's coming again?"

"It's a surprise. Trust me, you will be happy I made you stay for dinner. If you want to freshen up, there's plenty of time." He gave me a once-over, which made me glance down at the dress I'd just changed into.

"I did."

What was wrong with my outfit? It was a dress I liked, one of my favorites, in fact. It was also perfect for the time of year: a simple brown dress with long sleeves and cute ankle boots I picked up on sale. I refused to wear black, no matter the ridiculous custom, a custom that was more archaic than practical.

"Sorry, I didn't mean . . . you look fine, sis."

Fine? *Fine* was not a term anyone used to describe a woman, sister or not, when commenting on her outfit.

"Guess who I ran into on the way to grab the wine?" I leaned my hip against the counter and folded my arms over my chest.

"No idea," he said, not even glancing at me.

"Mr. Baxter, and he was asking about you."

"Me?" He gave me a side-eye. "Why?"

"Seems like there's been a lot of late-night activity I was unaware of."

His whole body paused for only a split second, but it was enough that I noticed. "Anything you want to tell me?"

He shook his head, but it wasn't a *there's nothing* type of shake, but more of a *crap — I need to think of an answer fast* type of gesture.

"It's them, isn't it? The Family, right?" A breath of anger blew on the glowing ember of frustration inside me. "Should I start calling you Brother?" My tone cut like the sharp knife in his hand.

"Don't do this, not now, okay?" Bryce wouldn't look at me. "Things are different, I promise."

"So you say, and yet, when Anthony wanted me present when a guest arrived, he always told me to freshen up and then said I looked fine, but with the same apparent disapproval in his tone that you just gave me."

Bryce dropped the knife and rounded the counter until he was in front of me. Placing his hands on my shoulders, he waited until I looked him directly in the eyes.

It took me a while.

"I will never treat you as our father did." His voice was sincere, and his gaze told me he'd never been more serious.

I believed him, even though I felt so frustrated with him.

"I'm not him, Brynn. I need you to hear me on that. I know your relationship with our father was different than my own. I wish we knew the same man. I wish we'd had the same experience with him. But I am not him. I won't treat you like he did. I see you, Brynn. I see you for who you are, for who you will become. I need—" his hands tightened on my shoulders — "I need you to trust me, okay?"

The truth of his words, of how different our lives were, weighed on me for longer than he knew. We were raised by a completely different man. Bryce knew a man who loved him and raised him to be the heir he needed.

I meant nothing to him other than the answer to some obscure prophecy steeped in some ridiculous fairytale only referenced with some secret books. He used and emotionally abused me . . . took what he needed, and then tossed me aside.

When Mother was alive, he paid me a little bit of attention. Once she died, the only attention I received was as if I were a servant, to do what he wanted, when he wanted it.

"I see Anthony more and more in you, and to be honest, Bryce, I don't like it. I don't understand what's happening, other than the fact you seem to have stepped into his shoes with an ease that shouldn't be possible." I laid it all out there, shared my thoughts and fears, and had no option but to trust him not to hurt me with it.

"I'm not him, but he wasn't all evil, Brynn. There was good in him; I've seen it."

"You might have, but I never did." I stepped away from his hold. I wanted, no, I needed some distance between us. Usually, we were on the same page, but tonight, we read from two different books in two different languages.

"I don't want to fight," Bryce said. "It's not what you think it is, okay?"

I didn't respond.

"You know, having our guest here will help, which I realize doesn't tell you much, but please, trust me? Just give me a little more time, okay?"

Without a response, he headed back to his dish.

Not wanting to be in the same room as him, I left the kitchen with more questions than answers and went to make sure the dining room table was ready.

"Oh, I thought we'd eat in the kitchen, if you're okay with that," Bryce called out. "Keep it informal and such."

With a guest?

Since Anthony's death, we ate our meals at the small breakfast nook.

"The kitchen is for family."

He shrugged, like he didn't get what I was trying to say. "Exactly. I told you things would be different, and this is just one of many changes I thought we'd make. This will make things more intimate instead of the charade our Father would put on."

I was torn. On one hand, his words lifted a weight from the base of my spine, as I realized I wasn't the only one who wanted to make changes happen. But at the same time, pressure around my rib cage intensified, with worry about what his words really meant.

The kitchen was for family, but our definition of family seemed very different.

# CHAPTER NINE

I needed space from Bryce and his words, so I spent the time in the front room, curled up in a cozy chair with a book I'd recently picked up from the library.

Our little library was one of my favorite places to visit. I believed in the power of what a library could do, so much so that I joined the board several years ago and volunteered to take on the yearly donation drive.

If I could have been a librarian rather than a funeral director . . . how different my life might have been.

Bryce walked into the room, wiping his hands on a dish towel. "What are you reading?"

I absentmindedly reached for a bookmark and slowly closed the book, sad to be leaving the world of romance and balls, of dukes and duchesses finding true love.

Holding up the cover, I waited for him to mock me.

"Does it feel nice to read those out in the open now, instead of having to hide them in your room?" He headed toward the window, hands clasped behind his back. "I know Father didn't always approve of your reading choices."

I wasn't sure where he was going with this, but the fact he didn't make fun of me said something.

"His approval was never needed," I answered. "I'm an adult. I'm free to choose whatever book I want. No one will ever tell me otherwise."

He was surprised by my words, if the raised brow was any indication.

"Is that why you'd always read those books supposedly banned on the internet?"

I nodded. Those banned book lists were something else, for sure. "Some people believe they have the right to decide for everyone what book should be read. It's ridiculous. Make that choice for yourself and your child, fine, but don't make that decision for me."

"Is that a banned book?"

I laughed. "What? No. If someone were to attempt to ban historical Regency romance, there would be quite the uproar."

Bryce glanced at his watch. "Our guest is fifteen minutes late." Tardiness was a sin, according to Anthony. He drilled in us that if we weren't at least fifteen minutes early to any appointment, then we were late. And being late was plain rudeness.

I reopened the book. "I'm sure they'll arrive soon," I said. "Male or female?"

"Male, and I hope you're right. Braised beef with mashed potatoes and vegetables isn't a dish to be enjoyed cold."

My stomach grumbled at the mention of dinner.

Fifteen minutes later, the headlights of a vehicle swinging into the driveway lit up the windows. Bryce was in the kitchen, so it was up to me to greet our guest.

I almost had a hard time getting the words out of my mouth after opening the door.

One of my favorite actors stood at the door — a Hollywood favorite who regularly graced tabloid magazines.

"Mr. Sawyer, hello," I mumbled the lamest of words. My throat was dry, my tongue swollen, and I probably sounded like an idiot.

The way he watched me proved it.

"You must be Brynn?"

Flabbergasted that he knew my name, I stared at him like a wide-eyed fan girl, drunk on his wickedly handsome good looks.

The smile on his face withered the longer we stood there, me being the fool, him being oh-so-patient.

*Get it together, Brynn.*

"My, uh . . . my brother is expecting you. Please, won't you come in?" I finally remembered to step back from the door, giving him space to enter.

Daniel Sawyer stood in my living room. I was about to have dinner with this Hollywood celebrity, and my freak-out meter was at a level of one hundred. *Keep it cool.*

"Bryce," I called out, hoping Daniel Sawyer hadn't noticed the hitch in my voice, "our guest has arrived."

"Please, call me Daniel." His rich, smooth voice was like melted chocolate on a luxurious bowl of fruit.

"Daniel," Bryce's voice boomed as he joined us. "Just in time, come, come." He shook hands with the star before pulling him in for a close hug, hands patting backs as if they knew one another.

Had they met previously and Bryce never told me? No, he wouldn't keep something like that from me.

"I'm late, aren't I?" Daniel smiled somewhat sheepishly.

"Well, you're not early, that's for sure, but you never are, are you?" Bryce laughed as he ushered our guest into the kitchen.

"Traffic out of the city was a nightmare."

"Excuses, excuses." Bryce pointed to the table and urged Daniel to sit. "Dinner is ready. Brynn, would you pour the wine while I serve?"

It was amazing my hands didn't shake as I filled everyone's glasses with the expensive wine. There wasn't enough room on the table for the wine decanter, so I headed back toward the counter where Bryce stood.

"Like my surprise?" he whispered.

"You ass, you could have given me some warning." I nudged him hard in the side.

"Ooof."

"That's for making me look like a fool when he first arrived."

"You still do." There was a twinkle in his eye as he grabbed the oven dish and headed toward the table.

I forced myself to breathe in deeply and find some focus. It wasn't easy, but I eventually found it. I pretended he was one of Anthony's regular guests, which instantly quelled any high-strung excitement inside me.

"I hope you don't mind the lack of formality," Bryce said as he dished out portions for everyone. "Brynn and I have been enjoying the coziness of the kitchen since our father's passing. It's helped us to find a way to rebuild what family now means for us, hasn't it?" He smiled over at me, which I returned.

"Not at all," Daniel said. "Actually, this is quite nice. My life is being wined and dined at fancy upscale restaurants, and I rarely eat a home-cooked meal anymore. I miss it and everything that it entails. Which, I guess, is why I'm here."

"Then let me offer an ongoing invitation to join us for a meal anytime you need to return to those roots." Bryce raised his glass in a toast.

I didn't say much throughout the dinner; I mainly enjoyed the company and watching Bryce in action. He was the gracious host, welcoming and open, and it was apparent he'd already fostered a friendship with Daniel before today.

How many other celebrities did my brother know?

"Tell me how you two met?" I finally managed to break into the conversation during a lull in their camaraderie.

"Your father was the one who introduced us, right? Last year, I think? Over a round of golf? Or was it afterward in the club lounge? I remember us laughing over drinks and nachos," Daniel said.

"If I recall, you complained about the nachos, stating it was the worst you'd ever had, and I said something about making a good plate of—"

"No, you boasted about making the best nachos a man had ever tasted," Daniel interjected, laughing at the same time, "and I told you to prove it. So off we went to the store, and then back to my place, where, yes indeed, you made the best nachos on this God-given earth."

Golf and nachos? My brother was keeping secrets from me.

"You know, I'm a little jealous," I kept my voice upbeat, as if I were teasing, but from the way Bryce swallowed, he knew we would have words later. "Don't tell me you've played more rounds together and not invited me."

"And get our asses kicked by you, no thanks." Bryce groaned playfully.

"No way, you play?" Daniel looked at me like he was surprised.

"My sister could have gone amateur if she'd wanted," Bryce bragged.

"Really? That's . . . interesting, considering . . ." He stopped as Bryce cleared his throat. "Why didn't you?" he asked instead.

Now that all the attention was focused on me, I was rather uncomfortable. How much did he know? More than me was the obvious answer.

"That wasn't where I was needed," I said softly, repeating words Anthony had repeatedly repeated. Mom was the one who encouraged me in my love for golf. She would take me to my lessons, practiced with me in the field, and spent Sunday afternoons with me at the driving range — never Anthony.

Like Bryce, following my dreams was never an option for him. To him, our lives had been mapped out since our birth.

Once, I thought for sure we'd find that freedom following Anthony's death, but more and more, the realization that I was wrong was being shoved into my face.

With Bryce taking on our father's mantle, the chains remained in place.

"So this funeral home is just a front, then?" Daniel directed his question toward Bryce.

"Oh, it's legit, if that's what you're asking. It's been a family-run home for generations now." Bryce leaned over and grabbed my hand. "Brynn here basically runs it herself."

"So what happens when . . ." Apparent confusion covered Daniel's features.

"Anthony took care of all those details, don't worry."

"What details?" I set my fork down on my plate, not following the conversation's lead.

My brother folded his hands on his lap.

"She doesn't know, does she? I'm sorry, man. I thought . . . I should have kept my mouth shut until we were alone." Daniel looked away as if embarrassed.

"No, no, it's fine. My sister is unaware of just how important she is; that is true." He glanced over at me, and I could tell he was struggling with how much to say. "Anthony tended to keep things tight to his chest, but the only way forward is together." Bryce reached for his wine glass and noticed it was empty. "Anyone like a top-up?" He stood and grabbed the decanter, filling all the glasses without waiting for an answer.

It was as if time stood still for me. I was so out of the loop, yet Bryce made it sound like all the puzzle pieces were right there for the taking. I was at the precipice of something that could or would change my life, yet I was numb — numb inside and out.

Why did he say I had no idea how important I was? Important for whom? Him, or that stupid cult he's a part of?

"Daniel, you know about the Family and the role we play at the end of days," Bryce said, not looking at me. "Having you come on board is something we value and honor, and your support means more than we could ever express." Bryce's words left me in a whirlwind of emotions.

The Family? End of days? My brother had really drunk the Kool-Aid, hadn't he?

"By doing this, I'm promised a spot, right? I'm taken care of and will be protected?" Daniel's sharp gaze transferred from Bryce to me, then back to Bryce, as if I had any clue what he was going on about. "This isn't some crazy cult that

I'm throwing money at and will end up on the front page of magazines, right?"

I couldn't wait to hear how my brother was going to respond.

"I promise you that will never happen. Unless you tell someone outside of the Family, no one will know of your involvement."

Interesting. Bryce had just told me more about the inner workings of the cult than Anthony ever had. Why?

"But I'm not just a silent partner, right? I want your word that I'm taken care of and protected."

"You have my word. In fact, we have documents ready for your signature that outline everything for you. Your space has been reserved in one of our centers of your choosing. We can go over the locations and your preferences later. After tonight, you are officially part of the Family."

That was it? That was all it took? Throw down some money, sign some papers, and one of the most famous actors in the world was now part of a super-secret cult?

How many other celebrities have joined? What was in it for them?

"When do I meet him?"

Him?

"Tomorrow. It's all been arranged."

Daniel leaned back in relief, all concerns and worries that had been etched on his face, gone.

"If things are going to be even half as bad as you say they are, I'm glad to be a member. I won't be called Brother or anything like that, will I?"

Bryce laughed. "No, and be thankful for that. The only Brother and Sister of the group are Brynn and I. And no, you don't have to call us that if you don't want to."

I didn't hide my sharp inhale at being called Sister. I hated that term. Every time someone came to the door and called me Sister, I recoiled with distaste.

It was a term placed on me by Anthony, one I never wanted and one I refused to accept. A term he used more

47

often after the death of our mother. Her death gave him the freedom to treat me the way he'd always wanted to.

Anthony kept me separate from his little group, which was good.

When Daniel excused himself to use the washroom, I turned toward Bryce with a wave of anger and betrayal that even shocked me.

"A heads-up would have been nice. Not just on our guest, but on this whole Final Family stupidity, too. I hate being called Sister and don't appreciate you bringing me along as if I'm a willing participant. You know how I've always felt about that stupid group of Anthony's. I want nothing to do with it. Nothing. And what's all that crap about details Anthony took care of? What are you keeping from me?"

"You're upset, and I don't blame you. You're right; I handled everything the wrong way," Bryce said, his voice lowered. "But this is our inheritance, Brynn. It's not what you think it is, I swear. I'm sorry Father kept you out of the loop. I won't do that. I want you to be as much a part of this life as I am." He reached across for my hand. "We're partners in this, I promise."

Nothing he said made any sense. Inheritance. Partners. That's what the funeral home was — our inheritance. We ran it together as partners.

That wasn't what he was talking about, though.

"I've made a mess of things, and I'm sorry. This is all my fault. Daniel and I can finish our business, and then we'll have dessert and talk about regular things, okay?"

Daniel returned before I could reply, so I finished the last bites on my plate and kept my peace as the two men talked more about an upcoming golf tournament they were both part of. I became a ghost at my own kitchen table, a familiar feeling I'd never thought to experience again.

If anything, tonight showed me just how wrong I'd been on so many levels about the life I thought I'd have following Anthony's death.

I remained just as much a prisoner with my brother as I had with my father.

# CHAPTER TEN

With my yoga mat rolled tight beneath my arm and my duffle bag hanging off my other shoulder, I struggled to press the buttons on the kitchen door's keypad.

A small package sat at my feet.

"Bryce?" I called out into an empty and dark house. I dropped my stuff down on the floor, went back for the package, and then checked my phone to see if Bryce had sent a message telling me where he was headed.

Nothing.

That bothered me more than it should. I wasn't his mother nor his keeper. We were roommates, and he was allowed to have his own life, so where did that controlling streak come from?

I needed to do sunset yoga more often. While I generally enjoyed starting my day with yoga, there was something to be said for ending the day perched on a hill, taking in the gorgeous sunset view while de-stressing my body with gentle movements and mindful breathing techniques.

With it being so late, my normal routine when I walked through the kitchen door was to go through the house and turn on the lights. If there was one thing I didn't like, it was being left in the dark. Call it a phobia or fear, but it was there and all too real.

My fear started as a child, when I was sure the dead spirits of the people in the caskets would find me; that one always lurked in the dark corners or shadowed hallway. Nothing my parents did or said convinced me otherwise. It wasn't so much that I was afraid of the monster in the closet or the one who hid beneath my bed — it was the ones who hovered around me in the night, emitting a glow that apparently only I saw.

Still, even now, the spirits were there. The only way I didn't see that glow was if a light was on.

Once, as a prank, Bryce told me where those spirits came from. When we were maybe eight years old, he walked me, hand in hand, to a secret passageway in our basement. He pushed a little button, and a door opened toward a dark hallway. He didn't turn on the flashlight until after pushing me inside and closing the door behind us. He had no idea just how real my fear was until I was frozen with fright, unable to move or even speak. He flashed the light around to prove there was nothing there, but I'd seen them — that passageway had been crowded with ghosts looking for a way to escape.

I never entered that passageway again, even though Bryce used it all the time to get to the embalming room.

Even at age eight, Anthony had begun preparing Bryce to take over, to learn the ropes of a mortician.

There are selected moments where my hatred for Anthony grew. That was one. I hated what he did to my twin, how he ignored his own son's passion and forced him to follow in his footsteps. All of Bryce's life, he'd wanted to be a chef. He'd never once mentioned wanting to follow in Anthony's footsteps.

Years of anger and resentment toward Anthony had built a solid foundation within the walls of my heart, and some days, I wondered if that was all I was — a woman with severe father issues, who only knew anger and disillusionment. I needed to let it go, especially now that he was gone. He couldn't hurt me anymore, and I needed to stop giving him the power to control me from the grave. I didn't need a therapist to tell me that holding on to the hatred I felt toward Anthony wasn't good for me. I didn't know how to do it, but I needed to try.

Back in the kitchen, with most of the lights now on, I looked at the package that had been left at the back door.

It was addressed to me and was from our guest last night.

I snapped a photo of the label. No one would believe a celebrity had sent little ol' me a gift. I wanted to show Mona, but then I'd have to explain why a Hollywood A-lister visited our home and ate dinner at our kitchen table. There was no explanation I could give, not even the truth, that would have her believing my story.

I called my brother instead, and when I got a voicemail, I taunted him that Daniel sent me a gift instead of him.

Inside was a wax-sealed envelope from Shinnecock Golf Course, one of the best private golf courses located in Southampton, New York, along with a box of chocolates from Jacques Torres, my favorite chocolatier, from the city.

Inside the envelope was a personal invitation to join Daniel Sawyer for a day at the Shinnecock Golf Course and dinner in a private lounge. I'd mentioned last night that playing those greens was a dream of mine, but I never thought or expected to actually be invited there and by someone like Daniel.

Giddy from excitement, it took everything inside me not to call Mona and blab the news. Instead, I checked the fridge in case we had any leftovers. Seeing nothing interesting, I grabbed cereal from the pantry and poured myself a big bowl of sugary cereal, something I never did when Bryce was around.

I checked Bryce's location and was surprised that it said he was at the house. Maybe he was over the Parlor, but then his location would show that, wouldn't it?

I finished my bowl of cereal, headed up the stairs, and knocked on his door, just in case.

"Bryce? You'll never guess what was at the back door . . ."

He didn't answer. I knocked again, louder in case he had his headphones on, and then I went to open his door, except I couldn't.

It was locked.

Not just locked, but I noticed the doorknob was new, with space for a key.

"What the . . ." When had he replaced the doorknob with that new one?

We'd never locked our bedroom doors before. Bathroom, sure, bedroom, no. I'd done that once as a teenager after getting in trouble with Anthony, and the next thing we knew, both mine and Bryce's doors had been changed with handles that were no longer lockable from the inside.

My phone rang. I expected it to be Bryce, but it was Mona.

"What are you doing?"

"Standing outside my brother's room, wondering when he put a lock on his door. Why?"

"A what?"

"A lock."

"Maybe he wants some privacy," she said. "Listen, a new bakery opened in Cedar Hills, and they're giving away free coffee and food to the first fifty customers tomorrow morning. Want to join me?"

Cedar Hills was a solid thirty-minute drive. "That depends," I answered. "What time are you planning on leaving?"

"They've been posting all over social media, so I want to be first in line," Mona warned.

It was on the tip of my tongue to say yes, but then I remembered we had a full day at the Parlor tomorrow. "I better not," I said. "But bring me back some pastries?"

"No way, sister. You snooze, you lose. Byyyyeeee."

I tried Bryce's door again, even though I knew it was pointless. I couldn't process the fact he'd lock his door on me. What was inside that was so secret? We respected each other's privacy, always had, so the lock was unnecessary.

What was my brother hiding that he couldn't risk me seeing?

## CHAPTER ELEVEN

It wasn't until the weekend that I had the chance to mention the lock to Bryce.

I was hunched over my steaming cup of coffee as Bryce's heavy footsteps thundered down the stairs. I woke up wanting an egg salad sandwich, and the eggs were boiling on the stove. The past few nights, I'd done nothing but toss and turn, and it felt like I'd barely slept a wink, probably because I'd been alone in the house and never slept when alone.

"Ahh, coffee. Thanks, sis," Bryce said, in a way-too-cheerful tone. Bryce had been away for two days, teaching at a local seminar about the ethics morticians faced, and didn't get home until sometime after midnight last night.

"How did you sleep?" He poured himself a cup, then came over to top mine off.

"Okay, once I fell asleep," I said, in between yawns.

Bryce glanced over at the stove. "What's happening with your eggs?"

"Just waiting for all the water to boil." I dropped my head into the crock of my arm and closed my eyes. "That's how you know the eggs are done, right?"

He laughed. "No, that's how you ruin pots, Brynn. How about I make you something?"

I peeked up at him with a smile. "Like I'm going to say no."

While I savored my much-needed cup of coffee, Bryce worked his magic in the kitchen while almost making a lot of noise.

"Do you honestly need to bang the pots and drawers?" I groaned. I had a headache in my eyes that shot splinters straight into the back of my brain. The book I had read last night had me crying by the time I finished it, and crying always gave me headaches.

"Ahh, someone having a rough morning? I promise breakfast will help. Give me a few minutes." He rummaged in his fridge and pulled out a bin. "How does a steak wrap sound with your eggs? I'll make a few extra, and we can eat them on the road."

On the road? "Where are we going?"

He wore an exuberant look on his face, a look he'd had since we were kids when he knew a secret I didn't. "We're playing hooky today. I have something I want to show you." His eyes lit up like spotlights. "Don't worry; it's all arranged with Merilyn. She's got things covered."

Merilyn Matthews was the shift supervisor at the Parlor. She'd been with us for almost eight years and taught me a lot about the industry that I would never have learned at school or from Anthony. I couldn't imagine running the place without her help.

"Merilyn deserves some time off, too."

He nods. "She's taking some time off this week. See, I've got it all taken care of, so you might as well accept it."

I wanted to argue. I wanted to tell him he was crazy, that I had too much work to take care of, but the fact I could barely keep myself awake stopped me from uttering anything more than a brief *uh-huh*.

Breakfast was delicious. I don't know how my brother managed to turn everything he made into magic, but he had those mad skills I wished he spent more time on.

"What kind of spice did you use on the beef? It's delicious. And oh my god, it melts in my mouth. How? How do you do that?"

His beaming smile had me returning a similar one. "Seriously, you need to figure out how to bottle and sell it," I said. "That, or start your own restaurant."

"Not this again," he says, but I heard the half-heartedness in his voice. "Maybe once upon a time, I thought I wanted to do that, but not anymore."

By now, I'd devoured my wrap and contemplated a second one, but his comment stopped me. "What do you mean, not anymore?" I didn't like the idea that he'd given up his dream.

He shrugged. "There are other things I want to do instead. Things that are more important to me than owning my own restaurant. And besides, I can't be in multiple places at the same time, right? We've got this place to run."

My smile remained while I savored the last bit of coffee in my cup.

"Hey, question," I said, unsure if now was the right time to discuss the lock.

"I might have an answer," Bryce said.

"When did you change the knob on your bedroom door?" I watched him out of the corner of my eye.

He pushed his chair back and headed over to the sink, where he rinsed his coffee mug. "The other day; didn't I mention it? I pulled too hard on the door and dislodged something inside the handle."

For excuses, that one sucked, but I let it slide.

"Nope, you didn't mention it. So why not just buy a regular handle? Why get one with a lock on it?"

He turned the water on and didn't answer right away. "It was on sale," he finally said.

"So you are keeping your door locked now? Are you afraid I'll go in and snoop or something?" My tone was upbeat and light, without any hint of hurt or accusation, I hoped.

"Well, actually . . . our birthday is coming up, and I don't want you to see your gift."

I was a little speechless at that. I hadn't even thought about his gift and what to get him, especially considering our birthday wasn't for six more months.

"That's not fair," I muttered.

"What? That I've already thought about your gift. Let me guess: it's too soon for you to think about mine," he teased. "Seriously though, are we all good now?"

I nodded. "Sorry, I just . . . we've never really been ones to keep secrets from each other, and when I noticed your door was locked, I got a little offended."

"And you've been stressing about it ever since? Next time, ask, okay? Now, do me a favor and get dressed, please. Meet me in the truck in twenty minutes," Bryce said. "Don't worry about wearing anything too fancy, just be comfy. We've got a bit of a drive, and it'll be a long day. I'll make fresh coffee and bring a thermos with us."

There was nothing I considered more comfy, especially for a drive, than leggings with a loose-fit dress. It was a simple design, cinched in a little at the waist, with long sleeves. It was stylish with an air of comfort, especially paired with running shoes. The look of appreciation Bryce gave me said he approved of the outfit, which rankled me a little.

I didn't need his approval. I liked and appreciated it, but that look reminded me too much of Anthony.

"So where are we headed?" I climbed into the front seat of his truck and buckled up. My headache was only a dull throb now.

"It's a bit of a drive," he reminded me. "But it's all back roads through the woods, so it'll be gorgeous."

"You didn't buy a cabin, did you?" My brother had more than enough money saved up that he could have, if he wanted to.

"No, I didn't buy a cabin, although I hear Dixon's cottage is up for sale."

"You've got to be kidding me." Shock and disgust were the only things I felt at that moment. Only someone as sick and perverse as Donald Dixon would ever consider buying that property.

"I am, actually. From what I heard, his ex-wife took over the deed. She tore down all the buildings and is creating a living garden on site."

That was a little better, at least. Everyone said Donald Dixon's ex was innocent, but there was always a niggle of doubt for me. I mean, she was married to the guy for how many years and even ran a business with him. Don't tell me she didn't at least suspect something was off.

"You know," Bryce said, changing the subject, "I think we need to give Merilyn a promotion that includes a raise. She's basically your right-hand woman, isn't she? Running things when you're busy?"

I nodded. Merilyn did deserve a promotion, I agreed. That was actually on my list of things to talk to him about. "Is that why you have her taking over today? Like a test run?"

He shrugged. "It's not like she has to prove herself or anything. She's been with us for a long time. I was thinking about what you'd said a while ago, about living lives outside of the death business. I know you were talking about me and going back to cooking, but it applies to you, too. What would you do if you're not working and taking care of others?"

I had to think about it, to be honest. What would I do? I'd read. I'd work in the garden. I'd go for walks through town and attend more yoga sessions. Was that enough?

"You should start a book club, or volunteer at the library more, or, I don't know, take some floral decorating, cake decorating, or even basket weaving classes." He laughed as if realizing how lame those suggestions sounded.

"I have taken a floral class. I don't bake, and basket weaving? Where did that come from? You should know me better than that." I jabbed him with my elbow. Thankfully, his left hand was on the wheel.

"How about knitting, then? You could knit me a Christmas sweater." His brows danced on his forehead, and I realized he was only half teasing. "Or officially join a yoga studio instead of doing those drop-in classes. I hear a new one outside of town will be opening up soon."

Out of all his ideas, the yoga one piqued my interest. I'd done several yoga retreats over the years and would have loved to do another one.

"Really? How come you know this and I don't?" Especially since I was the one into yoga, and he wasn't. "I'm surprised Mona hasn't said anything about it; she's been moaning over needing to find a new studio for ages." Mona was the one who introduced me to yoga. The studio we used to belong to recently shut down, another casualty of Donald Dixon, unfortunately.

"What's with all this sudden concern about what I do in my spare time?" I asked. "I belong to a book club already; I do ladies' nights at the town hall every month, and I sometimes join Mr. Baxter on his walks at night. It's not like I sit at home, withering away."

"I just worry about you, that's all. I want you to live a full life that is separate from the family business." There was something he wasn't saying, something he was trying to hide from me, but I knew from the tightness of his shoulders and the way he kept flexing his hand along the steering wheel he wasn't ready to share those things with me — not just yet.

"So what kind of promotion are you thinking for Merilyn?" I turned the topic around. I had no doubt we were on the same page regarding Merilyn's future with our company.

"I think we give her the manager position. We haven't had anyone in that role for the past year or two. I know Dad didn't think we needed anyone, especially with the two of us running things, but I'm of a different mind."

See, I knew we were on the same page. In fact, I'd mentioned that very idea in the past. Unfortunately, Bryce was the type of person who liked to have ideas come from him instead of others. He'd hear what you had to say, think about it for a bit, and when he was ready to act on it, he'd conveniently forget where the original idea came from. Or from whom.

"I think it's a great idea. How should we tell her?" I wanted to do something special for her, make it a real 'thing' rather than pull her aside with the news.

"Why don't we have her over for dinner sometime this week? I have some homemade sausage I need to use up, and if I remember correctly, she's a huge fan of my sausage." He wore the biggest smile on his face.

Once upon a time, years ago, in fact, Merilyn was interested in my brother. That wasn't the case anymore; she had a partner whom she met last year.

"You do remember she just moved in with her boyfriend, right?"

He shrugged. "That means she can look over a menu, but not order." The twinkle in his eye was brighter now, his tone upbeat and joking.

It was nice to be out and about with him, both happy and relaxed. He was right — it was nice to get out of the house, to play hooky for the day, and go for a drive.

We were definitely on the back roads, and I had no idea where we were. Cell service was iffy back here, and the map on the touchscreen only showed us a single road in a green field.

"You know where we're going, right?" The scenery was beautiful, with endless trees and wildflowers.

"Just enjoy the ride. I'm actually surprised you haven't guessed where we're headed." Bryce said. "Need more coffee? I filled up the thermos just in case."

I took another sip from my travel mug and realized I was empty.

"It's been a while since we've gone for a drive; I figured I'd just enjoy it." I just hoped that there was no backwater cabin involved.

His fingers drummed on the steering wheel and I caught him casting me side looks.

"Bryce?"

"Since Dad's passing . . . well, it's been going on for a few years now. I've been keeping a huge secret from you, and it's always bothered me, but Dad said it was necessary."

At his words, I froze. Any time the words *secrets* and *Anthony* were mentioned in the same sentence, I knew it wouldn't be good.

"Secret or lies?" I found myself asking. I turned to watch him. I knew him inside and out, that even the minuscule twitch of a muscle in his jaw would tell me everything I needed to know — and there it was, a slight throbbing on his jawline.

"I'm tired of living two lives and hiding things from you, Brynn. We're twins, and we shouldn't have secrets, right?"

## CHAPTER TWELVE

"What do you mean, a double life?" I half turned toward my brother, desperate for answers I knew he wouldn't give. Not all at once, at least.

The way his fingers gripped the steering wheel told me he was stressed, and my tone wasn't appreciated.

I didn't care.

Ever since Anthony's death, he'd been different. I felt us growing apart, little by little, and I didn't like it. The distance between us was something I'd expect if he'd met someone . . . unless that's what it was.

"It's not what you think, Brynn," he said. "I haven't told you because, well . . . it has to do with the Family, and let's face it, that's been a subject you never want to talk about."

The Family. Damn it. I didn't need him to say the words to know exactly what he was about to tell me.

"Let me guess. All those overnight and weekend trips you did with Anthony weren't all business-related, were they? And what about when you're gone for days at a time? Again, not business, right?" Why hadn't I seen it all sooner? "You've been going to their compound, haven't you?" I tried to keep an accusatory tone out of my voice, but failed.

He nodded.

"Turn the truck around. Now." There was no way in hell I was going to that place. I'd made my feelings crystal clear on the subject.

"I'm not going to do that."

"I don't want to go there, Bryce. You know that."

He glanced over at me with a frown. "You only think you don't want to go there because of what Mom told you. But it's not like that."

"And how would you know?"

"Because Dad has been taking me there for years. I know those people, Brynn."

That was a hard pill to swallow. Not news, but to hear him admit something I'd always known . . .

"You know I want nothing to do with that nonsense."

"It's not nonsense. The Family *are* different, and if you give them a chance, you'll see they are nothing like Mom built them up to be." I heard the pleading, and whatever words I wanted to say, I didn't.

"I can't believe you." I stared out my side of the window, no longer paying attention to the scenery. I was seething inside, my anger building until it was at a boil.

The Family. Anthony's cult. A group of people gathered with one singular focus — a focus that wasn't welcomed by the general populace.

Anthony's whole *end-of-the-world* bullshit wasn't a belief I ascribed to, and I couldn't believe my brother had been suckered in.

I wished he were taking me to meet a girlfriend or future in-laws.

"So it's real, then. You really are Brother, to them." The fulfiller of their doomsday prophecy.

"And you are Sister," he said, with a hint of caution.

I made my disgust known with my sigh.

"Let me guess, that would make Anthony what . . . Father?"

Bryce shook his head. "No. He was an Elder, just like Mom was."

"Really?" To say I was shocked was an understatement. "Didn't he have a hand in creating this group?"

Again with the head shake. "A lot of what you believe is wrong. Mom had as much to do with the Family as Dad, and you know that. I think, after seeing it up close, it's not what you're going to expect."

"There was a reason Mom walked away from it, Bryce. You remember that, right?"

"What I remember is that Mom never told us the full story," he said. "The picture she painted was skewed."

"Because she wanted to protect us." That was an argument we'd had time and time again, and I was getting tired of repeating the same thing.

He had to know I wouldn't go into whatever he had planned with an open heart. I'd already stated my feelings, made known I wanted to be as far removed from that whole group as much as possible, and told him over and over again that I didn't believe in any of their fundamental beliefs.

So why bring me out here? What was his goal?

He slowed the vehicle down and made a left turn into the middle of nowhere. There was no sign, placard, or mailbox to indicate that anyone lived down what looked to be an overgrown pathway.

"This isn't their driveway, right?" My right hand gripped the door handle as Bryce maneuvered around large divots in the ground.

"We're going in the back way," he said. He leaned over the steering wheel, focused on the ground and staying out of the potholes.

"Why?"

"Why what? Listen, give me a moment to concentrate, okay?" The stress level in his voice ramped up from a three to an eight, and my grip on the handle tightened.

"Last time I came this way, I missed—" he turned the wheel tight to the left — "a few of these holes and got stuck. Had to get an alignment done on the truck afterward." He turned the wheel back toward the right, and we did a half dip before it straightened out. "Shoot, that was close."

Those holes were terrible. They weren't your average dirt road with bumps along the way; some of these holes were huge, and I understood why Bryce was careful not to hit them.

"They should really get these fixed." I gritted my teeth as we took a deep dip and heard a *scraaatch* beneath the truck.

"I said the same thing," he said, "but they keep this condition on purpose. They don't want many to use it."

"I think they don't want *anyone* to use it," I winced as we hit another deep rut. "Why didn't we go in via the front entrance, again?"

"Yeah," Bryce said under his breath, "I should have insisted. This cloak and dagger stuff is ridiculous."

I turned at his words. "Um, this is because of me?"

He shrugged.

"And you don't find that a little ridiculous? Why not just blindfold me or stuff me in the trunk?" My sarcasm at that point was very loud and very, very clear.

A tic on the side of his face appeared, one that I didn't see too often.

"Are you for real right now? Don't tell me they wanted you to do that?" It amazed me that he could understand what I was saying with my gritted teeth.

"Their privacy is important. Don't take it personally; every outsider gets blindfolded. I even had to be for the longest time."

That was too much.

The roadway smoothed out, and Bryce's grip on the steering wheel relaxed. I looked out the windows, and I noticed something that was missing.

"Just how far away from civilization are we?" I asked, noting the lack of power lines. "Please tell me they don't live in the dark ages without electricity and running water."

He barked out something resembling a chuckle. "They're self-sustained," he said. "They are completely autonomous, Brynn. It's really cool once you understand it. They rely on solar and wind energy, they have their own rainwater collection that gets filtered out, and they live off that for the most part. They do have large water tanks for dry spells and whatnot, but seriously, they are, for the most part, self-sustained. They grow their own food, and their protein is locally sourced. Most of their livable buildings have green roofs, too."

He was trying really hard to sell me on them, but it wasn't working. Didn't he understand that? Probably not. The more he talked, the more excitement filled his voice. What was it about those people to have grabbed his attention with such strength?

"Bryce, I hate to be the one to say this, but you drank their nasty Kool-Aid, and it's done a number on you. Don't expect me to do the same."

He remained silent, but his hands were tightly gripped around the steering wheel, knuckle-white. Considering the road was smoothing out, he probably regretted bringing me today.

I regretted coming, that was for sure.

# CHAPTER THIRTEEN

We arrived at a large metal gate, and Bryce entered a code at the keypad. I leaned forward and gazed up at the tall fence, immediately noticing the security cameras.

Did farms typically have surveillance and electronic keypads?

"Just keep an open mind, please," Bryce's voice was low, but he kept his gaze forward.

I said nothing. I did, however, take note of everything around me as we slowly drove through the opening gates.

I had a checklist in mind with everything that made The Final Family a legit cult. I was one hundred percent positive I'd be checking off all the little boxes by the end of this trip, too.

A few months ago, I started researching cults and how to know if you were in one. The stuff out there was crazy and made my skin crawl. I found a website that offered ten signs one might be living in a cult or commune and printed it off. The more research I did, the more I added things to that checklist. My goal was to provide my normally fact-driven brother with a list of irrefutable proof that he was involved in a doomsday cult.

The fencing and security cameras deserved a definite check mark.

On our left were half a dozen small cottages, each with wrap-around porches and what looked like a small shared playground in the backyard with picnic tables and swing sets. To our right was a large garden area behind a very long building with a covered porch on the front, where a group of children sat at tables. The building was massive, and the outdoor area was equally so.

"Does any of this look familiar? I mean, things have changed for sure, but anything?"

The lid of that memory box closed well and tight, and I didn't even have the key to open it if I wanted to. To be honest, I didn't want anything from this place to look familiar to me — not the picnic tables and playground, not the gardens, and definitely not the large building we were driving up to.

The second a memory sneaked in, it was pushed away without any help from me. Something blocked my childhood memories, and I always assumed there was a reason for it.

Sometimes, it was best not to hunt the monsters beneath the bed.

"That's the communal housing, with the main kitchen area and everyday rooms. The homestead is quite large, as you can see," Bryce said.

I caught a hint of something in his voice that had my nose turning up like I smelled a rotten apple. "Communal housing? So that's where everyone lives?"

He shrugged. "Honestly, you don't remember any of this? I mean, the cabins have all been renovated, and the communal building is new, but . . ." He passed me a glance, and the hope that I recognized the place was written all over his face.

I couldn't give him that satisfaction.

"Explain all this to me. That long rectangular building is the communal housing where everyone lives. But then there are those buildings . . ." I pointed toward some small cottages all lined in a row. "What are they for?"

He followed my gaze. "If you're a family unit, you live in the cottages, and if you're an elder, you live in the

Elder Home, but everyone else sleeps there in the communal housing."

*Sleeps.* Not *lives.* I noticed the wording and added another check on the cult form.

"Don't tell me, men and women are separated, right?" Was my sarcasm loud enough? "Like summer camp or something, I imagine."

I caught his questioning glance. "What's with the attitude? Wouldn't you want your privacy?"

I shrugged. He had a point. "So, does everyone get their own room, or is it one big happy family?"

He let out what resembled a huff and didn't respond as he drove around the homestead, compound, farm . . . what was it officially called?

It resembled a big farm with many buildings, similar to what you'd see on any drive through the countryside, only larger. Fenced and open gardens were everywhere, along with pickup trucks, rain barrels, wood crates, and general farm equipment. A few dogs roamed around, along with more free-roaming chickens than I could count.

There were *so* many chickens. Was that part of the communal living or regular farm living?

"Where are we headed?" I glanced back toward the crowd gathering. "What's with all the people?"

Bryce adjusted his mirror. "They're all excited to have you back."

I let the comment slide. "Hmm." He wanted me to keep an open mind, and I was trying. I expected to see everyone wear last-century clothing, with women in pioneer skirts and dresses and men looking like they just came out from hand plowing the fields. But instead, I saw lots of jeans and T-shirts. Sure, some women wore dresses with aprons tied tight around their waists, but for the most part, everything looked up-to-date and modern.

Not cultish at all. I was a little disappointed I couldn't check that off my list.

"All those kids? Shouldn't they be in school?"

"They probably were. They focus on homeschooling here."

But that, I could. I mentally added another check mark.

Someone off to the side waved us down. Bryce slowed and rolled down his window.

"Brother, you made it. I know you're to head to the main house, but why don't you go ahead and park over there for now? I can get one of the boys to move your vehicle to your spot up front later." He gave me a shy smile. "Nice to see you, Sister."

I thought I recognized him as someone who had come by the house a few times, but honestly, I wasn't sure.

Bryce slowly moved to the side and parked beside a massive black Ford F-450. Next to that truck, I felt like a dwarf sitting in a clown car.

"Whoa, hold on a second," I said, grabbing Bryce's arm. "Care to explain what exactly is happening?"

"Everyone is just excited to have you back," he repeated, condescendingly patting my hand. "Nothing crazy is going on, I promise." He opened his door. "Remember, you said you'd keep an open mind."

*Have me back.* My heart sank with a thud. Our mother would be rolling in her grave. She'd made me promise never to set foot on this land or allow Anthony to bring me here, for whatever reason. She told me if I did, I'd never leave. To say she'd scared me away from this place was an understatement.

"You made me break a promise I made to Mom; I hope you realize that," I muttered.

"What was that?" he asked over his shoulder.

I waved him off. It may have been my first time back in years, but he was a regular fixture here. My words and thoughts wouldn't matter. They certainly wouldn't move the mark at all, would they?

He led me back to the main area and introduced me to Uncle So-and-So and Aunt What's-Her-Name. The smile pasted on my face stretched my skin uncomfortably. The way they introduced themselves, they expected me to remember who they were. Didn't they realize I had no memories of my time here? That part of my memory was scrubbed away, wiped clean with bleach.

I pretended to ignore all the farm smells of manure and grime, taking tiny breaths as I focused on inhaling through my mouth and not my nose. I would never complain about the smells at work again.

My smile was more genuine, along with my interest, as a group of children came over with some drawings they'd made for me. One little girl in pigtails and a soft yellow dress handed me a picture of what I assumed was this farm, complete with all the buildings and gardens, and even what I thought was a dog. Another girl, a little younger, with dimples, drew a beautiful sunflower garden. She stood in the middle, and beneath her feet, she pulled the dirt and the roots of the flowers, with dots of colors in the roots.

I squatted down so I was eye to eye with her. "These are beautiful flowers, but what are these?"

Pointing to the dots, she giggled before whispering into the other girl's ear.

"She says those are the blessing jewels that give life to the flowers." She gave the little girl a side eye before blushing. "Mine is of our home. I hope you like it."

I looked at both the drawings and then at the girls, and my heart warmed in a way that surprised me. "I love them, thank you. I'll take them home and put them on my fridge, if that's okay."

Both girls nodded with enthusiasm.

"Here, let me take those and place them in your vehicle." Someone came over and took the pictures from my hand.

"Um, thanks."

"Would you like a tour?" Another girl stepped forward. "My name is Lily."

Lily had to be close to sixteen, older than the other two by years. She was almost as tall as me, wearing jeans and a strawberry shortcake T-shirt. Her hair was pulled back in a ponytail tied tight by a thick scrunchie. She was innocence and awkwardness rolled into one, and I saw a little bit of myself in her. I was the same at that age, unsure of how to straddle the difference between keeping my naivety and wanting to be seen as an adult.

A group of men surrounded Bryce, and he barely paid me any attention. So, was that how it was going to be? He brought me here to show me the place; now, he'd leave me alone while he did who knew what, with who knew whom?

I realized something: I was seeing a side of my brother I almost didn't recognize. With his shoulders dropped, his hands rested at his sides, and the way he stood, he had morphed into someone so different than the man I knew. He was relaxed, but with a sense of authority.

"Bryce?" I raised my voice just loud enough that he heard me.

"Go ahead. I'll meet you back here when the tour is done." Bryce smiled at Lily and nodded, almost as if he gave her permission.

A group of women stood off to the side, all watching me. Why? To see if I would turn down their offered hospitality? My mother raised me better than that.

One lady, in particular, was looking at me with a sense of worry or fear. When she realized I had noticed her, she quickly busied herself with whatever was in the basket she held tight against her hip.

"Sister?"

I gave Lily my full attention. "Lead the way," I told her. Just then, a tiny hand took hold of mine and tugged.

"Cousin Bea, you did your part," Lily leaned down and hissed softly. A blush bloomed along her face and neck when she realized I had heard. "Why don't you go draw Sister another picture for her fridge? Maybe one she can keep here to see when she returns?"

Little Bea's hand slowly slid from mine, and with a downcast face, she inched away from me until she was back at her picnic table.

To say I felt terrible was an understatement. "It's all right," I told Lily. "I don't mind if she joins us."

There was a tightening to Lily's lips as she glanced over her shoulder to a woman who stood at the front of the group. There was a slight shake of a head, a clear indication she was in charge, maybe not of everyone, but of the children at least.

"It's my honor to show you around," Lily said. "Things probably look different now than when you were here last." She gave me a side-eye. "Elder Faye told us that when you were little, there were only a few buildings, the gardens, and the farm."

"And Elder Faye is . . ." I asked.

"The mean-looking one wearing the pink apron," Lily said. "Don't look, though; she's watching us."

I casually glanced over my shoulder as if looking toward my brother. Sure enough, Elder Faye was watching us, and was the same woman who had shaken her head regarding little Bea joining our tour.

"Truth be told," I said, "I don't remember much from when I was little."

Lily had a puzzled look on her face. I expected her to question me, but she just shrugged. "Well, would you like to see the gardens or the communal home first?"

"How about you decide."

Lily led the way down a stone pathway that wound through a home garden and disappeared around the corner in the distance.

"This is the children's garden." She pointed to a strawberry patch. "Everyone has a role in our community, and the responsibility rests upon all our shoulders. We grow our own food, and we learn early on just how important it is to tend to the gifts God has given us through nature."

I mentally added another check to my cult theory on my list.

"We have all sorts of berries that we enjoy. Once we're inside, we have a little tasting tray the children have set up for you with items they've made themselves." Lily sounded very grown up just now, and I appreciated just how seriously she took her responsibility of being my tour guide.

After winding through the garden walkway, she directed me toward a back patio with a few tables and potted plants. "This is my area," she claimed. "It was my idea to create a little reading nook out here."

"It's quite lovely."

Before I could adequately take it all in, she opened a door into what looked like a great hall.

"This is our home," Lily announced.

The area was massive, so much more than I had expected when looking from the outside in. It reminded me of those photos of winter ski resorts, with huge main social areas, complete with two enormous fireplaces, seating everywhere from couches to sections to chairs and rockers, and bookshelves full of reading material and games. The one thing I noticed right away was the lack of television screens.

So, was this a secular-free zone? No TVs, no computers, no electronic devices at all? Another check on my cult list, if it was.

"This is where we spend our evenings. The family unit dynamic is important to us, so we like to socialize as a group. We're all on this journey together, and we can only become stronger if our core base is impenetrable."

Okay, now that sounded like something someone wrote for her.

"So, you spend time together in the evenings. Got it. What if you want some alone time? Like, to read or watch videos or . . ." My shoulder lifted with a *you-know* shrug.

Lily pointed to a corner with four seats, tables, and lamps. "We have a reading area for that. You can take books back to your room if you desire. It's not like you can't be alone," she said, with a tone of disgust that only a teenager could give. "We don't watch videos or have electronics, though. Our souls must be clean for the rebirth, and most outside influences are stained with evil." She glanced around, and I noticed a few adults off down the hall, watching us.

73

Clean souls for the rebirth: sure sounded like a cult to me. And I was raised in that? No wonder Mom took me out as soon as possible. "Got it. Cell phones are bad. Books are good." I was definitely adding another check to my list.

Lily continued the tour toward the main dining hall, where long rows of tables were set up. It looked like they ate family style, which was fine, and I couldn't really dock them for that.

"So, who does all the cooking? Do you all take turns?"

The way she gazed at me, I knew she was surprised at my lack of knowledge. "Preparing our food is only allowed among the anointed. Aunt Elise is in charge, and she has a core group she trusts to work with her in the kitchens. I hope to one day earn that privilege," Lily said.

Anointed to cook? Sounded like a bunch of crock to me.

"You like to cook? Bryce does, too. I'd eat grilled cheese and cereal for most of my meals if left to me. Or I'd order in." I tried to be personable with Lily; I could see that much of what she was saying was a front, an act for those listening in.

"Yes, Brother often comes down and prepares meals for us. He says it gives him great pleasure to use his gifts. In our old life, my mother cooked for a fine dining restaurant. I know she'd hoped I'd follow her path, but I must first prove myself."

I caught how she said *in our old life*, like it was something she missed dearly.

"How long have you been here?" I added a softness to my voice I knew couldn't be overheard.

"Almost three years. My mother died last year." Lily kept her gaze downward.

My heart broke for the girl, for the grief she must have gone through. Losing a mother, no matter the age, was never easy. "What about your father?"

She shrugged. "He died when I was young. This is all I have now."

"I'm so sorry." There was nothing I could have said to ease the hurt, to numb the pain, to change her life course,

74

even if I wished I could. I wanted to ask how her mother died, but I didn't.

"Sister!" A loud voice filled the room, and it took Lily nudging me to turn in response.

"That's Elder Elise," Lily whispered. "She's going to finish the tour."

I gave the woman a small wave. She stood in the distance, a dish towel flung over her shoulder, and nodded toward me as she wiped her hands on her apron.

Lily moved so she stood before me, her back to everyone else.

"You need to leave." The urgency in her voice was palpable. "They think you're here to fulfill the prophecy. Leave and never come back. It's not safe for you." She held out her hand and slightly twisted her body so that she was no longer facing me directly.

"Sister, come join me, will you?" Elder Elise called out, her voice loud and authoritative. "Lily, if you'd like to join the others in the kitchen, you can help the little ones with the tasting event."

"Remember what I said," Lily hissed before she walked away.

Remember what she said? How could I forget it? Her words were burned in my brain, her warning searing like fire.

# CHAPTER FOURTEEN

Aunt Elise was a battleaxe with a knife in her apron that she didn't hesitate to show me as she led me out of the great hall. She had a thing with flipping her utility knife open and closed, making me nervous.

"I trust your tour with Lily was nice," she said, her voice a little rough and hoarse, similar to what you'd hear from someone who grew up smoking a few packs of cigarettes on a daily basis.

"She was a sweetheart," I said. "I was sorry to hear that she lost her mother recently."

"She lost a member of her family, yes, it's sad. But she's not alone, and I hope you aren't implying she is."

Taken back by her abruptness, I struggled to find the words to respond. I opted to say nothing.

"Family is important to us. If your mother had stayed, you would understand that."

"You knew my mother?" For some reason, this surprised me.

"Of course I did. I'm one of the originals, thus an Elder." The way she said it, it was like I should have understood that by now.

"My apologies," I said, trying to be respectful even though inside, all my bristles were up. "I'm really not all that familiar with your way of life. Neither my mother nor Anthony shared much about my time here as a child."

By her look, I knew right away she found that hard to believe.

"That is unfortunate for you, then. I assume you'll be joining the initiates group. They'll be meeting in a few hours."

Initiates group?

"I'm really not sure how long we're here for. I know Bryce wanted to show me around a bit."

"Which is what we are doing right now," she tsked. "He has other business to attend to, and we don't need to bother him."

My hackles were up now, on the inside and out. "Actually, if I want to bother him, I will." Regardless of who she was within the group, she meant nothing to me, and I wasn't about to be cowed by her — Elder or not.

"Sister—" she stopped and turned, hands behind her back — "I am sorry. I'm treating you like a cousin; you are more than that. Please accept my apologies."

"No apologies are needed," I said to keep the peace. Her smile felt slightly forced, but I ignored it. "Why don't we start over?" I continued. "And maybe you could explain the titles used within the . . ."

"The Family. That's what we call ourselves. The official name is The Final Family, but that's rarely used."

I cocked my head as if I was intrigued. "Why The Final Family?" I already knew the answer, I thought, at least.

"Your mother really secluded you from all of this, didn't she? Elder Anthony, as well? To say that's a disappointment is an understatement. With Brother's involvement, we all assumed that you would at least have the basic understanding of something you're so integral to."

She sighed deeply, her ample chest heaving. "We are called The Final Family because we are the last true family God has created before the rebirth will occur."

I wanted her to clarify exactly what the rebirth was, but she held up her hand, her mute instruction to remain silent.

"As for our titles, they are more like designations. Being called an Elder bears the heavy weight of responsibility. We were here from the beginning and are responsible for those beneath us. We are the leadership, the ones who ensure our community standards are kept and that we don't allow secularism to encroach and rob us of our future joy. We deal with the conflicts and the decisions. Aunts and Uncles have joined together to build up our community. We disagree with the legalized version of marriage, but we instead embrace the full family dynamic. Once you have a child, you become an Aunt or Uncle. Cousin belongs to everyone else — from the youngest child to the oldest single adult among us."

The idea seemed very basic and undoubtedly carried more nuance than she was explaining.

"You will learn more in the initiate class," Elder Elise said.

I only nodded. I had no intention of taking part in that class, *thank you very much*, but there was no reason she needed to know that.

"Let's walk, shall we? There's something I would like to show you." She led the way down a pathway of white stones that wound through a field of wildflowers. At the crest of a hill, some white crosses stood.

"We created a place of honor for your mother and father," she said. "Your father provided us with some of your mother's ashes, and we celebrated her life and blessing here. We did the same with your father when he passed. Your brother was kind enough to share his ashes with us, too."

Excuse me?

"We have a family mausoleum in Bervie Springs," I said, staring at the crosses. "I'm not sure whose ashes you buried, but they are not my parents."

"The one in town is only for show." She dismissed my words. "There is a spot beside each parent for you and Brother," Elder Elise continued.

For show? What was she talking about?

"My mother and father are buried in Bervie Springs," I reiterated. "I'm sorry to disappoint you, but I won't be buried here."

I noticed the other crosses beside where we stood. "Who are those for?"

"Those are Elders who have given their blessings," she said. "All of this will be explained . . ."

"In the initiates' class, yes, so you've said. I want to know why you believe my parents are buried here when I know they aren't." If Anthony had made last-minute wishes and told Bryce, that I could understand. But my mother walked away from all of this, so why dishonor her choice by placing a cross in her memory in a graveyard on a hill?

Unless it was all Anthony, once again showing his true colors. He'd wanted her here, plain and simple. He'd probably also discussed that with Bryce, and no one bothered to fill me in.

"This is a place of honor, where we come and remember their blessings," Elder Elise continued, either oblivious to my anger and shock or not caring that I had no idea about any of it.

On the crosses were small white pebbles. Elder Elise took one and brought it to her lips before she laid it back down. "I honor your blessing," she said in a whisper.

My hands fisted at my side as I struggled to contain the words I wanted to say. Unloading on her wouldn't be fair; it was my brother who deserved to feel the full force of my emotional turmoil.

A bell sounded in the distance. Elder Elise gave a little clap, and a smile appeared. "The little ones are ready to treat you to their desserts. Will you join us? They've put a lot of effort into this moment for you."

We slowly walked back along the pathway. It wasn't until we were well away from the small cemetery that I finally spoke.

"Why?"

"Why what?" A crack in her usual calm composure appeared, an exasperation, but I didn't feel it was toward me. "So many of your questions should already have been answered by either your mother, your father, or even Brother. I'm very disappointed, not in you, but for you."

I didn't care about her disappointment, to be honest. "Why did the children put in a lot of effort for me? It's obvious I'm not a part of this life, of this family—"

Elder Elise paused and reached out toward me. "Surely you don't believe that? You are the very foundation of this Family," she said. "Not just that, but you are also the fulfillment of the prophecy," she continued. "As to why the effort, that's not even something that should have to be explained. As soon as Brother told us you were coming, the preparations began. We have all been waiting for you to finally return home to where you belong. You must understand that."

That was the problem. I didn't understand. But it wasn't for Elder Elise to explain anything to me. That was on my brother.

She brought me back into the great hall and led me to a table. A handful of children lined up against a wall, each with a plate in their hand.

For the next twenty minutes, I sampled every fruit dessert made for me while I fawned over the children responsible for the treat.

When Bryce joined us, the smile on my face was real.

"I hate to interrupt," he said, concern written all over his face, "but we need to leave."

Immediately, anyone near me backed away, and the children were sent off to another room. Elder Elise appeared at my side, her hand on my elbow, forcing me to stand.

"Already?" she asked.

He nodded.

"What? What's going on?" I asked him.

Aunt Elise clapped her hands together three times, the clap-clap-clap echoing in the room. "The time for the preparation is now." Her voice thundered through the room.

80

"What is she talking about?" I whispered to Bryce.

"We need to leave, Brynn. Please don't make a scene. I'll explain it all later." I heard the lie in his voice, and I knew he knew it.

We stood silently at the walkway's edge while waiting for someone to bring up his truck. When it arrived, I noticed a blindfold on the passenger seat.

"Is that for me?"

"We don't have time to leave the back way," Bryce said, opening the door for me. "I hate asking it of you, but please?"

I swallowed hard. I would have argued, but everyone was watching us, and causing a scene was the last thing Bryce wanted.

"Of course," I said, my voice soft with a bit of bitterness added to it. I sat down, adjusted the seatbelt, and pulled the blindfold over my eyes.

I hated the dark. I developed the phobia as a small child, always afraid of a ghost or dead person waiting around the corner to attack me. I needed a nightlight to sleep as a child, and even now, I still had one out in the hallway and hated sleeping with my door closed.

"Bryce, what is going on?" I sat there, hands clamped tightly in my lap, and tried to envision the scenery as we drove on the gravel road.

"It's the time for preparation," he said, his voice taut and full of stress.

"What does that even mean?"

He remained silent for the longest time before I heard him exhale through his nose. "You're not going to understand, and you're going to inundate me with a million questions, but I don't have the emotional or mental capacity for that right now, okay? I need to get you home, and then I need to get ready."

"Get ready? Do you mean you're coming back here?"

"No, not today. Just . . . can you let it be for now? I promise I'll explain everything later, but right now I just . . ."

I knew from his tone that he wasn't going to say more, so I didn't push it.

"Fine. Keep your damn secrets. Just let me know when I can take this stupid blindfold off, please."

He turned on some music, and we sat silently for what felt like forever, but it was probably only fifteen minutes.

My anger and anxiety grew the longer we sat in silence. Ants crawled along my skin, my throat a Sahara, and my insides twisted every which way. I knew all of this was from being in the dark, from the panic attack I struggled to hold off from hitting me full force.

"Now?" I practically begged to have the blindfold removed.

"Yes, sorry."

I tore the fabric off and tossed it to the ground. It took three long inhales, each breath held for a count of five, before I felt any semblance of calmness.

"Sorry, Brynn. I hated asking that of you." He sincerely sounded apologetic.

We were now on the main road, and I recognized the scenery from earlier.

I reached for a water bottle and drank until the dryness in my throat disappeared.

"Then why did you?"

"They're really serious when it comes to their privacy."

I snorted. "Fine, but why make me keep it on for so long? I could have removed it once they couldn't see the truck, right?" It was just him and me — no one would have known.

"That's not how they do things."

I bit my lip while I ran that through a few times. "They or we?"

"I'm sorry?" He glanced over.

"They are really serious about their privacy or we are?"

He shook his head. "I don't understand."

I sighed. "You know how claustrophobic I get, especially in the dark, so you could have had me take the blindfold off a long time ago. Instead, you made me sit here in fear, almost having a panic attack, for what?"

"Because . . ." he didn't finish. "Yeah, I see what you're saying."

"Why?" I wasn't about to let it go, even though I knew he wanted me to. I had a point to make and needed him to understand it.

"I said I was sorry."

"Yep, you did." I nodded. "But if I wanted to return, would I have to be blindfolded again, or would we go the back way like earlier?"

His fingers drummed on the steering wheel, and I knew the hamster wheel in his brain was working overtime. "Are you saying you want to go back?"

Hmm. What a great question. Would I go back? I was curious, for sure. Curious about the people there who knew Mom, who had known me when I was younger, and about the pull they seemed to have on Bryce. About what it all meant.

Going back meant getting answers, answers no one had ever wanted to provide.

"Elder Elise said I should join the initiate class."

The grin that grew on his face quickly disappeared when he glanced over at me and caught my frown.

"It would help to explain a lot of things," he said with caution.

"I'd rather you just explained them to me. Like what a blessing is, and why ashes from our parents are in a home-made cemetery back at that farm."

His inhale came from a dark place I knew nothing about. "That was one of Father's instructions to me," he said. "He knew you wouldn't understand, so . . ."

"So I was kept out of the loop." I clamped my lips together and counted to five. "Kept out of the loop, and never told about another resting place designated not just for our parents, but for us as well. Except I never expressed any interest in being buried there, Bryce." I worried my hands together, the need to focus on something other than the anger building inside of me, stronger than I'd ever felt.

"The initiate class does a great job of laying the ground-work for why the Family exists and why we are so important," he said, ignoring my comment. "Especially now. Especially us."

He kept his focus straight ahead, but he white-knuckled the steering wheel.

"Riiighht. Us. The prophecy." It was the bane of my existence, the lie I grew up with, the one Mom tried to shield me from. "The one where you and I are twin flames, and we'll bring in the utter destruction of humankind, and only those who join the Family will be saved? That prophecy?"

"It's true, you know. All of it is true."

I closed my eyes to his words. I wished there was a word for the emotion I felt. Still, the kaleidoscope of hurt, fear, unease, anger, bitterness, and worry all morphed into some-thing stronger, something more palpable, with sharp edges that cut into the fabric of our twin bond.

# CHAPTER FIFTEEN

*Present Day*

The darkness around me is smothering, like a weighted blanket around my neck suffocating me.

I try to see past the blackness circling me, and I'm instantly hit with pangs of pain, filling my brain and surging through my veins like bolts of lightning.

The darkness swallows my gasp.

I've been moved. There's a dank smell coming from beneath me, around me, and the bed I used to be on is gone.

I'm scared.

"Brother? Elder Allison? Anyone? Someone help me, please?" Every word I scream out tears through me, slicing my throat one syllable at a time.

My cries are met with silence.

I lift my head only an inch and get hit by even more pain, but this time around my neck.

My hands race to my throat, but they stop before I can barely lift them. I pull, yank, and use every ounce of strength in my arms until I grasp the futility. My wrists are bound by coarse rope, just like my neck. My whimper breaks that silence.

I hear a slight click, and then a flare of light in a corner illuminates the room.

Not just the room, but the fact that I'm not alone.

Sir is here. The shadows lingering around his illuminated area move around him. He's sitting on what looks like a wood crate, and beside him is an old camp lantern. His legs are crossed, and I can't read the look on his face.

"I wish it hadn't come to this." He tsks, like I'm a child getting disciplined. Everything about him projects danger, that I'm in danger. "But you went after someone dear to me, and well, let's face it, you've proven you can no longer be trusted."

My arms drop to my sides, the rope loosening with the action. I move one arm up and feel the hold tighten against my other wrist. It must be one single piece of rope binding me, running beneath the cot I'm on.

"A blessing is best given when it's a choice, but let's be honest, I'll take what I can get."

I ask the only question I have. "Why?"

He waves his hand in dismissal. "You already know the answer to that. Do better."

Do better? What's better than asking why is my life so important?

"You may not believe in the prophecy, but everyone up there—" he points upward — "does. Why else would you be raised to believe you and Brother are so important? Your destiny is here, and yet, you're willing to condemn us all, aren't you?"

I want to believe him. I hear the sincerity in his voice, but this isn't something I can or want to be a part of.

"We're about to ascend, to be reborn . . . you don't want to take that away from us, do you?"

He's placing this all on me, and yet he's the one doing this. He's the one forcing this on me.

"I don't want to die," I say. It hurts to speak, but the pain reminds me I'm still alive, that there is still a chance of staying that way.

"No one wants to die, and yet, death is inevitable. You, of all people, know that. In fact, you make your living based on that simple, universal fact, don't you?"

"I don't want to die for a lie."

"Tsk, tsk, you honestly don't believe that, do you? The foundation of our belief isn't a lie. Every belief system started somewhere, Sister." He shrugs. "Whether it's psychedelics, entheogens, or even cannabis, they've all been used since the beginning of time when it comes to establishing religious beliefs. I won't even get into the Abrahamic faiths using substances to elicit spiritual awareness and experiences. Even the symbolic holy anointing oil used on Jesus had medicinal plants in its substance." He's got a grin on his face that tells me he's enjoying this.

I don't know how to respond, what words to say to argue against him and his logic.

"You are the blessing. There is no running from that."

An invisible rope wraps around my chest and tightens until the pain echoes throughout my body. "I don't want to be the blessing."

"It's not up to you to decide, though, is it?" Sir's voice rings hollow. "God has said that it's time, and it's all working out just perfectly, don't you think?"

The brutal realization of what's going to happen to me hits home. My decision, my choice, my right to existence is being taken away, and there's nothing I can do about it.

Mom tried to protect me from this. She wanted me to live and embrace everything life offers, but I threw that all away when I agreed to come back here.

This is what Anthony destroyed me for. He wanted me broken, a husk of a person who followed orders and never fought for herself.

In the end, he won.

# CHAPTER SIXTEEN

*Then*

If ever there was a day from hell, it was today.

By the time I locked the kitchen door behind me, the clock on the stove said it was after midnight. For the past three hours, all I had wanted to do was soak in the tub and be surrounded by absolute peace.

My brain felt like a symphony of caterwauling kittens begging for food on repeat. I couldn't do it anymore. I needed silence.

I was used to subdued settings, soft classical music playing in the background, the hushed tap-tap-tap of shoes on the carpet, sniffled sobs, and whispered words of comfort from loved ones.

All my life, a low cadence of somberness surrounded me.

But tonight, I needed to be embraced by stillness, to have the quiet cleanse me from the sludge of heaviness that coated me today.

Today was not a day I wanted to repeat ever again.

First, my staff abandoned me during a service, and then we had a later-than-normal viewing tonight with a family reeling from the death of their teenage son. Their grief had not only been palpable, but it had been draining, too.

Some families were like that. Some wore their grief like clothing; it was part of who they were, and their aura was subdued and somber. Others wore their grief like an accessory, loud and recognizable, something to be felt by everyone around them. The family tonight needed to express their loss loudly, and that loudness was draining for someone who was an introvert.

I noticed a low hum in the house coming from upstairs. Bryce's truck wasn't outside, unless he had parked it in the garage. I stood still and listened. The hum now included a voice — his voice.

I took the steps, one at a time. Exhaustion settled deep into my bones like it belonged there. I was tempted to call out, but something stopped me.

A sliver of light filled the darkened hallway from his room. The hum was louder now, almost melodic, with Bryce speaking over the top of it.

"This helps, thank you," he said. "I appreciate you sending this; it'll help me know what to expect. I wish I'd been able to be there for the last one, but . . ." He paused, nodding as he listened to whomever was speaking. "Yeah, no copies will be made, and I'll return the USB drive this weekend."

I stood just outside his door and peered in. Bryce's back was to me, phone up to his ear, and he stood at his desk, staring at a video on the screen.

That was where the hum came from.

At first, the images didn't make sense. Whatever he was watching was dark, with shades of light that came and went. Was he watching a movie? A clip of something? My brother was not into horror movies or intrigued by things that went bump in the night, so I had a hard time imagining he'd be watching anything remotely scary.

And scary was exactly what I was seeing on the computer screen.

The humming intensified as the scene expanded, so it became clear that a group of people, all in hooded robes, were walking through the woods at night, with lanterns lighting the way at their feet.

They came to a building with a large closed barnwood door and stood there, the volume of whatever they were humming or chanting growing. Nothing happened; there was no movement, and no one even spoke, but suddenly, the doors creaked open as if of their own volition, and a pathway of candles led the way further into the building.

The vibe was very ceremonial. Dark ceremonial.

Bryce leaned forward, the palms of his hands planted on his desk. He blocked my view, so I couldn't see what happened as the people walked inside the building.

I couldn't see it, but I heard it.

A man's voice rose above the noise, eerily familiar and yet . . . not. There was an authority to his voice, a charismatic pull that made you want to listen to him.

The chanting continued, building to a crescendo until a high shriek broke through the noise, followed by a piercing cry that was quickly drowned out by the group.

And then there was nothing.

No sound, no humming, no chanting, no crying. Just deadly silence.

My stomach knotted and twisted, and images played in my mind of what could be happening on that screen — images I wanted nothing to do with.

The following sounds had me backtracking toward the stairs, everything inside me roiling with fear and disgust. I was careful that my steps wouldn't alert Bryce to my presence.

I tried to push those sounds, the images, from my mind. If there was one thing I was good at, it was compartmentalization, and if ever I needed a night to excel at that skill, it was tonight.

Once downstairs, I did my best to make my presence known. I banged the cupboard doors. I turned on the kettle and emptied the dishwasher with a heavy hand. It didn't take long for the sounds to reach Bryce, and the thump-thump-thump of his footsteps down the stairs alerted me to his presence.

"When did you get home?" The fact my voice hid the revulsion that skimmed over my body was a miracle.

"An hour or so," he said, as he began helping me unload the dishwasher.

"Where's your truck?" What a stupid question to ask, because the answer was obvious, but I was at a loss for what else to say to fill the awkward void between us.

"In the garage. Sorry, I should have texted you. I saw the lights on over in the office and figured you were working late, and didn't want to disturb you."

My brow arched.

"Then you would have noticed the staff vehicles, too, right? You didn't think to come over and see if we needed help?" While he put the silverware away, I grabbed a lemon, cut it in half, and squeezed one half into my cup and the other into his. I then added a bit of honey, stirring the two while waiting for the kettle to boil. My throat was a little scratchy from all the talking today, and nothing sounded better than a hot mug of honey and lemon tea.

"I should have. I'm sorry," Bryce said, turning the boiling kettle off and pouring the water into our waiting mugs. "I guess I just figured you had it all under control."

I couldn't have hidden my snort if I'd wanted to.

"What happened?"

"What didn't? The Miles service was this morning." I sipped my tea, letting the sweet honey liquid swirl on my tongue.

"Okay?" From Bryce's expression, he had no idea of the issue.

"Almost everyone called in sick. Guess there was a twenty-four hour flu going around that miraculously cleared up in time for tonight's viewing."

"Damn," Bryce said, rubbing the back of his neck. "That or they were making a statement," he said.

I shrugged. That was precisely what they were doing, and I got the message loud and clear. Devon Miles, an associate of Donald Dixon, had been found guilty for his involvement in Dixon's criminal activities. Years ago, at the time of his parents' passing, he'd pre-paid for his own funeral service, so whether or not I wanted our funeral home to be the one responsible for his burial preparations, I had no choice.

Not that I would have said no, anyway. I believed that everyone deserved a proper funeral, regardless of who they were or what they'd done.

Not everyone on our staff agreed with me, which they made very clear today.

"I forgot that was today," Bryce said. "You should have reminded me."

"It's in the business calendar," I reminded him.

He bowed his head and stared down into his cup of tea. "You're right. I've been . . . slacking, haven't I?"

I didn't answer. My brother wanted me to absolve him, and that wasn't something I was willing to do.

I knew him too well. If I let him off too easy, he would continue to take off and leave me to deal with things.

Running the funeral home was supposed to be a joint thing. We were full partners, helping one another and supporting each other. Yet more and more, he was ditching those responsibilities and leaving me to run the viewings and services.

"So, where did you go? What emergency happened that you had to take off without any warning? And please don't tell me you were invited to play golf with some celebrity or something."

I didn't even know why I asked. The obvious answer for why he left was, of course, because of the Family. It was the answer that made sense.

More and more, Bryce was turning into Anthony, and I hated it.

Hated. It.

"Not quite," he said. "I was issued a last-minute invitation to join someone at a seminar, and I couldn't say no."

Another seminar? He could read the skepticism on my face.

"I should have told you about it, rather than rushing off so quickly."

"You think?" I said. "What was it on?"

Bryce grabbed his leather bag, pulled out a bunch of papers and brochures, and set them out on the island so I could see them.

I'd expected to see information related to cooking, or something for our business, but instead, he showed me information regarding solar panels and wind turbines, a checklist of one hundred things required to live off the grid, and price comparison lists for a whole slew of other things.

Did he want to add more solar panels to the property? The roofs of both buildings were already covered in them.

"Going off the grid?" I grabbed one of the brochures and held it up, extremely puzzled.

"Cool, right? It's all I can think about lately."

"Care to share?"

The grin on his face confirmed I had asked the right question. "Have you ever thought about living off the grid? I mean . . . what it would take to do it? Think about it. The government wouldn't control how you live, and you wouldn't be helping huge corporations line their pockets . . . you'd be in control of your destiny." The level of excitement in his voice raised the longer he spoke.

"Living off the grid?" Of all the things he could have said, that surprised me the most. "No, Bryce, it's not something I've actively considered. I like my comfort, thank you very much. That includes knowing I'll always have running water, a toilet to flush, and the ability to let someone else fix the problem if a wire is down or something. Seriously, can you see me living off the grid in the middle of the woods?"

He must have heard the disapproval and doubt because the smile etched on his face disappeared.

"You're not serious, right?"

93

He shrugged. "I find it intriguing, to be honest. It would be different, sure, but I think I could do it."

My eyebrows trudged upward as I struggled to process his new interest.

"Okay, well . . . um . . ." For whatever reason, there was a sense of uncomfortableness between us now. I didn't miss the way he'd personalized his interest. "It's not really my cup of tea, I guess," I said.

"Yeah, I guess. I find it interesting." He sounded like a small child who was told the picture he drew was ugly.

I didn't know what to say. Of all the reasons why he'd taken off so suddenly, going to a seminar about living off the grid was not what I'd expected. If he'd told me an old friend had an emergency, then okay, I could understand that, but a seminar about a subject he'd never once mentioned to me before? I wasn't buying it.

"So, who was it that invited you?"

He didn't answer.

"Let me guess, this is a new interest because of them, isn't it?" I didn't need to clarify who *them* were.

He again didn't answer, which made my blood boil, but I knew I needed to remain calm. Today had been a day, and my body was exhausted. That had to be why I felt so cranky.

I wanted to ask about the video he'd been watching, but I wasn't ready to go there. Not yet.

"You'll be around tomorrow, right?" I changed the subject for both our sakes. "We've got that viewing for eleven, and I could use your help."

He nodded. "I'll be there. Listen, I am sorry for my slack. It's not fair to leave everything to you all the time. I think . . . I think we should hire more support."

"Why? So you can have more time off?" I wasn't sure how I felt about that. I never took time off, rarely took a sick day, and the last vacation I had was . . . oh, *never*.

"No, no. To give us both some breathing room. This shouldn't be a twenty-four/seven job for us. We should be able to have lives outside of the funeral business, right? At least, think about it, okay?"

He yawned, which had me yawning.

"Let's chat about this another day, maybe?" I suggested, ready for bed. "When it's not after midnight, and we don't have to get up early the next day?"

I left him without waiting for his reply, not liking the change in the dynamic between us.

# CHAPTER SEVENTEEN

The past few nights, I tossed and turned. Every time my eyes closed, imagined scenarios played out in the dark, my mind piecing together fragmented images to accompany the sounds I'd heard.

I was exhausted from the lack of sleep.

I thought of bringing it up with Bryce, but I never did. Deep down, I knew the reason why I didn't ask about that video or why I caught him watching it again the next day, too: I was afraid of the answer.

I rubbed the bridge of my nose, yawned, and reached for my now-empty coffee cup. How many of these had I drunk today? Three? Four? The way my stomach felt, it was at least two too many.

The numbers on the screen in front of me swam, and no matter how many hours I spent at this desk, I wouldn't get any more work done today. The idea of being curled up in my chair at home with a hot mug of tea and a good book sounded more appealing than remaining here.

My phone rang. I wanted to ignore it, have the call go to voicemail, and call it a day. But life as a funeral home owner was never simple. Our business relied on one inescapable fact — the need for people to die.

"Good afternoon, Kern Family Funeral Home. Brynn speaking, how may I help you?"

"Hey, Brynn, it's Elizabeth Fields." The exhaustion in the woman's voice on the other end of the line prepared me for what I was about to hear.

Elizabeth Fields ran the local retirement home. She only ever called me directly when something was wrong.

"Elizabeth, I take it this isn't a call to grab a coffee, is it?"

"I wish. We've got a case of pneumonia running through here, and I wanted to give you a heads-up, so you can be prepared."

My heart sank at her words.

"How bad is it?" Now wide awake, I scrolled through a file on my computer and pulled up a document used for situations like this in the past. This was one of the first things I'd done after school: create a standard protocol for different situations we might face as a business.

This file included a series of checklists, not just for me, but also for the staff. It was easy to forget things and to let standards slide when things got busy, but just because it happened didn't mean it was right or necessary.

"Two residents won't last the night, and I've already started a list of others who are sick."

"I'm sorry to hear that. Is there anything we can do, besides the obvious? Are you okay?" I considered Elizabeth a friend, and I knew how personally she took every loss at her workplace.

"It's never easy when one of my own passes, you know that. They are like family to me."

As I hung up, any hope of taking a day off disappeared. The next few weeks could get chaotic, and there was no time like the present to prepare. The last time something like this had happened, Anthony had been alive.

If there was one thing Anthony excelled at, it was finding calm in the chaos. I never quite knew how he did it, never understood how he could remain so at peace when everyone else was stressed, and yet, he did.

It was something I wished to emulate.

There weren't many qualities within Anthony that I liked, but that was one of them. It had been almost four months since he'd passed, and while Bryce still mentioned him and said often how he missed him, I didn't.

Truth be told, I didn't miss him, didn't miss his presence, didn't miss his constant barrage about every aspect of my life — when he took notice.

But I didn't miss him mainly because his presence wasn't gone.

I felt him more and more as the days went on. I felt and saw him embodied within my brother, and I hated it.

The brother I once knew was a mirage.

There was a photo of the two of us on my office desk. That one would always be my favorite of all the pictures we'd taken together. There was a carefree vibe between us, and taken just moments before we burst out laughing at some inside joke. That vibrancy, visible on our faces, that shared intimacy only twins could know . . . it was all there in that photo. We'd never been closer.

Now, we'd never been so far apart.

I rarely saw him anymore. If he wasn't in the basement working, he went off to who knew where, with one person or another. We'd sip our coffee together in the morning, and that was about it. Often, I'd walk into the house late at night, and he'd leave me a dish of something delicious, but it was rare that we'd share a meal together.

Where once our conversation had been easygoing and open, now he was cryptic when answering questions, or he'd change the subject completely, brushing off any of my inquiries, especially when I asked where he was going or if it had anything to do with that group.

"Hey, Brynn?"

Merilyn poked her head into my office and waved a sheet of paper at me.

"You mentioned you wanted to know when that shipment arrived from the new vendor," she said. "I think you'll be impressed."

"Good, because I just got off the phone with Elizabeth Fields. Several of their residents have pneumonia."

"Oh no," Merilyn said. "Okay, tell me what you need from me, and I'll do it."

I appreciated her words more than she probably knew. I felt a deep need to prove that I could handle this, not only handle it but also do it better than Anthony.

Stupid and prideful, but it was my time to prove I was more than he ever gave me credit for.

"I'd like to sit down with you and Bryce later and go through some things, if that works for you?"

She nodded. "Just tell me when."

We walked together through the building, down to the loading dock, where staff unloaded a van full of flowers. The assortment was a little overwhelming: everything from casket and standing sprays to simple floor and table arrangements.

"So, what do you think?" Merilyn asked, while I took in the plethora of flowers filling the platform.

"Let me see that invoice again." I grabbed the sheet from her hand and tallied everything up. I couldn't believe the price.

"Hey, Brynn, thanks again for ordering these." Krissy Barns was a local florist. She set down another box of smaller arrangements. "We've been trying for years to work with you, but there were never any openings."

"Are you sure you charged me correctly?" I asked. There was no way she had, considering how much product she was dropping off.

"Of course. It's what we agreed upon, isn't it?" She looked at the invoice in my hand and nodded. "Is there an issue?"

Issue? Not at all. I was just surprised. For years, we'd used a floral company from out of town to provide all the arrangements for the services and weekly refreshers for the vases within the funeral home. Fresh flowers were a necessity to help mask the other odors. Their prices were more than double what Krissy charged.

"Honestly, I can't tell you how much I appreciate you giving us a chance. If you're happy with these, I will email you photos so you can update your catalog."

"Oh, I think I'm more than happy, Krissy," I said. "You did exactly what I'd hoped — created something elegant and warm, with a fresh twist. We've had the same dated look with our arrangements for too long."

Anthony had set up the contract with the other florist. When I was researching ways to cut costs, I'd been shocked at the monthly price tag we'd been paying. The delivery cost alone had been ridiculous.

It didn't take me long to put out feelers for new bids. As soon as word got out, I was inundated with proposal after proposal. I finally selected a local florist, thrilled to help out a fellow community member, and loved the idea that it would save us money as well.

"Hey, what's going on here?" Bryce's voice called out from the loading bay door.

Surprised, I turned with a questioning look on my face. "Well, hello, stranger. I thought you were gone for the day?"

"Oh, yeah, something came up, so here I am," he said, his brows knitted in confusion. "Um, why all the flowers? I thought we were having a slow week?"

"We are. Rather, we were. We need to chat about that afterward, but," I motioned for him to stand beside me. "You know Krissy."

"Of course I do," he said, finally putting a smile into his voice.

"Well, you remember how I put out a request for new bids for florals? I'm thrilled to say she's hit it out of the ball-park and is now officially our new supplier."

"New supplier?" He stepped back, pulling me with him. "What was wrong with our regular one?"

I gave him a look that hopefully told him to shut up before I turned back to Krissy. "I'll get this to our accountant, and they'll get in touch to set up the account with you."

I nudged Bryce to follow me back into the building, leaving Merilyn to deal with the flowers, but first, I snagged a smaller arrangement for my desk.

"Seriously, what are you doing?" Bryce asked, as we walked through the hallway.

"Have you ever looked at the books? We are overpaying for so many services, it's ridiculous." I lowered my voice so as not to be overheard.

"But why did we change suppliers for the flowers? What was wrong with using the other?"

"The other is more than double what Krissy will charge us. Seriously, Bryce, we talked about this. With Krissy being local, we don't have that ridiculous delivery fee, for one. I swear the other increased their prices every quarter."

Bryce shrugged. "Everything is more expensive nowadays, but that doesn't mean you cancel contracts. You should have told me, and I would have seen what I could do to renegotiate things."

"Negotiate things?" Was he serious? "We've had nothing but issues with them for ages now. I've been complaining for at least the past year."

"And Dad took care of things, didn't he?"

Took care of things? No. What Anthony did was tell me to leave the running of the business to him. He didn't care that we frequently received wrong orders or, even better, sometimes those orders never showed up, period. I was the one who had to frantically call every florist shop around to find replacements at the very last minute.

"What's the issue here?" I asked him, as we approached my office.

Bryce shrugged before he flopped down on my couch. "I don't think you should make all these changes without consulting me first."

It took me a sweet second to regroup after that comment.

"Which was exactly what I did, thank you very much," I said, biting my tongue from saying more.

He snorted, which was all it took.

"I'm sorry, but it's not my fault that you ignore my emails and are hardly around anymore. For us to run this place together, that means you actually need to be here."

"That's a low blow."

"Is it, though?" All pretense was gone. I sunk down in my chair, the weight of exhaustion hitting me. "You can't deny that you're hardly around, can you? Someone has to run this business, Bryce. If you're not here to do it, then you can't get upset at me for picking up your slack."

He jumped to his feet at my words, his face turning red from anger.

"Whoa," I said, needing to calm him down. "What's going on, Bryce?"

His hands clenched at his sides, and I could almost see the words he wanted to throw at me forming on his lips — words he wanted to rip through the air to mark me. I prepared myself for the onslaught.

Instead of the arguments, he breathed in deep, once, twice, three times before he stuffed his hands in his pants pockets.

"Listen, some of our contracts are in place for a reason. They're also important connections. You can't just make these decisions on your own, okay? You have no idea what you're doing, how you're hurting us. Anthony had those in place and would have wanted them to remain that way."

He'd made me feel like a child, channeling Anthony, figuring if it worked for our father, it would work for him.

"Anthony isn't here to run the business. And frankly, neither are you. Again, it's not my fault you ignored my emails."

"You're also not the one in charge. I am."

The second he uttered those words, I knew he regretted it. Not because of what he said, but because now I knew how he truly felt.

He was the one in charge? Him, not me, not the partnership of siblings running the family business. Just . . . him.

A puddle of tears formed in my eyes, and everything in the room swam until Bryce resembled a drowned rat. I quickly swiped at my face.

"Listen, that came out wrong." Bryce sounded apologetic, at least.

I scoffed. "No, that came out exactly as you meant." I leaned back and closed my eyes, swallowing past the pain forming in my throat. I hated being a weak crier, how my face would go all red, my eyes would swell, and my throat would tighten to the point where it hurt to swallow. Anthony always laughed at me and called me spineless.

I wasn't spineless in that moment. I was hurt. I was angry. I was . . . so beyond frustrated. Who was this man in front of me? Certainly not the brother I grew up with, the man who always had my back and supported me through everything life threw our way. This man . . . this man was a stranger wearing my brother's face, a face I no longer recognized.

"I don't know what is going on with you," I continued, once I could speak past the ball of wounded pride, "but I'm at the point where I don't care either. You've got a choice to make — either be present and help me run our business together, or get out of my way. I'm not arguing with you about this." It felt so good to get that off my chest.

"You have no idea what you've done, Brynn. That's what I'm trying to say." Bryce sounded a little frazzled as he rubbed his face with the palm of his hand.

"Then explain it to me." I struggled to keep my voice calm, unguarded, without hinting at the hostility I felt.

"There are certain key . . . figures in The Family that—"

"Nope." I cut him right off. "I don't want to hear about Anthony's stupid group. Our business has nothing to do with them."

Our funeral home should have nothing to do with Anthony's little side project. And if it did, it was my mission to eradicate any trace left. If that meant I had to cancel every single contract and start fresh, then that was what I would do.

"That's not how things work, Brynn. You should know that. Dad's reach was . . . impressive. It still is, actually. The more I learn, the more amazed I am at what he accomplished."

"That makes no sense, Bryce. None."

The look he gave me said I should have known better.

Okay, fine. Maybe I've had my head in the sand for years, but it was easier that way. It was the only way I could survive Anthony. The man undermined me at every turn and never treated me like a daughter — I was just a *thing* to him. Why didn't Bryce understand that?

"Just . . . just don't make any more changes without my input, okay? I'll pay more attention, I promise. Dad did business with many people who were also part of The Family. It goes hand in hand, Brynn. And what you've done, it could hurt everything." Bryce's eyes closed as if he could see the ramifications of my decisions play out.

It still didn't make sense. "So we went with a cheaper vendor. Who cares? What is that going to do?"

"I guess we'll see, won't we? Hopefully, I can fix this before it goes too far." Bryce's lips pursed in disappointment before he walked away, leaving me with more questions than I knew I'd ever get answers to.

# CHAPTER EIGHTEEN

I was curled in a chair with the latest Jane Porter book on my lap when Bryce interrupted my reading.

At first, I thought he was talking to me. It was one of his rare nights at home, and he was making dinner. I had offered to help, but he shooed me out of the kitchen and told me to relax.

Like I was going to say no to that.

We were into week two of the chaos with viewings and funeral services. So far, there had been at least five deaths at the retirement home, and that was five too many. Our town had gone through so much in the past few years that having an illness run through our town like that was difficult.

It didn't take long to realize Bryce wasn't talking to me, but to someone else. I heard a tinge of excitement as his voice rose. Curious, I set the book on the coffee table next to me and listened in, even though I shouldn't have. Not that I felt guilty, because I didn't. Well, maybe a little, but Bryce had been so secretive lately that if a bit of eavesdropping was what I needed to do, then so be it.

I stood in the kitchen's entranceway and leaned against the frame. His back was turned as he hunched over the stove.

"Don't worry; I'll take care of everything. How soon until he gets here?" There was a pause, and he nodded. "Yeah, okay, that works. And he stays as an observer, correct? Is there anything special I need to know? Okay, yeah, Anthony told me about that." There was another pause. "What time for the ceremony? Sounds good; see you then." He raised his hand to his ear and dropped his earpiece onto the counter.

His shoulders slumped, and the way his chin dropped to his chest, concerned me.

"Hey," I said softly. "Everything okay in here? Who were you talking to?"

He tried to mask the emotions on his face, but he didn't do a great job.

"Listen, I won't be able to eat dinner with you tonight," he said. "It's almost done; it needs twenty minutes in the oven. Sorry about this." He started cleaning up, but I noticed his hand shaking slightly.

"Who were you talking to?"

"No one."

"Really?" My sarcasm hit a new level, and I was quite proud of how he winced. Why lie to me? "That didn't sound like no one. What are you taking care of, who is observing you, and what's this about a ceremony?"

He ran his hands through his hair, making a mess of things.

"Fine." He took a deep breath. "That was Kylian."

"Who?" That name meant nothing to me.

"Elder Kylian."

"Okay . . ." Elder. I got it — someone from the cult had called him up. Did I want more information? No, but deep down, I needed it.

He rubbed his face with his hands, smearing sauce along his forehead.

I grabbed a paper towel and ran it beneath the water for a few seconds before I handed it to him, indicating the mess he'd made. "And what did Elder Kylian want or need?"

He hesitated, biting his lip, a tell-tale sign.

"Just spill it, would you?"

"You know how Dad always handled the late-night emergencies?" He wiped his hands on the towel slung over his shoulder. "Especially when it came to the Family? Well, now it's my turn, that's all."

Anthony had taken care of the night shift. He kept a business line in his office and answered all the midnight calls from the police or hospital whenever a death occurred, and they needed to move the body to the funeral home.

I also remembered how he was when it came to his little cult, too. He was secretive in his correspondence, the phone calls, and how he played with the accounting so their invoices, if any, were never on the books.

"So now you are The Family's personal mortician?"

If he noticed my eye roll, he didn't comment on it. "Don't be like that, please." There was an exhausted desperation in his voice, which left me with a load of guilt. For what, though? For not being on board with his new 'life goals,' or whatever he was calling it? He was the one pulling away from me. He was the one following in Anthony's footsteps. If anyone should feel guilty, it was him.

"I hate that we're on opposite sides of something important to me."

Like a dull knife through the heart, that hurt.

"Do you need any help?" The words came out before I could stop them. The second they did, I wanted to take them back. I didn't want to help with whatever he was doing; that would give the impression that I was on board with all the craziness, and we both knew I was not.

When he shook his head, I felt a semblance of relief.

"They have some religious requirements for their deceased, and other than the person who stands as an observer, they only allow one other person to handle the body. Don't worry, it's fine. Anthony left me detailed instructions on what is required, so I'll take care of everything, just like he did. You don't need to worry about anything."

"That's not how we work." Why was I reminding him of that simple fact? "We're partners, Bryce, and we agreed there would be no secrets. That included all this with the Family, too. I never liked that Anthony kept them off the books. It's an accounting nightmare, and we have to do better."

A shade of red climbed from Bryce's collarbone to the crown of his hairline as he crossed his arms. "There are no secrets, Brynn. I wish you'd stop being so paranoid. They need to remain off the grid, and the less people know about them, the better. As far as they're concerned, society must have no idea they even exist."

That made no sense at all.

"Then explain Daniel Sawyer. How is it that he knew about the Family? Or anyone else who becomes involved, for that matter?"

Bryce checked his watch and glanced out the door. "With Daniel, that's different. People like him are personally invited. A cultivated relationship is made months before there's ever any mention of the Family. It's not like they hand out flyers on street corners or sponsor soup kitchens, inviting the masses to join them. Listen, I need to run and get things set up before they arrive."

He leaned over and gave me a quick peck on the cheek. "Again, I'm sorry about dinner. I set the timer, and if you could leave me some, that would be great." He pocketed his phone and earbuds and grabbed the keys hanging from the wall.

"And the ceremony tomorrow?" My words stopped him from leaving. "Do you need help with that? What time should I have staff come in?"

He waved a hand in dismissal. "No, the time of preparation is over, so there's nothing left to do. I've got it all covered."

The time of preparation. That phrase sounded familiar — why?

"What does that mean? You said that when we were at the farm, too . . . when you made us leave so abruptly."

He nodded, stuffing his hands into his jeans pockets. "Yeah, that's the term they use when someone is dying. It's a time for them to prepare as a community for the loss of one of their own, to make way for the blessing to occur, and find the appropriate person to fill that position."

"So someone was dying?"

"Just like someone is now dead, and I need to prepare for their arrival. Brynn, this is the first time they've asked me to step in. It's a big deal; until now, Anthony always took care of it. Now it's my turn."

"But it shouldn't be." Before, Anthony personally oversaw all the funeral needs from the Farm. In my opinion, that place had way too many deaths, but whenever I mentioned it to Anthony, he shut me down.

"We're a team, remember," I continued. "You just said this is the first death from there since Anthony's passing that you've been asked to assist in. At least let me help you get the permit, since you need that before you can do anything else. I'm assuming they'll bring a death certificate with them?"

He paused and cocked his head, as if trying to read the meaning behind my words.

"They do things a little differently," he said, his voice very hesitant.

"There are steps that need to be followed, legally. You know that."

According to the state of New York, when a death occurred, the authorities were the first to be notified. After that fact, we were able to transport the body and obtain a death certificate before filing for a burial permit.

He shrugged. "They have a little more leeway under the Religious Freedom Act."

"You need to be careful." The law was the law, and when it came to death and burial practices, there was a fine line between what was acceptable and what was not.

"I know what I'm doing, okay? Now, if you don't mind, I need to go and get things ready before they arrive."

I checked the time. "You can spare me a few more minutes. It's not like they'll be here within the hour."

The exasperation pouring off him had me a little worried.

"Anthony trained me in what needed to be done, and since this will be my first time, I want to ensure I do it properly. I appreciate the offer of help, but we both know you hate being in the dungeon." He air-quoted that last word, and I attempted a smile.

"Fine." Any further arguments would only push him away more. "But I'd really like to sit down and go over all these different rules Anthony had for that group compared to everyone else, okay? How he handled things and how we handle them need to be different." I refused to back down from this.

He nodded, but I knew he was placating me. He had no intention of sitting down with me.

"Sure, sure," he said. "Don't wait for me, okay? I don't know how long I'll be."

"I'll leave you a plate in the oven, but Bryce, I'm serious, okay? I'm here to help if you need me."

"This is my responsibility, not yours," he said, one hand on the doorknob. "Besides, aren't you the one always telling me you want nothing to do with the Family?"

He was right, and I still felt that way, but the bottom line was that if I wanted him to work with me and be a partner in our family business, then the same had to be true for me. "This is important to you." I swallowed hard. "So it needs to be important to me."

My gut wrenched and twisted, working itself into a tight knot. I wanted to vomit at the smile that grew on my brother's face.

"I'll take care of things tonight. Next time, you for sure can help, okay?"

"Thanks. Hey," I called out, just as he was about to open the door. "What happened to the last one? Why didn't they ask for your help then?"

He ran his hand through his pale hair and winced. "The blessing wasn't willing." Without saying anything more, he left me alone, with only the sound of the oven timer going off like a siren calling to her victims.

110

# CHAPTER NINETEEN

There was a quick *knock-knock-knock* on the kitchen door. A glance at the time said it was too early for anyone to be knocking, so I had half a mind to ignore whoever was on the other side. If it were important, they'd head over to the Parlor to find me or Bryce.

Except today, they wouldn't find either of us.

I sat at the kitchen table, wound into a pretzel position with one leg tucked beneath me, the other hooked over my knee, and held a warm cup of coffee as the door opened.

How was it not locked?

"Hey beautiful, any plans for the day?" Mona waltzed in with a smile.

I glanced down at the lazy outfit I'd thrown on — leggings and a hooded sweatshirt with a gardening gnome holding a sunflower. After the craziness of the past few weeks, I had officially taken the weekend off. "It's overcast today, so I figured I'd work in the garden a little, maybe bug my neighbor. Mr. Baxter tends to get grouchy if I don't stop in for a chat."

"Can that wait?"

"It could. Why?"

"I'm feeling antsy and needed to get out of the house, so I figured I'd grab you, go for a drive, and maybe check out a new bakery I heard about."

Another one? It was like they were popping up all over the place.

"Is there any coffee left?" She headed over to the pot, grabbed a cup off the counter, and poured the last of the coffee. "Go get dressed, will you? Bring your hat — we'll be doing some walking."

"Is the bakery in the middle of the woods?" I downed the last mouthful from my cup.

"Just go." She pointed toward the stairs. "You've got the time it takes me to finish this cup, and considering there wasn't much left, this won't take me long."

I saluted, which earned me a saucy grin before I ran up the stairs.

It didn't take me long to get dressed. I tended to wear a simple black uniform for work, so my weekend wear was more relaxed. Leggings and long, simple dresses with long sleeves were my usual go-to, so I grabbed a dress from the closet and one of my hats.

I knocked on Bryce's door, but when he didn't answer, I pulled out my phone and texted him to tell him I was headed out for the day. He'd promised me he'd take care of things in my absence. In fact, it was his idea that I take the weekend off.

"Okay, I'm ready." I bounced down the stairs, set the hat on my head, and grabbed my purse before I followed Mona out the door. "So, where are we headed?"

Once in Mona's car, she handed me a pamphlet for a yoga retreat center located forty-five minutes from town.

"We're headed there?"

"Yeah, I thought we could check it out. Read it over — their retreat weekends sound great, plus they have ones for a week, or even a month."

The pamphlet was intriguing. The place was called FAM Casa, and their schedule had the right amount of sessions, combined with other activities for the senses.

"FAM Casa, the family home. Sounds cozy," I said. "It says here to come and enjoy a holistic experience that creates a deeper connection with your mind, body, and spirit in our beautiful outdoor areas." I laid the pamphlet down on my lap.

"I'm sure they do some indoors as well. That's why I wanted us to visit it in person. Scope it out, ask the questions, and if it works out that it's something you can do . . . awesome, right? And if not, well, at least we can enjoy lunch at their cafe."

True enough. Road trips were always fun. Mom and I used to do them on the weekends. We'd head out with no destination in mind and would make split-second decisions on which way to turn and what store to stop at. It always ended up as a fun day. I missed those trips with her.

When we arrived, we pulled into what looked like a luxury cottage resort, which was completely out of my price range.

"Wow," Mona said. She leaned forward in her seat and took it all in as we drove through the open gates.

The resort was full of white cabins of different sizes, connected by stone walkways. Tall trees lined the path; at their base were garden areas, some with herbs and flowers. Water fountains, bird baths, benches, and white lantern-type statues were everywhere.

I pictured what this place would look like at night, with those lanterns lit up, and I imagined it to be beautiful and cozy at the same time — a picture-perfect resort to escape and refocus.

Mona drove slowly until she came to a line of stone planters full of greenery marking the end of the driveway.

"Are you sure this place is open to the public? It looks like it's one of those spa resorts celebrities escape to, you know?" I glanced back at the pamphlet on my lap and looked it over. Sure enough, there was an official opening date on the bottom.

"Mona," I said, slapping her lightly on the arm, "it doesn't officially open till next month."

"No way." She grabbed the paper from my hand and looked it over. "Then why is the cafe open? See?" She pointed to the graphic that, sure enough, said to come and try their farm-to-table items, open now.

A woman in linen white pants and top stepped out of what was probably the main office and waited for us at the base of the walkway. Her silver-stranded hair was pulled back into a loose ponytail over her shoulder.

"How old do you think she is?" Mona whispered as we walked toward her. "They must have amazing skin care products here," she continued. "She's smiling, and there are no wrinkles. I want whatever they're selling."

An ethereal vibrancy surrounded her, a glow I could sense even with my sunglasses on.

"Hello," the woman said, her hands clasped behind her back. "I am Allison. Welcome to FAM Casa, your home away from home." She directed her words to Mona, but she stared at me like she saw a ghost.

Was I supposed to know her? There was a hint of a smile that spoke of familiarity, one that made me uncomfortable.

"We came for the fresh pastries, but actually, I'm kind of hoping for a little tour," Mona said, oblivious to whatever undercurrents swirled around us.

I wanted to tear my eyes away, but I stood mesmerized, pulled in, and felt a deep, overwhelming need to know who she was.

"Sister, I can't tell you what an honor it is to have you here," Allison said, her gaze deeply penetrating.

Sister. My heart sank at the term. There was no way that woman called me that name by accident.

I was the first to break eye contact.

"Of course, we can give you both a tour," Allison continued as she glanced at Mona. "I wasn't expecting you for a few more weeks, but everything is in place now, so it's perfect timing."

Mona glanced my way and mouthed *WTF?* to me. I only shrugged.

We walked by a large FAM Casa sign made out of wood with a simplistic font, and it was like things clicked into place: the Family ran this yoga retreat.

"It sounds like this isn't the best time for a tour." I placed a hand on Mona's arm, stopping her from moving forward. "Why don't we just come back another time?"

If this was indeed something the Family owned, I wanted nothing to do with it.

Mona looked at me strangely, and as hard as I tried to signify that I wanted us to leave and that I needed her to trust me right then, I knew she didn't understand.

Despite our years of friendship, Mona wasn't the most intuitive of people, despite her line of work.

"I apologize if I insinuated you weren't welcome," Allison said. Her voice remained calm and soothing, without a hint of any type of emotion other than peace. "Please, it would be my honor to give you a tour."

"Come on, let's check it out." A large smile grew on Mona's face, and I saw my mischievous and always ready-for-fun friend emerge. She entwined her arm with mine and pulled me forward. "And look at all this shade. It's like this place was made for you in mind."

That was a little extreme, but I understood what she was saying. There were pockets of space full of sun, but there were also clear pathways beneath the full shade, not something one would expect at a wellness retreat center.

"Honestly, Mona, I'd rather come back another time," I whispered, hoping she heard the sense of urgency in my voice. I really wanted to leave.

"Nope. I'm not letting you do this," Mona said. She turned us both around, so we spoke in private. "Listen, you need time away from that place. Always being surrounded by death, it's not healthy, and you know it. The past few weeks have been crazy for obvious reasons, and you need a breather." She glanced over her shoulder toward Allison. "You made me promise to ensure you took breaks when things got chaotic, so this is me making sure you take at least a day. All right? I'm not taking you back, and that's final. Not until after the tour and after we at least eat some of that farm-to-table food." Despite the smile she gave me, I knew she was serious.

There wasn't much I could do other than look like a fool. Mona had no idea who the Family was, nor would she understand my hesitation about being here.

Which meant it was time for me to give in, take the tour, eat the food, and hope I was overreacting.

I breathed in deeply, which she took as my acceptance.

"Allison, please lead the way," Mona said, doubling down on her hold of my arm. "I have to ask: I heard rumors that this used to be an A-list retreat location for celebrities. Is that true?"

Allison slowed as she led us along one of the pebble-lined pathways. "That's true. FAM Casa has been a private yoga retreat for many years and was invitation-only. We recently decided to make it open to the public."

"Why is that?" I asked.

Allison's gaze on me was warm and inviting, with a disconcerting familiarity. "What we offer here at FAM Casa is more than just a wellness retreat. We don't only focus on the physical well-being of those who come, but also the mental and spiritual. Most people claim they have life-altering experiences here through our personalized sessions, and our founder realized that it was time to open the doors and help as many people as possible before the opportunity is lost for good."

Life-altering experiences?

"So you utilize drugs here?" Mona said, not holding back.

Allison gave a little chuckle. "We use a holistic approach here."

"That wasn't a no. Did you hear that?" Mona said after giving me a wink. "Sign me up."

"You are already on our invitation list, Mona," Allison said. "You should be receiving it in the mail shortly." She led us to one of the cabins and pulled out a key card. "This is one of the cabins you will be staying in. We have different-sized cabins, depending on whether you are here alone or with friends. Each suite has a spa bathroom, fireplace, comfortable seating, and all the luxuries you would expect at a five-star resort on any tropical island. We cater to all your senses here at FAM Casa."

Mona walked into the cabin, her mouth gaping open, oblivious to what Allison had said earlier, but I heard her.

I heard her loud and clear.

We never gave Allison our names when we arrived.

# CHAPTER TWENTY

While we walked, I listened and cataloged everything Allison said, including all the times she spoke directly to me.

While Mona only heard the generalization of everything the wellness center stood for and offered, I heard everything else.

"We believe that the way to heal one's whole self is not to just focus on eating the right foods or doing the proper exercise techniques, but it's a matter of healing the wounded soul within as well," Allison said, her hands still clasped tight behind her back, her footsteps measured and unhurried.

"We offer a variety of tracks, depending on your level and length of stay," she continued.

"What does that mean?" Mona asked.

Allison turned and smiled. "Some only want a weekend getaway, a detox from life and screens. That would be our basic membership. Then, some want to take an enhanced journey and stay for either a week or often two weeks, where they will focus on their core values and strengths, leaving with the proper steps to a better nutritional understanding as well as physical well-being and mental health. That would be either our silver or gold levels, probably something you yourself would be interested in," Allison said to Mona, who nodded. "Then there is our platinum and star level, where we offer anywhere from one- to six-month stays that include a variety of treatments, where you can go deeper into your psyche and connect with your inner child, begin the journey toward inner healing, and have a greater self-awareness of who you not only are but who you can become."

"Oh, I don't know. Escape life for at least a month at a place like this—" Mona waved her hands around — "where my every need is catered to, and I can leave feeling well-rested for the first time in my life. I might be interested in that." She turned to me. "What do you think, Brynn? Of all the people I know, you for sure could use at least a two-week vacation here."

"When you put it that way . . ." I gave a half-smile. "Although the business won't run itself, and now really isn't the best time for a vacation."

"Which is why you need to come here more than me," Mona said, not letting go of the idea. Knowing Mona like I did, she'd hound me until I agreed to at least one weekend together here.

"And it's exactly that reason we decided to open our doors to the public," Allison interjected.

She wasn't saying that they were also opening it to the public for financial reasons.

Sometimes, after I'd been dismissed and sent off to bed, I eavesdropped on Anthony and his guests late at night. I heard how they spoke about their group, the people who belonged to it, and those in leadership positions.

What I remember the most, however, was how they discussed future recruitment to grow their ranks and bank accounts.

Truth be told, at the time, I didn't pay too much attention to any of it, but the more Allison said, the more it all came back.

Some in leadership didn't want to recruit openly, and they preferred the way things had always run. It had been successful and profitable to go after the Hollywood crowd, to promise them protection and anonymity, plus all the perks of joining the most exclusive club possible.

However, others believed they needed to grow beyond their borders and extend their reach.

Anthony wanted to keep things as they were.

Now that he was dead, a new guard was in charge, one who apparently believed in that second way of business.

I didn't want to believe my brother was involved in that change.

"This is pretty awesome, don't you think?" Mona said, turning when she realized I'd been walking behind and wasn't being an active participant.

I nodded.

"Beats going to the hilltop for sunrise or sunset yoga sessions." Mona nudged me lightly in the side.

"I've been saving the best for last," Allison said, focusing on me. "Mona, would you do the honor?" She handed her key card over. Mona, like she'd been given a one-way ticket to paradise, ran ahead and opened the door to a larger cottage with a wrap-around porch.

"This is a recent addition, and one we created specifically for you, Sister." Allison held me back with a light touch. "We still have a few final touches I'd wanted to add, but this would be your own personal suite, a home away from home, if you will."

It sounded like she was saying this was mine, something created specifically for me, but why?

"Surely Brother explained all of this to you?"

My eyes closed with frustration; everything was confirmed with that one question.

"Why?" Of all the things I could have asked, my brother was the only one I wanted to answer my questions.

The way she smiled felt condescending. She seemed to view me as a child, explaining something only an adult would understand.

"I will leave that for Brother to explain," she said, "but please, let me show you around. He was very specific on how he wanted everything for you." She held out her hand, indicating I should go ahead of her.

Bryce designed this for me? Why?

I pulled out my phone, intending to ask him specifically.

"This is a device-free zone."

"I'm sorry?"

"Surely you've seen our signs." She pointed to one just off the side.

With a sigh, I returned the phone to my purse.

Inside the cottage, now that I knew specifically what to look for, I saw my brother's hand in almost every touch.

"Brynn, look at this reading room. I swear, isn't this like that photo we saw on social media? The only difference was the view of the ocean, where there is a little Zen garden."

It was gorgeous, and exactly what Bryce would have known I'd like. There was even a screened-in studio area at the back and then a shaded pathway that led into a garden area, leading to an outdoor covered yoga area with a view over hilly fields.

"You can see yourself here, can't you?" Mona said, standing beside me.

"Why do I feel like you have an ulterior motive?" While Mona was normally bright, bubbly, and persistent to a fault, something was off. "My brother asked you to bring me here, didn't he?" I knew right away I was right.

"Going out was my idea," Mona admitted. "He was the one who handed me the brochure and mentioned the cafe. I swear."

My brow arched as she squirmed beside me.

"Fine," she huffed. "He might have said something about donating some funds, which meant you get priority for retreats or something. I asked if it was like a timeshare you can buy in Florida, but he laughed me off. It totally is like a timeshare thing, isn't it?" She directed this toward Allison.

"I don't know who I'm more upset with," I told her. "Him for keeping this a secret, or you for helping him with that."

Deep down, I was most upset with the Family, who had dug their claws into my brother and wouldn't let go.

"All our members are like family to us," Allison said, her voice bright and full of smiles I'd like to slap off her face. "FAM Casa, the Family Home — and Mona is correct, this indeed is your home, Sister."

The emphasis on the word *Sister* wasn't lost on me. Nor was it on Mona, from the confused look she gave me.

Mona said nothing about it until we were seated at the cafe, a quaint spot that was half full by the time we arrived.

"Don't you think it's weird how they call everyone Sister? I mean, this isn't a woman's-only club, right? So are the men called Brother, then? That's a little woo-woo, don't you think?"

"What I think is that I don't like you not being honest with me." I changed the subject, hoping she wouldn't catch on.

"Yeah, I'm sorry. I should have been upfront from the beginning. We were going for a drive, though; that was true. I'd found a charming little river cafe that just opened up, so I thought we'd try it. We'll have to go another day. It's only an hour away, but in the opposite direction of this place."

"Sounds great." I leaned back in my chair and looked around. All of the staff wore the same outfit as Allison. I wonder how involved she was with the Family. Had she known Anthony?

"You know, I overheard Maximus Rutledge used to visit here before he died in that big explosion on his mega yacht. I bet he was in a suite like the last one we saw. I can't believe your brother donated all that money, right? I mean . . . was it something Anthony had wanted? I find that hard to believe, though, don't you?"

"Anthony donating money to a wellness center? If it were his money Bryce used, he'd be rolling in his grave." I couldn't help but snicker, if that were the case. If this was an idea Anthony had been against, I was more inclined to be okay with it.

We shared a smile.

"Sister, so nice to see you today." A server approached our table and placed a large Cobb salad in front of me and a strawberry spinach salad in front of Mona.

"Again, with the whole 'Sister' thing. But only directed to you, so weird," Mona said. "I will say this place is nice, and I'm not surprised this was a secret among A-list celebrities. Maybe we should book a weekend; what do you think? Who knows who we might meet."

"You just want to experience their spa, to get some of their magic skincare," I teased. Until I spoke with my brother, I had no intention of booking anything here.

In fact, I had no intention of booking anything here, regardless of my discussion with Bryce.

My phone buzzed. I peeked at it quickly and saw an SOS text from Merilyn. Her message was cryptic, but I knew Merilyn wouldn't get in touch if it weren't necessary.

"Would you mind if we headed back after our lunch? There's an emergency at the funeral home, and Merilyn can't reach Bryce." I couldn't hide my eye roll. Of course, Bryce wouldn't be around; that was starting to be his pattern.

"What kind of emergency could happen at a funeral home? Did they cremate the wrong person? Lose someone's ashes? Stuff like that doesn't happen, right?"

I laughed it off. "Not with us, it doesn't. I've heard horror stories of other places, but so far, knock on wood—" I gave our table three solid knocks with my knuckle — "stuff like that never happens at our place."

That didn't stop me from glancing at the text message again.

*Sorry to bother you, but Bryce isn't around, and I think your worst nightmare just came true. Need you back ASAP.*

# CHAPTER TWENTY-ONE

On the whole drive back, I pictured various scenarios about what could be happening and why I needed to be there ASAP.

Merilyn said my worst nightmare was coming true. I had a lot of nightmares, so as much as I tried to narrow it down, I couldn't.

Had someone claimed to have seen a ghost? Had a decedent fallen off a gurney or, God forbid, had a casket toppled over in front of a family member? Had someone called in for a body pickup, but the person was still alive? Was there a sudden bug infestation because of improper cleanup?

I promised to call Mona later, and even suggested we do a dessert night soon when she dropped me off. Then, I dashed through the back door of the Parlor and headed up to my office. Merilyn agreed to meet me up there, claiming the fewer ears, the better.

When Merilyn walked into my office, her movements were heavy as she closed the door behind her and sat in front of my desk.

"What's up?" Of all the times for Bryce to go missing, now was possibly the worst time.

The last time Merilyn came in here like this, I'd had to fire staff members and pray we didn't get sued by a family.

One of our new employees had been caught fondling one of the deceased during the casketing process. It would be one thing if Merilyn or I had caught them doing that; they would have been fired on the spot, but it would have remained an in-house issue. Unfortunately, a family member had been there and witnessed the whole thing. Not only did we comp that service and all costs pertaining to it, but we also had to bring in outside support and redo training with all the employees.

I was still surprised the family didn't sue us, despite their threats.

"I'm sorry I had to call you in on your day off," Merilyn said, worrying her hands together.

"You have nothing to apologize for. The only one to be apologizing is Bryce. He promised to be here. I've texted him, but he must be out of cell range."

She nodded. "I texted and called, too, multiple times. I really didn't want to bother you. You've been working so hard; you deserved at least a full day off." She swallowed hard, but looked me straight on with a determination that told me whatever she was about to say would be bad.

"I don't know how to say this, so I'll just come out with it: we cremated the wrong person."

Of all my nightmares, that was one I didn't want to acknowledge as possible.

"Excuse me?" I didn't need her to repeat it; I needed her to take back her words and say something else.

"We cremated the wrong person yesterday. The Morgans were given Mrs. Strutt's remains."

My stomach twisted into a million little knots as her words sunk in.

We cremated the wrong person.

Not only that, but we gave a bereaved family the remains of the wrong person.

Stuff like that didn't happen in my funeral home. I'd heard of it occurring at other locations, the horror stories of mismanagement and lack of proper processes, the undue anguish families went through because of someone's careless mistakes.

"How?" It took me a moment to ask the question, but when I did, I saw the same horrific look on Merilyn's face as she sat across from me in my office.

"I honestly don't know, Brynn. This has never happened before, at least not while I've been here." There were genuine tears in Merilyn's eyes, and I knew she was taking this personally.

"Since you've been here? How about never, in the history of the funeral home?" I ran my hands through my hair. "Let me get this straight: we somehow not only managed to mix up caskets, but we cremated the wrong person, too? We have systems in place so this doesn't happen, Merilyn."

"I know, I know." She leaned back in her chair, her gaze turned toward her lap. "It's my fault, let's be clear on that."

"Oh, we're clear." The ramifications of this circled round and round in my head until the beginning of a headache formed.

"Walk me through it, please," I asked. I knew the steps that were supposed to take place, the systems and precautions that were set up to ensure that exact scenario didn't happen. For the life of me, I couldn't understand why it had.

"The two funerals were back to back, and with neither you nor Bryce here—"

I stopped her there. "Don't blame us for your mistake. You assured me you had everything under control, that you could handle it," I reminded her.

It wasn't the first time she'd been in charge of a service and cremation, so there had been no reason to question whether I needed to be there.

I believed in building a team around me good enough that I wasn't needed.

"I know, and you're right," she said. "That's why I wrote up my letter of resignation." She laid it on my desk and slid it across to me.

I glanced at it but didn't pick it up. "And I don't accept it. Let me be clear about that." Mistakes happened — that was a given — but not like that. Never as bad as what happened.

"Have the families been informed?"

She shook her head.

"Are we sure that the remains we gave the Morgan family are Mrs. Strutt?"

She nodded. "They were the only two scheduled for cremation this week."

"So, the Morgan family is downstairs waiting for the cremation to begin, except we've already cremated their grandmother, and it's actually Mrs. Strutt who is in the casket?" I slowly pushed my chair back. If anyone was apologizing to the Morgan and the Strutt family, it was me.

There was a knock on the door, and Bryce walked in.

"Hey, just the person I wanted to see. I was wondering . . . um, is everything okay?" He glanced from me to Merilyn and then back to me. "Is this a bad time?"

"Where have you been?" I waved him in and motioned for him to close the door.

"Yeah, I saw you both tried to get in touch. That's why I'm here."

"Where have you been?" It was a simple question, so why wouldn't he answer it?

"Why do I feel like I've just walked in on something I don't want to be a part of?" Bryce tried to make light of the tension in the room, but it fell flat.

"You were supposed to be here. You promised me you would be here to take care of things, to support Merilyn."

"And I have been. I just had to run out for a bit today, and my phone battery died." His voice was nonchalant, as if he didn't see the issue.

"We cremated the wrong body yesterday."

"Okaaaayyy . . ." he said. "So, who did we cremate, how did we figure this out, and whose ass are we firing?"

"No one is getting fired." I swallowed back tears that came out of nowhere. "Merilyn discovered the mistake this morning."

The way my brother looked at Merilyn surprised me. There was a mixture of distrust and anger, two emotions that shouldn't have been there, since I hadn't even said this was her fault.

"And who did we cremate?"

"Morgan, when it should have been Strutt. Morgan is supposed to be happening right now." Merilyn answered.

He processed that for a hot minute. "No one noticed it was Mrs. Morgan before placing her in the chamber? Did no one look? No one thought to double-check the codes, lift the lid, and look at the body?"

The silence in the room stretched long and thin.

"Again, let me ask the obvious question: who are we firing?" His arms crossed over his chest, and I did the same.

"And again, no one is getting fired. It was an honest mistake. A horrible one, but—"

"Is that what we're going to tell the family? Is that what we're going to say to the Morgans, downstairs? I'm sorry, but we accidentally already cremated your grandmother yesterday. We'll try to get her remains back, though; just be patient with us while we track down the family who flew to Europe to bury her in their family plot over there?" He threw his hands up in anger, and I totally got it. It was all I'd been thinking about, too.

The Strutts caught their flight last night after we ensured that the box the ashes were in was airline-approved and that they had the necessary paperwork. Taking cremated remains on a plane wasn't a problem as long as they were in the correct container with the proper documentation.

I plopped back in my chair and let out a small groan.

"It's my fault," Merilyn repeated, locking her gaze with Bryce. "I should have checked. I thought I did, to be honest. I went in the day before and noticed the boxes had been moved, so I rearranged them so that something like this wouldn't happen."

I leaned forward with interest. "The boxes had been moved?"

Merilyn nodded. "I thought it weird, too, right? I mean, we were all there when they were brought up from downstairs. We went through the process like always and placed them against the wall, and I added the proper tags to each box." She lifted one shoulder. "When I noticed that one of the boxes wasn't in the right spot, I moved it back and didn't think of it."

"That room should have been locked. The three of us in this room are the only ones with keys, so . . ." The question settled between us. "I wasn't here. Did you, Bryce?"

"No, why would I?" His gaze slid from mine.

"Is it possible one of the staff took your keys?" I asked this question to Merilyn. I had a feeling I knew her answer, but I still needed to ask the question.

"The keys remain on me at all times; you know that. I didn't hand them out to anyone."

I did know that. She was pretty militant about her keys and who had access to what in the Parlor, which I always appreciated.

But if she didn't hand out her keys, and I knew I didn't, that only left Bryce.

"Oh, wait," my brother said, noting how I looked at him. "I did have to go back in. I realized I'd forgotten to make some notes regarding Mrs. Strutt's autopsy. I brought her downstairs to finish up and then returned her. I could have sworn I returned her to the right spot, though."

"Obviously, you didn't." I noticed the emotions rolling across Merilyn's face, from relief to disbelief to anger.

"No, but this isn't on me," he said. "Who checked off on the caskets before they went into the chamber?"

I obviously couldn't answer, so I looked at Merilyn. She stared down at her lap.

"Yeah, so again, this is on me," she whispered. "I had one of the other staff take care of that, using it as a teaching moment, you know? Carol Ann wants more responsibilities, so I thought . . ." She trailed off, not finishing, because we all got it.

*Damn it.*

"This definitely was a teaching moment." I swallowed hard. "So, how do we handle this now?" I looked to Bryce for help.

"Well," he said, as he sat down, "it's not like this hasn't happened before. We just need to make sure no one sees the body inside the box before it's placed in the chamber."

"Wait, what?" I did *not* just hear him say what I thought he said.

"You didn't know?" Bryce leaned forward, arms resting on his knees. "Yeah, it's not the first time. Dad never sweated over it, though. I mean, remains are remains, and it's not like the families are going to know those ashes aren't their loved ones."

My stomach rolled with disgust.

"Are you saying Anthony . . ." I didn't finish. I couldn't.

Merilyn popped up to her feet. "I'm not hearing this." She waved her hands around with the same tension I felt. "If you do this, I don't want to be a part of it. For the record, I'm not okay with this at all."

She shot me a gaze full of daggers before she stormed out of the room.

"She won't say anything, right?"

I blinked at my brother in disbelief. "You can't be serious?"

"About what?"

My mouth gaped open, and I struggled to get the words out. "This has happened before?"

The way he waved his hands, it was like he waved away my concerns. "More than you want to know. But seriously, our father didn't sweat over it. It wasn't like anyone would ever find out, as long as it's between us."

Obviously, I was not okay with the deception, but how could I get my brother to understand the seriousness of the situation?

"What didn't you fill out?" The question came before I had a chance to think it through.

"What?"

"On the form? You said you missed some things from the autopsy. Why did you need to bring Mrs. Strutt back downstairs? Couldn't you have filled in whatever right there in the cold room?"

"I, uh." He paused, brows furrowed. "I just needed some measurements, and my tools were downstairs." He wouldn't look at me.

"That seems odd."

"It happens." Again, with a nonchalant attitude. "I was probably a little distracted or something."

"Or rushing?" I tried very hard not to come across as accusing, but the truth was, looking back, he'd been in and out of the Parlor all day for one reason or another. I'd had to call him to remind him to come home and finish his job.

He thrust his shoulders back, ready for a fight. Except I wasn't his opponent, not today.

"I think you should be the one to go down and explain. It's only right." I rested my elbows on the desk. "It might not be what Anthony would do, but we're doing things differently, remember?"

I knew he wanted to argue. His mouth opened, and his hand rose, finger pointed at me.

"Not today, please, Bryce?"

Mouth closed, he pushed himself out of his seat. "Sure, no problem."

Except it was a problem, and we both knew it.

"Listen," he said. "Apart from all this, I wanted to see if you had dinner plans tonight. I was able to stock up my fridge with meat and wanted to make you something special. Is that okay?"

"Mona and I had to cut our day short, so we were going to grab some dessert tonight." My eyes narrowed. "By the way, we need to discuss the FAM Casa, don't you think?"

He rubbed his face with the palm of his hand and shuffled his feet in place, clearly feeling uncomfortable. Interesting.

"Yeah, uh . . . what did you think?"

"Are you sure you want to know?"

The question hung there between us. He finally nodded.

"Whose money was donated?"

I doubted that was the question he thought I'd ask first.
"Mine, why?"

I shrugged. "I figured, since it was all Family-related,
maybe Anthony had left you more instructions I was unaware of."

"No, no, that was all my money." He swallowed hard.

"Impressive. I didn't realize you had that much to throw
away toward a wellness retreat center."

His brow furrowed. "I didn't throw anything away. It's
a solid investment. They catered to the rich and famous, and
are now expanding. It's a win-win to me."

"As long as you did your research. I didn't need my own
cabin, though."

A slight smile played on his lips. "Well, it's for both of
us, really. We both need time away from this place, and yet
it's close enough if we need to rush back."

"And it's Family-run?"

"Is that a problem?" From the look on his face, he wouldn't
understand if it was. He went on, "Listen, would you mind if I
took a few days this week to myself?"

I wanted to say no, that all he'd been doing lately was
'taking time' for himself, but that wouldn't be fair. He'd been
here most of the time over these past few weeks, pitching in
where he could, being present.

"Sure," I said. "Any specific days?"

He shook his head. "No, I was thinking maybe tomorrow and Tuesday, but . . . it's only fair I'm here to deal with
the Morgan and Strutt fallout."

I breathed a sigh of relief, thankful it wouldn't all be left
on my shoulders.

"Doing anything specific?" I kept my tone upbeat and
curious.

"Nothing too interesting." His reply was very cryptic.

132

"You know, we've hardly hung out since Anthony died. With all the craziness of the past few weeks, we haven't had time to relax and check in with each other."

His eyes twinkled as he stepped around my desk and leaned down for a hug.

"That's why I thought we could have dinner tonight. It'll be ready for around five o'clock, okay? Does that still give you time for dessert with Mona?"

"That's fine," I said. "Now go; the family is waiting downstairs. Do you promise you'll take care of things?"

"Promise." He held out his hand for a pinkie promise, and I couldn't help but smile.

Of course he would take care of it; why did I doubt him?

## CHAPTER TWENTY-TWO

I stayed at the Parlor for the rest of the day, working in my office and researching the FAM Casa. Something Mona had said about it sparked my interest, so I delved deep into past celebrities linked with the wellness center, especially Maximus Rutledge.

I remembered the day his mega yacht exploded in the Caribbean, off the coast of a private island he owned. His name was linked to everyone and anyone important in the world. It was said he had all the connections to make or break a person.

To know he had been less than an hour away intrigued me. For a man who could have gone anywhere, why there, at FAM Casa?

He had to be involved with the Family, or had been, before his death. Had Anthony known him?

Nine out of ten reviews about the wellness center were off-the-chart positive. A few spouted some crazy nonsense about the cult-like atmosphere and weird rituals they witnessed in the dark of night, or how they didn't like feeling cut off from their life due to the cellular and device-free rules. Still, those were buried at the bottom of the review listing.

I'd set an alarm on my phone to remind me of dinner with Bryce. By the time I left, the Parlor had been locked up tight, with all the staff having left hours ago.

I padded my way across the yard and opened the kitchen door.

"Hey twinny, I'm home." I shucked off my shoes and walked barefoot toward Bryce, whose head was buried in his fridge. Peering over his shoulder, I was surprised at how stocked it was. There was hardly an inch of space in there.

"Now that's a lot of meat. I didn't realize you'd been out hunting. Was that why you weren't around today?" I dropped my bag on the counter.

He pulled out a container of what looked like beef in a marinade. "Yeah, I had to grab the stuff from the butcher, and he was in the next town over. The hunting trip was last week. You should come with me next time." He laughed, knowing that was far-fetched. Hunting was an activity shared between him and Anthony. I'd never been invited, nor had I ever wanted to be, truth be told. He could find someone else to fill those shoes, if he hadn't already.

"The only hunting for meat I'll be doing is walking to the local butcher in town and filling up a shopping cart. You know that."

He rolled his eyes. "Yeah, yeah, and how often do you have to do that? I keep our freezer well stocked, and you know it. I assume you want to shower first, so if you go now, dinner will be ready by the time you're done."

"Any hints to what you're making?"

"Something I think you'll enjoy. I thought I'd try something a little different tonight. Are you game?"

His hand rested on a container, his finger tap-tap-tapping the top of the lid.

"You should know by now you never have to ask me twice."

"Good. Go. And wear something nice, will you?"

I sighed as I headed up the stairs. Here, I'd thought we would have a nice dinner where we'd catch up, talk about today's mess-up, and figure out how not to have it happen again. But instead, I was probably playing hostess with someone from the Family.

"I'm not here for dessert, in case you forgot," I said over my shoulder, not bothering to wait for his reply. While he chatted with whomever was coming, I would head over to Mona's for our dessert night.

I took my time getting changed. There was nothing I loved more after work than having a hot shower where I rinsed the smell of death off my skin. The almond-scented shampoo, soap, and moisturizer enveloped my senses, and I tried to bolster myself for company.

Today had not been easy, especially with the mix-up between the Strutts and the Morgans. After Bryce left my office, I went through the records to see if I could find any hints of history repeating itself, but if there was one thing about Anthony that I should have considered, it was that he knew how to keep a secret.

I planned on going through his desk tonight and pulling out some of the boxes that contain his old planners. Something wasn't sitting right with me, and I needed to figure it out.

Back downstairs, Bryce had already poured a glass of wine that waited on the counter for me.

"By the way, it's just you and I tonight. No guests," Bryce said.

"Then why tell me to dress up?"

He nudged the glass close. The wine was excellent, vibrant, and probably too expensive.

"I didn't say dress up; I said wear something nice. I should have realized you'd assume we were having guests." Bryce reached for his glass and sipped.

"And I could have clarified with you first."

He patted my hand. "I should have communicated better with you, so that's my fault. I guess I was thinking that since we've barely seen each other lately, it would be nice to . . ."

"I get it," I said, interrupting him. "It's all good. And you're right. If it's not work, you're at the Farm, and we haven't spent any time as just you and me, brother and sister, siblings trying to navigate this new world together without any parental figures in our lives."

"About that." Bryce drummed his fingers on the counter. "I know it's been a hard adjustment for me since Dad's death, and I haven't thought much about your feelings, have I?"

I didn't know what to say about that. "Maybe it's more me who hasn't considered your grief. With Anthony being gone—"

"Dad."

I sighed. "He was a father to you. Not to me."

"Doesn't negate the fact that he was your father, Brynn. It's okay to give yourself permission to grieve."

He wanted me to grieve?

"I grew up with an absent father most of my life, Bryce. Just because he was so present in your life doesn't mean he was in mine, and you know it. You know how he treated me, how he viewed me. I'm not going to sugarcoat any of that just because he's dead."

His lips tightened at my words. "He had a different parenting style with you, yes, but it was because he expected so much from you. Don't you get that?"

I laughed; there was no other option. "The only thing Anthony expected from me was to fulfill some stupid prophecy we both know is ridiculous. I was a means to an end for him, a vehicle of some twisted belief he couldn't admit was false."

"The prophecy isn't false." An undercurrent of hostility and frustration seeped out with his words. They were said quietly, but with enough force, I had to step back from him.

"You're clinging to that group because you miss him." I hadn't fully realized this until I heard myself say it.

"I'm not clinging to anything," he said dismissively. "It's a part of my life, something you've always turned a blind eye

137

to." Bryce refused to look me in the eye. "You say that Mom was trying to protect you, but all she did was brainwash you. All you know is what she's told you. You refuse to listen to both sides, to decide the truth for yourself. Mom wasn't perfect, and she was more of a mother to you than she was to me."

That hurt. I wanted to argue, to defend her, but the truth was, our parents had a fight long ago and picked a child they wanted to raise. Anthony chose Bryce. Mom chose me.

"You're right."

He glanced at me with surprise.

"Our parents weren't perfect, and the decisions they made weren't the best." It wasn't difficult to admit that. "But that's all in the past now. We need to focus on the present, how we are as adults, and our future, and give each other the space to be who we want to be."

I wanted to run our funeral business. I wanted to continue with the family legacy and be successful at it, continuing to build on that strong foundation to one day pass on to my own children.

Bryce, well, maybe it was time for him to accept our family business wasn't for him. Now was the time for him to pursue his passion for cooking.

My brother nodded. "Yes, about that," he said, looking around the kitchen. "Truth be told, this doesn't feel like home to me anymore, Brynn. It's just a place now. It's your place, and I don't feel like I belong here."

"What are you talking about?" I reached my hand out to his. "Of course, this is your home, that's not what I meant—"

"No, it's not. Not really."

My heart dropped as I heard the truth in his voice.

"Is it something I've done?" If he said yes, then I could try to fix it. But he was going to say no, and the massive gulf growing between us wasn't something we could easily repair.

"Why am I not enough?" The words spilled from me, along with a torrent of childhood pain that I'd kept locked up inside: all the years of trying to be good enough, of trying to be seen, of wanting to be worthy of something that should have been given unconditionally.

"I've never been enough. Not for you. Not for Anthony. I always come in second place, don't I?" I fought to control the tears, but lost the fight as they trickled down my cheeks.

"That's . . . that's not it, Brynn." My brother swallowed hard, staring at me like a deer who realized it was too late to run from the oncoming vehicle, but ran anyway.

I wiped my face with my sleeve and forced myself to look at him. To really look at him.

"Then what is it? Will you tell me?" I pulled out a chair from the table and sat hard.

"Will you listen without judging me?"

*Ouch.* That hurt.

Bryce sat next to me and reached for my hand. "You are more than enough, and I hate that you don't see it. But this life, there's more to it than this. Come on, we've always known that, right?"

"Are you going to open your own restaurant? Is that what tonight is about?" It was naive, and I knew it the moment the words slipped out, yet he didn't say no. "The special dinner, the new recipe you're trying out, the stocked fridge?" My lips slowly turned upward as an image of him working in a real kitchen took hold. "I'm happy for you, Bryce; it's about time."

He slowly shook his head.

"Not a restaurant. But I do want to try out new recipes, and eventually, I'll be cooking them in a new kitchen." He said the words slowly, taking his time to let the message come across.

His message came across loud and clear. I knew exactly what he was talking about.

He pulled out his phone and showed me a photo. It was a kitchen that could be found in any food or architectural magazine, with a large gas range, gorgeous cabinets, a waterfall island, a water tap over the stovetop, and more.

"I designed this," he said. "Spent months making sure it was perfect, and it's almost done. It's the kitchen of my dreams."

"So when are you moving out there?" The words tore through my throat, and my heart broke into tiny little pieces. If that was a kitchen he'd designed, the kitchen of his dreams, then there was only one place he could have built it.

Clearly stalling, he took out a dish from the oven.

"Oh, come on, Bryce." I struggled to withhold the hurt and pain I felt from my voice. "That's what you're trying to tell me, isn't it? I always assumed you'd move out for love, but it's for the Family, right?"

When he turned, I couldn't read him.

"Come with me."

I laughed. Of all the things I thought he'd say, that wasn't even on the list of possibilities.

"There's a house they built for us, Brynn. I wanted to show it to you when we were there. The kitchen is amazing, and the library . . . you'll fall in love and not want to leave. You could write that book you said you wanted to write one day. Well, now is the day. There aren't many left, and we should—"

I held up my hand. "Whoa, slow down. What are you talking about?" There was a house built for us? Not many days left? Nothing he said made sense.

Rather than answer, Bryce pulled some plates from the cupboard and set them on the counter.

"Dinner is ready."

Whatever he had made smelled absolutely amazing. I waited until we were at the table before I answered his question.

"I can't move out there with you. It's a cult, Bryce, don't you see that?"

He dropped his fork on his plate. "It's not a cult. Why can't you see that?"

"Do you know what the definition of a cult is?" I asked. He rolled his eyes at me, but I decided to ignore it. "I looked it up the other day, and a cult is basically a small group of people, led by a charismatic leader, who hold beliefs that others view as extreme and dangerous."

He shook his head, and I knew continuing to argue was a losing battle. But I had to say something, try to get him to see, to understand.

"You've got all the check marks for a cult with that group, Bryce. First, let's start with the name they use for themselves. The Final Family? Really? Elders, Aunts, Uncles, Cousins . . . it's a little weird, don't you think? Then, there's the whole doomsday thing that really—"

"Stop. Just . . . stop, please." Bryce pushed his seat back. I half thought he would get up and walk away from me.

"I can't." I leaned forward, pushing my plate away. "You want to move there and do what, exactly? They're too far out to make driving back and forth work, so you're what, going to be their chef? They already have someone for that. Will you create products and sell them at farmers' markets? Maybe work at the FAM Casa? I don't understand what your end goal is, Bryce. You used to have such plans; do you remember that? Where did those hopes and dreams go? We're free now to follow our own lives. If you don't want to be part of the funeral business, that's fine; I can run it. But what will you do? Because living on a farm in the middle of nowhere doesn't sound like much of a life to me. That's not you, Bryce."

"What I do here isn't me either, you get that, right?" There was a sense of anguish in his voice, in the stoop of his shoulders, and I wondered if he harbored doubts he didn't want to admit.

"I do," I told him. "I hated that you were made to take those courses and get a degree you never wanted."

"Dad—"

"Anthony didn't need you to," I cut him off. "He wanted you to. He didn't care about your passion or what you wanted for your life. He just wanted you to follow his." A rope of twined exasperation and irritation knotted within me. It was because of Anthony that Bryce was part of that group. It was because of Anthony that he gave up his dream of owning his own restaurant. It was because of Anthony that I was losing my brother.

"Do you actually believe that the world is ending?"

No reply.

"What about that stupid prophecy of theirs? You honestly can't believe in that." I needed to get through to him. "We're not special, Bryce. We have less melanin in our system than everyone else, that's all. We have lighter hair, eyes, and skin. We are more prone to burning. We are not special." I repeated. "We are not the fulfillment of some drug-created prophecy, and the world for sure is not ending."

"You don't know that."

I laughed. I couldn't help it. "Don't you think we'd know, as a society, if it was? Don't you think the scientific community would be shouting it from the rooftops? And that the stock market would crash, and everything would go in a tailspin like it did when the world stopped because of a virus? Come on, Bryce. You're smarter than this."

He rubbed his face with his hands, and what I hoped to see wasn't there.

There was no understanding. There was no acceptance. The brother I'd grown up with my whole life, who I would have sworn I knew better than even myself, was gone.

What I saw was someone unrecognizable, and I had to swallow back the fear rising like a snake in a basket with its lid removed.

"I've tried. I've really tried to get you on the same page, to see what I see and know. I've taken you there, introduced you to people who are important to me, and wanted to share that part of my life with you, a part that is important to me, and all you've done is throw it back in my face. Who are you? You're sure not the sister I thought I knew."

No matter how much that hurt, I couldn't back down.

"You've tried?" My voice leveled up a notch with active frustration. "All you've done is shove something — something you know I've hated by the way — down my throat while trying to tell me it's for my own good." I clenched my hands and my joints popped one by one as I tightened my fists. "I hated that group when Anthony was a part of it, and I sincerely despise it now that you are. It's a cult, Bryce. A cult that has managed to pull the wool over your eyes and make you believe in something that is one hundred percent make-believe. I don't get it."

Bryce picked up his dish and dropped it in the sink. "I'm not doing this with you," he said. The red rising on his skin, trailing like scratches against his pale features, said I'd pushed too far.

Or maybe I hadn't pushed far enough.

"That *Family*—" I used air quotes, something I knew he hated — "destroyed our family. It started with Anthony, and now it has you in its clutches. I can't believe you would leave me, leave our family business, for them. Do it because you're pursuing your passion, fine, I want that for you. But don't do it because someone's made you believe you're the savior of a doomed world."

I tossed my napkin on the table. I sucked a breath through my teeth and forced the knotted ball of emotions to remain in place and not spill out. Tears would not help here. I wasn't sure my brother understood where I was coming from, but I was at a loss of what else to say and how to say it.

How did I get him to understand he was involved in a cult?

What could be said to break the power of the so-called prophecy that had hung over our lives, and to make him understand we were not as unique as that cult said we were?

I was too late. I knew from how he held himself, the shuttered look in his gaze, and the sudden distance between us.

"What if you are wrong?" His five simple words strung into a sentence that shattered me. He was broken. I heard it in his voice. He was broken, but it wasn't because of some-thing they'd done to him.

I was the one who broke him, because I didn't believe in him or trust him, and realizing that ripped me apart.

# CHAPTER TWENTY-THREE

Life was all about balance. Mom used to say it was important to set aside time for yourself, to not always be about work and doing things for other people all the time.

That was why I tried to keep Sundays as 'me' days. These were the days when I headed to the local farmers' market, spent time at the library finding books to read, and stopped in at my favorite cafe for a freshly made donut and latte. Sundays were days when I left my job behind and embraced life as best I could.

Armed with a list of produce from Bryce to grab at the market, I headed out for a walk, enjoying the fresh air against my face. Despite the clouded sky, I wore a large hat to protect my skin, as well as a light, long-sleeve sun shirt that paired well with jeans.

Like most other small towns, Bervie Springs came to life on the weekends, and today was no different. The sidewalks bustled with families and couples, the shops had their signs out by their doors to entice customers to stop in, and the traffic was quite heavy, which was surprising for a late Sunday morning.

"Hey, Brynn, wait up."

Mona rushed across the street, sidestepping puddles while holding onto a coffee tray.

"I grabbed you a vanilla cream cold brew." She handed me one of the cups.

"I thought we were going to meet for coffee." I glanced over to Sweet Beans, our to-go coffee shop.

"I figured we'd do that after the market and library. I was chatting with Nancy, and she let it slip she'll be making fresh choux pastry for cream puffs later, and I know how much you love those." She tossed the tray into a recycling bin and sipped her coffee. "These will do until then."

"These will definitely do until then, thank you." We took our time walking down the street, window shopping along the way.

"Anything in particular you're looking for today?" She glanced at the bags I carried. "Let me guess, Bryce gave you a list?"

"It's a long one, too. I might see if someone can drop my bags off at the house rather than lug them around if they become too heavy."

"I'm sure Trevor would. He'll be there today, selling his comics and toys," she said, winking at me.

I ignored her comment. She had been trying to hook me up with her brother for years, but that ship sailed long ago, and she knew it.

Trevor and I were friends, and that was it. We tried going on dates a few times, but the chemistry wasn't there. Not for lack of trying, that's for sure. Personally, I think my profession was an issue for him, not that I blamed him. Dealing with death daily wasn't for everyone.

The town square was ahead, where the weekend market was set up. "I'm really hoping my skincare person is here this weekend. It's been two weeks in a row I haven't seen her." I did a cursory glance toward the stalls I could see, but they were for honey, quilts, and fresh bread.

"She does have a store, you know."

"In the city." Nothing more needed to be said, not really. I was not a fan of the city, where everyone stopped and stared as I walked through the stores. At least here, no one looked at me as a freak, mainly because I'd grown up with most people in Bervie Springs. They knew me as more than just 'the albino.'

"I have to run in for a doctor's appointment this week," Mona said. "If she's not here today, I'll stop and grab you your skin care products, okay?"

I smiled, thankful that she understood just how important my skincare products were to me. I couldn't use regular drugstore brands. I needed the highest SPF available, plus one that was good for my sensitive skin and wouldn't clog the pores. I always bought double, because Bryce used them, too.

We walked around, filling our bags as we shopped and sipped. I found my skincare, and after spending some extra time chatting with the vendor and looking over some new products she had to offer, I headed to the produce stalls to grab the items Bryce had specifically asked for.

His items filled both bags that I'd brought, and they weren't light. When I saw Trevor, he took the bags from my hands and plopped them down behind his table.

"I see your sister talked to you already."

"I would have offered anyway, and you know it." He directed the words to me, but he focused on the vendor next to him.

"Don't look," he said with a slight hiss.

"Why?" Despite what he said, I did exactly that. I glanced over my shoulder and instantly smiled.

"Hey." I waved over at the girls standing in a circle. I recognized them from the Farm.

"Do you know them?" Trevor asked.

"Kind of." My voice trailed off.

He groaned. "You're kidding me, right? Please tell me you're not involved with them." He ran his hands through his already disheveled hair.

"What are they doing here?" I couldn't recall if I'd seen them at any past markets.

"Same thing we all are, I guess. Selling their home-grown produce and handmade goods, from the looks of it.

And, apparently, promoting a new wellness retreat center. Yoga, meditation, tea, and crap." Trevor's disdain didn't go unnoticed.

"Your sister took me to that place. It's nice," I said. "It will probably bring in more business to Bervie Springs, too, considering it's close enough."

"Don't tell me you're drinking that Kool-Aid, too," he grumbled. "I've already had this talk with Mona. Places like that, they suck you in and then steal your money, your identity and your whole life. Next thing I know, I'll be forced to do an intervention, so that you both don't end up joining some kooky cult."

I laughed, not because of how absurd he sounded but because of how close to the truth he was. "Mona in a cult? They wouldn't keep her much past a one-month initiation, and we both know it."

"They would if they fed her fresh baked goods every day. That sister of mine has a fetish for bakeries, in case you haven't noticed."

"It could be worse." Bryce instantly came to mind.

"True, yet I will never understand you two. Your idea of a vacation involves sunrise stretching and long hikes in the middle of nowhere, followed by some nasty herbal tea, not to mention being electronic device-free. You're hopeless. Give me an all-inclusive on a beach, some water skis, and unlimited alcohol any day." His shrug, along with a dimpled smile, was meant to soften the harshness of his words.

"You know those don't work on me." I pointed to his dimples.

"Really? So, when we were on our first date, and I asked you why you loved your job so much and then didn't hear a word you said . . ."

"I knew the second your eyes glazed over you'd tuned me out." I sighed. "I let it slide because of that smile." I shook my finger at him. "Those dimples get you out of so many things, don't they?"

"Just don't tell my mom, okay?"

I sidestepped as customers approached his stall to look through the comics he had on display.

I noticed the group of girls in a circle kept looking my way.

"Sister, you're here." One stepped toward me as I approached. She clasped her hands behind her back and gave me a deep nod.

I needed to ask Bryce what the Family had against shaking hands. Everyone I'd met so far clasped their hands behind their back when around me.

"Hey, ladies, it's a surprise seeing you here." I glanced at their stall, taking in the wicker baskets of carrots, cucumbers, radishes, and lettuce. Quilts hung on wooden stands, along with some amazing watercolors that stole my breath away.

I gravitated toward them, mesmerized by what I saw. I found myself lost within the swipes and swirls between the shading and the detail. Those were gorgeous works of art, and I wanted one.

I wasn't an art person. I didn't generally get lost in the underlying detail, notes, and meaning, but . . . these pictures spoke to me in a way I never knew was possible.

"They're beautiful, aren't they? The artist is one of ours."

I turned to find someone standing directly behind me, someone I recognized, a tall woman with silver-stranded hair.

"Sister," she greeted me. It was Allison from the FAM Casa. "It's so nice to see you again. Imagine my delight to see you twice in such a short time, especially since it's been years since . . . well, I took it from the last time we met that you didn't recognize me."

A wisp of remembrance in her voice had me struggling to place her in my memories. I wanted to say she was there, somewhere in the fog of my childhood . . . there was something about her smile that put me at ease, just like at the retreat center.

"I knew your mother and miss her dearly," she continued. "I was supposed to be there when you were at the Farm, but something came up, and I was called away."

I heard the disappointment in her voice, and there was a tug inside me, like a knot tying up a memory I couldn't hold on to was about to unravel.

Something inside me told me I knew her or that I should have remembered her, and there was a twinge of regret that I couldn't.

"You knew my mother?" Others at the farm had said the same thing, even going as far as to share stories from the past, but there'd been a distance between them and me. Now, I felt the pull to know more, where before, I didn't.

"She was the sister of my heart," Allison said, touching her chest with the palm of her hand. "Even when she left, we stayed in touch. She never came back to the Farm, but we'd meet up whenever I was in town." She glanced off into the distance with a faraway look in her eyes.

I wish I knew what she was recalling, what memory made her lips turn upward with a wistful smile.

"Well, maybe the next time you come to the Farm, we can sit and chat, and I can share some stories with you?"

"Or the next time you come into town, we could go for coffee," I suggested. I wasn't sure how much of a rush I was in to return to that place.

My gaze returned to a painting of a girl and her mother sitting in a field. The little girl wore a hat and leaned against her mother as she was being read a story. Despite the fact that the faces aren't visible, there was a sense of vulnerability and comfort. I felt the warmth on my skin, the sun's heat, as I sat there in a sundress with my arms exposed, and there was a longing in me, a choking feeling that I struggled to swallow.

"Do you recognize it?" Allison asked, her voice soft.

I didn't, but I felt like I should have. Regardless, I wanted it. I needed to have it.

"It's you and your mother," she said.

I gasped involuntarily as I turned to look at her.

"I painted that," she went on, her head tilted, her smile full of memories. "Your mother never saw this one. I always meant it to be a surprise, but then she left, and well, I never quite got over it, to be honest. But by the time I was ready to give it to her, it was too late . . ." She turned with tears in her eyes. "I would love for you to have it, please."

Composing myself in that moment was difficult. There were no words as I continued to stare at the painting. I wished I could remember that day, hold the memory of Mom and me in the field as she read to me . . . I wished I had those memories to hold on to. Mom never liked to talk about that time. She always told me none of it mattered, that it was a time best left forgotten, even though Anthony continued to be involved.

"If that is me, why aren't my arms covered from the sun?"

"You noticed," she said. "That was something your mother always . . . wished had been different for you and your brother. That you could feel the sun on your skin without any fear, so that's how I wanted to paint you . . . if that makes any sense."

It did. Mom hated that we couldn't enjoy the outdoors like others could and that we always had to be careful about our skin, no matter the season. She called it a curse.

For reasons I couldn't explain, I grabbed a quilted throw and a crocheted basket and placed them on the counter. "I'll grab these, too," I said, pulling my wallet out of my purse.

"No, please. Consider these a gift," Allison said, laying her hand over mine. "You are family. We don't charge family."

My instinct was to correct her, but I swallowed my reply. Behind us, excited whispers caught my attention. I turned slightly and noticed the teenagers huddled together.

I couldn't make out everything they said, but I felt instantly uncomfortable, and Allison recognized it.

"Girls," she called out.

"Sorry, Elder Allison," one of the girls said. All heads bowed as they turned away.

"I would rather purchase these. Consider it my contri-bution." I pulled out my bank card and handed it over.

I knew she wanted to argue with me, but instead, she gave the girls a look that needed no translation. They all bowed their heads and separated.

"Sister, please." She placed my bank card on the table and pushed it toward me.

I pushed it back. She sighed, but I smiled: I doubted many won an argument with her.

"Have you considered returning to the wellness center?" she asked. "I would love for you and your friend to join us for our upcoming three-day retreat."

"That is a kind offer." I was intrigued, and I knew Mona would be too. "Let's do that."

"I'll set it up and get in touch," she said.

I glanced up toward the other paintings. "Are these all yours as well? They're quite remarkable."

She laughed. "Oh no. I only dabbled. We have a true artist, one quite gifted. I'll introduce you when you return to the Farm. She has a studio she works in. In fact, she'll probably ask you to sit for her." Her smile was one I couldn't help but return.

"I would love to meet her." My gaze returned to the paintings once more. "These are excellent pieces. They deserve to be in a gallery."

She nodded. "They are. She's highly sought after as an artist, so we recognize her gift and treasure that she's chosen to share her talent with us." The commanding tone in her voice also held an air of pride. "I'll make sure to set the introduction up. I'll connect with Brother and set a date."

The idea excited me, to be honest.

"We can drop this off at your home later today if you'd like. It won't be an issue."

The word 'sure' was on the tip of my tongue, but I refused to let it slip out. "That's okay. I'll take care of it getting home. Thanks so much." I grabbed the bag with the quilt and the basket in one hand and held the painting tight to my chest with my other arm. "This was such a pleasant surprise," I admitted. "I hope we can have coffee soon."

"I'll make sure it happens," Allison said as a goodbye.

Trevor waited for me.

"I wasn't sure I should come in and rescue you or . . ." He peered over my shoulder and exaggerated a shudder.

"Seriously, they creep me out. And why do they keep calling you Sister?"

I closed my eyes. "I thought you tuned them out."

"I did, but ignorance isn't always bliss, you know? What if they're like another Waco or something? Our town doesn't need a fire or a huge poisoning tragedy. Bervie Springs has been through enough, don't you think?"

"They're not like that." I felt a need to defend them — something I noticed I did earlier, too. What was with the sudden change of heart?

"Seriously—" he placed his hands on my shoulders — "you are not involved with them, right?"

I weighed the pros and cons of telling him the truth, as opposed to smoothing things over with a lie. If I told him, Mona deserved to know as well, and I'd done everything I could to keep all of that separate from our friendship. "Would that be such a bad thing?" I said, finally.

"You're kidding me, right?"

I shrugged. "My parents were a long time ago, I guess." There it was, out in the open.

"You guess? Or you know? And that wasn't exactly answering the question, Brynn."

I looked around to make sure no one was listening. "This stays between us, please? I haven't even told Mona . . . yet, but I will. Anthony was, and now . . . well, Bryce has taken his place, I guess you could say."

The way his eyes widened while his lips quirked, I knew he wanted to laugh. "That's absurd. And too crazy to be a lie. So why all the secrecy?"

"Because I didn't want to be lumped in with that group, since I've never . . . I'm not a part of it."

"Yeah, I get that. They are pretty out there. But Bryce? I thought he was smarter than that."

I didn't know how to answer that, so I didn't.

"Wait." Trevor tapped his thigh with his fingers. "Is that what all the stupid prophecy crap comes from? Your brother? But that would make you . . . no way! Tell me I'm overthinking this."

"You're overthinking this." My voice was deadpan and straight. How did he even know about the prophecy?

"Not cool, Brynn." He pulled me out of their line of sight. "Listen, between us — and don't you dare tell my sister — I went to a few of their *get-to-know-us* meetings," he said, air quoting with his fingers. "You need to be careful. Seriously, they're nuts. You know? Have you heard some of the stuff they say? The world is ending, and all that crap. It would be one thing if they were just a yoga and sex cult—"

"Sex cult?" Where did he come up with that? Or did he know something I didn't?

"Aren't most cults about sex? I don't know; I just figured it was a given."

I wanted to roll my eyes, but I didn't.

"Seriously, there's something off about them, don't you think?"

# CHAPTER TWENTY-FOUR

Golfing at Shinnecock Golf Course was a dream come true.

The greens were perfection, and my partner equally so. Through all eighteen holes, Daniel Sawyer was witty, charming, and full of stories too salacious to be anything but true.

"You never did finish telling me that pool party story," I reminded him as our caddy placed our golf bags in the cart.

"Considering how you just whipped my butt, I'm not sure I want to. My pride needs a little healing."

He grinned, the same smile he flashed at me this morning when I met him in the lobby. It had the same effect: My knees went a little weak, my stomach flip-flopped, and I had to remind myself he was way out of my league.

Not that I won't return to this day in my memories for a lifetime to come.

"You were warned." My smile was wide and bright. It had been a while since I'd taken a day to play golf, but it was good to know I hadn't lost my touch.

"Between you and me, I thought your brother was exaggerating about your skill level. I mean, my bad and all that, but you are definitely not what I expected."

He'd mentioned that a few times during the day. At first, I wrote it off as Anthony being Anthony, never giving me credit, but now I was starting to wonder.

"What *did* you expect?" The wind blew through my hair as we made our way down the path toward the clubhouse.

He glanced over, and I knew he wanted to say something, but stopped himself.

"Let me guess," I said, deciding to make it easier on him. "A good daughter, a supporting sister, a helper when needed." I counted off each demeaning quality I could think of. "Someone with mouse-like qualities who does as she's told. A woman with no personality." A coil of disappointment settled in my stomach at each nod of his head.

"Definitely a mouse," he confirmed, rubbing at the slight stubble on his face. "But you're more than that, and I shouldn't have judged you before even knowing you."

At least he was being honest.

"But next time I see your brother, I'll have a talk with him about how he portrays you to others."

"My brother?"

"Yeah, sorry," he said. "You were probably hoping it was your father, right?"

He was right. Hearing my brother was the source sunk my heart like a bag of bricks dropped into the ocean. But I shrugged, like his words weren't destroying me piece by piece. "Anthony and I had a . . . challenging relationship."

He was silent as he navigated us toward the patio.

"Not all parental relationships are healthy; I get that. My mother died when I was young, and I don't talk to my father. I haven't in years, truth be told." He waited until our bags were taken away, and we stood alone on the sidewalk. "I was just a paycheck for him. Once I was old enough, I made sure he didn't have access to me or my bank account anymore." He held out his hand, suggesting I lead the way into the clubhouse.

"I'm really sorry to hear that," I told him. My instinct was to reach out and touch him, to offer some comfort, but I'd done that once earlier today and he'd flinched, saying he had a thing about being touched, and not to take it personally.

I didn't. I did, however, feel bad for him. I couldn't imagine what he must have gone through to not like being physically touched.

He'd also made it very clear that he wasn't romantically available — which was fine. He was in a league I could never aim for, nor would I want to.

He stared intently off into the distance, before forcing whatever memory played with his emotions away.

"We can freshen up, and then I have a room reserved for dinner," he said. "No promises that the food can compete against your brother's culinary skill, but one of the chefs has won a few awards."

It was on the tip of my tongue to make a sarcastic comment about my brother's cooking, but I knew those words only came out of hurt, so I forced them back and just smiled.

The women's area was one of the fanciest spa lounges I'd ever seen, let alone been in. I had my own basket of toiletries with top-of-the-line products that were out of my budget, and the shower was a pampering experience all on its own.

By the time I met Daniel in the lounge, I was relaxed and ready to eat.

I thought he'd been teasing when he said he'd reserved a private room, but sure enough, there was one table with two chairs waiting for us when we walked in.

"I hope you don't mind," Daniel said. "If we ate in the main room, I'd be inundated with people wanting to say hi, take selfies and ask for autographs."

"Does that happen a lot?"

He grimaced. "All the time. It comes with the territory, though, and it is a give-and-take relationship when it comes to the paparazzi and fans. But," he spread his arms out, "there are perks, too."

"I guess you never really think about what real life will be like when you wish to be rich and famous," I said.

He gave me a half-smile. "The golden age of Hollywood, when being aloof and maintaining your privacy was a benefit to your stardom. Now, if you're out of the public eye, you get forgotten."

"That has to be exhausting." I dealt with people on a regular basis, but nothing compared to his life.

"It can be. That's why it's important to surround yourself with people who won't always be kissing your ass and aren't afraid to tell you no. Like your father."

My brows shot up, and I knew he saw the skepticism on my face.

"I have a feeling the man you grew up with was very different than the man I knew and trusted. I'm hoping your brother can take his place, but your father was one of a kind."

Now, I was intrigued. Everyone had always been so hush-hush with me regarding Anthony and his role in the Family.

"What did Anthony do that earned your trust?" I reached for a glass of wine and held it in my hands. I couldn't recall the name of the wine, but I did catch the nod of approval from Daniel when the sommelier presented it to us.

"He got me out of a jam that I thought for sure would ruin my career. That's what convinced me to join the Family." He leaned forward, his voice lowered. "When they say they'll protect you, they mean it. No questions asked."

I leaned back in my chair and finally took a sip; Daniel was already on his second glass. What sway had Anthony held within his group, that he could protect a big-name Hollywood star? And what kind of trouble had Anthony saved Daniel from?

I did my best to hide my curiosity. At least I hoped I had.

"You don't believe me," Daniel said, proving I'd done a poor job.

I lifted a shoulder. "My father owned a funeral home. What protection could he offer you in LA?" I gave up trying to hide any skepticism from my voice.

"You really don't know, do you?" He sounded incredulous.

"To be honest, I keep my distance from that group as much as possible." I sighed. "Anthony generally respected that, to a point."

"I figured," Daniel said. "Probably for the best, either way. There's no going back for me now, whether I wanted to distance myself or not. Your father was connected with some very powerful men in our country. There was nothing he couldn't hide or make disappear, or so I was told when your brother first approached me with the offer to help me out of my . . . jam."

I wanted to ask what exactly my brother and Anthony had done for him, but I had a feeling he wouldn't tell me.

"So you regret it now?"

He half snorted. "If by 'regret,' you mean I don't like having something hanging over my head, knowing that one wrong misstep could result in blackmail, hell yeah, I regret it. But, I also wouldn't be where I am today if it wasn't for that group, so . . ."

I blinked slowly and did my best to read between the lines, but I knew I'd failed miserably.

"Between you and me—" Daniel drank the last of his wine in two swallows — "you know how you hear about whispered cults and ceremonies held within Hollywood? They're closer to the truth than anyone wants to admit. To make it in this business, you have to be willing to sacrifice something . . . or someone."

I watched as he poured the rest of the wine into his glass, and did my best not to focus on his words. That life wasn't something I wanted to be a part of, including knowing anything about how it ran.

Nor did I want to know just how embedded my brother was in that life.

"Between you and me," I said, echoing him, "I'm glad I've kept my distance, if everything you're saying is true."

He laughed. Not a full belly laugh, but more of a sarcastic, caught-in-the-chest snicker. "You may think you're not part of that group, but that's only because they let you believe that. The best thing you could do, if you really want to keep your distance and stay alive, is to run and hide. But that's easier said than done, because they have the resources to find you . . . and you are the one person I've heard they'll never let out from under their control."

Run and hide? Stay alive? Was that the wine talking, or was he actually trying to warn me?

Servers approached our table with our meal.

"The chef has prepared a special menu for your tasting tonight," the head server said as he placed a plate down in front of me.

My stomach growled, and the only thing I could do was blush.

A new bottle of wine was placed on our table.

"Enough talk about business. You fascinate me, Brynn Kern. You're so much more than anyone has ever said, and I'd like to get to know the woman behind the legend."

# CHAPTER TWENTY-FIVE

My drive home from the golf course was a fog. I remember leaving and I remember arriving home, but nothing in between. Maybe because I was riding a high from spending the day at a golf course I'd only ever dreamed of playing, maybe because I enjoyed the time with Daniel Sawyer even though I knew it would never happen again, or maybe because the warnings behind his words played over and over in my brain. I wished I'd had the chance to ask him for more clarification.

When that server arrived at our table, all talk of the Family or my brother and father disappeared. He asked me question after question about myself until his phone rang and he had to leave, but not before he thanked me for the escape today gave him.

I mumbled something like 'Don't mention it' then mentally kicked myself as he walked away, but not before he'd made me promise to stay and enjoy dessert.

I stayed. I enjoyed. I savored every moment until it was burned into my memories.

I stood at our mailbox, music blasting through my earbuds, when a car behind me honked.

I jumped, dropping everything I held to the ground before I turned and was about to give whomever the culprit was the finger.

Mona waved at me, her face full of laughter.

"I hate you," I said, projecting my voice so I knew she heard. I pulled out my earbuds and stuck them in my pocket.

She inched her vehicle forward. "That was hilarious," she said. "Sorry. I thought you heard me pull up."

"What are you doing here?" I asked, walking alongside her.

"Can't a friend drop in for a visit?"

I glanced at my watch. "Did you leave work early?"

"Did you?"

That was a fair point. I didn't want to lie, but I couldn't tell her the full truth, either. Besides, she'd ask for proof, and I was the idiot who didn't ask for a selfie with Daniel Sawyer.

I pointed toward the Parlor, where a plume of smoke filled the air. Merilyn was taking care of the cremations today. "That was happening today, so I went and played golf." That was only a half-lie, or half-truth, depending on how you looked at it.

"Wow, I'm impressed you actually took my advice. How many years now have I told you to go golfing while the fire was burning?" She shuddered before she tore her gaze from the building smoke. "Whenever I see that, it creeps me out." She parked beside Bryce's truck and joined me at the kitchen door.

"So you've said, numerous times. It's a natural part of life, Mona."

"So *you've* said, over and over and over. Just bury me, okay? And no, I don't want to think about what happens with my body as it decomposes. Now, can we talk about something else, please? Like this invitation." She waved an envelope in the air. "Did you get one?"

Sure enough, there it was deep in my pile of junk mail, bills, and bank statements.

"Looks so fancy, doesn't it?" Mona's face was alight with excitement as she rubbed her hand over her linen envelope. "Go ahead and open it. I wonder how they got our addresses."

Inside was a white card, the paper heavy and velvety soft, giving off the aura of 'expensive and exclusive.' On the card was a simple message: I was invited to an exclusive three-day soul-intensive retreat at the FAM Casa Wellness Center in three weeks. The retreat was a gift from an unknown benefactor. There was a QR code with which I could RSVP.

"I have no idea what a 'soul-intensive retreat' is, but if some fancy rich person wants to pay my way, I'm in." The smile on Mona's face grew. "Regardless of what your calendar says, I think we should go. Say yes, please?"

I re-read the invitation and wondered if the unknown benefactor was my brother. If so, why keep it a secret?

"You did say you wanted to check it out, and it's only for three days, so . . ." My own smile slowly edged upward.

"Good," Mona said, her eyes twinkling. "I've already RSVP'd."

I chuckled. "Of course you did."

"I figured I had three weeks to bug you into going, if you were reluctant. We were going to do it anyway, so why not go when it's free, right?"

"Why not, indeed." I breathed a long sigh before heading to the fridge. "Sticking around, or are you heading home right away?"

"Is there a bottle of rosé and a charcuterie board already prepared in that vast fridge of yours?" She pulled out a stool from the island.

"Did I hear the term 'charcuterie board'?" Bryce walked through the kitchen door and gave Mona a side hug. "Hey you, good to see you."

"Hey, you too," she said. She paused for a heartbeat before she slid her invitation toward him.

"What's this?" He picked up the card and gave it a brief perusal. "Nice! And already paid for — how sweet is that? Are you going to go? You should. Take Brynn with you," he said.

He came around and pushed me away from the fridge. "I wasn't sure what to make for dinner tonight, but something low-key like charcuterie sounds perfect."

While he rummaged around in the fridge, I grabbed a bottle of wine and poured us all a glass.

"Hey, how was golf?" Bryce asked over his shoulder.

"It was . . . good to be out on the greens again. Didn't beat my personal best, but considering that was the first I'd been out all season, I was happy."

"I'm glad. You deserved the day." Bryce turned with his hands full of packages of meat and cheese. He gave me a look that said he had a lot of questions.

*You're not the only one*, my expression said.

One of his brows perched upward as he stared at me. *What does that mean?*

I rolled my eyes in response.

"I wish Trevor knew his way around a kitchen," Mona said, unaware of the silent conversation Bryce and I had. "Have you ever thought of doing some cooking lessons for guys like him? Or creating your own video channel where you teach Neanderthals the basics of boiling water and how to marinate a steak?"

"Trevor can barbecue." Bryce sounded surprised. "I've been over, and he's cooked mean burgers on that grill of his."

"He's good at burning chicken, undercooking pork chops, and charring steaks, if that's what you mean." Mona swirled her wine in her glass. "I'm serious. I know at least a dozen, if not more, guys who would take a class from you in a heartbeat."

Bryce was in the middle of organizing the meat, vegetables, and cheese he'd pulled out of the fridge. "It's something to think about," he said. "My plate is a little full at the moment, but I'll keep that idea on the back burner."

"Full plate? You? Doing what?" Mona glanced at me, then back to Bryce before she grinned. "Ahhh, you've met someone, haven't you? Why didn't you tell me?" Mona directed that question to me. I shrugged.

"Something like that," Bryce said. He didn't look up, didn't send a glance my way.

"Funny enough," I piped in, steering the conversation away from just how full my brother's plate actually was, and the reason for that. "I received an invitation, too. Compliments from a mysterious benefactor. You wouldn't happen to have any ideas on who that could be, would you?"

He glanced up then. "Not me, if that's what you're insinuating."

"Honest?" I wasn't sure if I believed him or not.

"I swear on the Family," he said, one hand held up high.

"Well, I would have sworn to God, but whatever, family works too . . ." Mona mumbled before she stole a piece of salami off the tray Bryce was in the middle of arranging with food.

"So, are you two going to go? Sounds like a perfect weekend of relaxation and whatever else they'll be offering."

"I've got lots of vacation time lined up," Mona said, "so I'm in. Actually, I was going to suggest we maybe look for some deals in the Caribbean. It's not Italy," she says glancing at me, "but Trevor won't shut up about doing an all-inclusive and he keeps forwarding me some really great deals. Surely the two of you have some vacation time to use," Mona said.

"I haven't taken a vacation in years." My sigh was both wistful and wishful.

"Exactly." Mona raised her glass and clinked it against mine. "Nothing right now; we'll wait till mid-winter, but what do you say?"

"My calendar is currently free, so why not? I'll mention it to Merilyn to make sure she can cover for me, but sure." Vacations were never in our family repertoire unless it was camping in a tent, with nature as our outhouse. Mom's stress level was always higher than a ten because of all the preparation, packing, cleaning, and cooking. To her, it was never a vacation; it was more like a prison sentence. Looking back, I'd have felt the same way, too.

"Bryce, what do you say?" Mona asked. "Will you be my brother's wingman and keep him out of trouble?"

"First, you want me to teach him how to cook; now, you want me to keep him out of trouble. The guy owns a comic book and toy shop. How much trouble do you think he will get into?" he teased her. "Let's circle back to this as we get closer."

I noticed that wasn't a yes, which surprised me. If there was one thing my brother loved to do, it was travel, and the old Bryce would have jumped at the idea. So much about him had changed since Anthony's death.

## CHAPTER TWENTY-SIX

My mother loved bucket lists. She was always adding and checking things off, but they weren't the 'over-the-top/never-to-be-accomplished' type of lists like some people make. She would add simple things, like taking a gardening class or visiting a popular garden exhibit, to them.

She always told me that whenever you added one item, you checked off two others.

Over the past few years, I'd kept a running list of all the things I wanted to do, and one by one, albeit very slowly, I checked them off my list.

For example, when I took a baking class and learned how to make macarons. Sure, Bryce probably could have taught me, but pastry wasn't his specialty. Besides, there was a little shop in town where the baker was classically trained, and she offered workshops throughout the year in her shop.

Today's project was to go through the basement and empty it out. There was so much down there — boxes, garbage bags, old furniture, and old Christmas decorations. Anthony had been a hoarder. He kept everything unless it was broken beyond repair, but it was one of his embarrassing habits, so he kept everything he hoarded down in the basement.

I'd already filled three garbage bags with items intended for the dump and two boxes with items that would be donated. These included clothing, bed sheets, old pots and pans still in usable condition, a stovetop kettle that our current electric one replaced, a set of dishes, some baskets, and other items.

Music blasted from my phone as I worked, so I didn't hear the obvious squeak of the door opening up, but the clop-clop-clop of my brother's heavy shoes as he stomped down the stairs was unmistakable.

I pushed back some tendrils of hair off my face and wiped my dirty hands on my jeans.

"Having fun?" He turned in a half circle, taking in the mess I'd made.

Everything was everywhere.

"Having time to help?" I knew the answer would be a fat resounding no, but trying didn't hurt. No doubt he was about to leave for the Farm, and he would offer his apologies and blah blah blah.

At least, that was what usually happened whenever I attempted to steal some time with him.

"Well, that depends. Are you purposely trying to make a mess, or is there a plan behind all this chaos?"

"Oh, there's definitely a plan. That pile over there is for the garbage. That pile there is for donations. And this pile is for me to reorganize once I go through everything."

"Donations?" He headed over to the boxes and started rifling through them.

"Yeah, I thought maybe we could donate them to the Family. Do you think they could use them?"

I knew by the brow arch that I had piqued his interest.

It hit me that morning that it was time to stop fighting Bryce about the Family, and while not about to give in completely, I was, at least, willing to come to a truce. I wasn't ready to join him, but there had to be something to the Family that had him so involved, something I was missing, something beyond ties with Anthony. Fighting with him wasn't going to get me the answers I needed, and if I continued to dig in my heels, I was only going to push him further away than I already had.

Losing my brother was not an option.

So I would play nice, be interested and open-minded, and see where that led. Who knew, maybe they weren't as bad as I'd made them out to be.

"That's an excellent idea. I can take inventory and see if they'd like anything." He started to go through the boxes, sifting through what was in there and making voice notes on his phone.

"Or," I let the word draw out as if it was one of those it-just-hit-me ideas. "We could just go and take them there ourselves? Our visit was cut short last time, and you mentioned there was more for me to see."

When Bryce took me to the Farm to meet the Family, we left early for some still unknown reason. He had been apologetic but also nervous, and despite my insisting I wanted to stay, his insistence worried me.

I hated wearing that blindfold, hated that he made me wear it for longer than was needed, and hated the distance that whole episode had created between us. But what I hated more was seeing my brother rattled like he'd been.

I wished he'd been honest with me then about the reason for our abrupt departure. Someone was dying — I could have handled that information better than being left in the dark like I'd been.

"I'm surprised you want to return," Bryce said, his voice super neutral, but I knew better. From the slight rise of his right eyebrow and the small waver of a smile he quickly hid, the idea I'd willingly return made him happy.

"We haven't really talked much about that visit." If I was going to do it, I needed to be smart about how I worded things. "I felt bad leaving without tasting everything the children had made for me. That was such a sweet gesture."

I knew my words had caught him off guard by the double take he gave me.

"They did go all out, didn't they? They were so excited to have you there."

"And Lily was such a sweetheart," I continued. "I was sad when she mentioned her mother had passed, and she was all alone."

His brows furrowed at my words. "She's not alone, though, Brynn. Family surrounds her. They would never leave her orphaned, I promise."

"But they're not her real family."

By his quick frown, I realized I'd said the wrong thing. "I mean, they're not blood," I amended. "I'm sure they've gathered her within their fold and love her, but well . . . you know. Losing your mom, the one who knows you best, there's no replacing that." I made my meaning personal, and it seemed to work. His frown disappeared.

I squatted down, resting on my heels, as I went through another box. It was full of toys that deserved to be played with rather than kept hidden in a dark basement.

"Hey, look, the kids there would love these, don't you think?" I beckoned him to come over and look.

He rifled through the box and only pulled out a handful of things. "Most of this doesn't align with the teachings for the children. They don't believe in teaching violence, especially through toys like this." He pulled out his action figure dolls and played with their arms and legs.

"What about my dolls?" The box also contained a slew of dolls, ponies, and fancy dress clothes.

"They're kind of iffy on those as well. I mean, of course, the kids have dolls and play dress-up, but they don't like to give the girls the wrong impression about what's appropriate to wear and such, you know? Maybe you should donate the dolls, but we can see about the horses and other animals in there."

I swallowed any words I wanted to say, because I knew they would only cause an argument, but what was wrong with my Barbie dolls and the clothing? What child didn't like to play dress-up and pretend to be someone they weren't,

169

or even possibly act out the future life they wanted to have? What was wrong with that? And why could only girls play with dolls, but not boys?

"Do you remember the tea parties we used to have? With my dolls and your action figures? Didn't I have a dollhouse someone made for me somewhere down here?" I climbed to my feet, hands on hips, and swiveled around, looking for that house.

I couldn't remember who made it. It sure wasn't Anthony or even our grandfather.

"The one old man Baxter made for you? Dad always hated him, you know that, right? Something about the man acting like he was more of a father to you than he had the right to."

I shrugged. Anthony not liking anyone who gave me attention wasn't new, and I'd always viewed Mr. Baxter as a pseudo-grandfather anyway.

"He wouldn't have gotten rid of it, though?" I headed to the far back corner of the basement, a section I hadn't gotten to yet, and peered around the boxes to see if it was there in the back, but there were too many boxes in the way. They were stacked just high enough to block my view.

I nudged a stack to the side with my hip, taking the lazy way of moving them, but damn, they were heavy.

"Want some help?" Bryce grabbed the boxes individually, setting them off to the side. "Bet you these are all full of books; they're so heavy."

Sure enough, I opened a few, and that was exactly what was inside. "These must be Mom's," I said. I took a few out and looked them over.

"Mom had books?" Bryce sounded surprised.

I shook my head as I went through the boxes. They contained a wide variety of genres, from fantasy to romance to literary, sprinkled with some really old covers and even a few children's books.

"Of course, she had books. Mom loved to read, don't you remember that? She'd always read to us at bedtime, then close the book and say it was her turn to read her 'mommy' stories." At the time I hadn't known what she'd meant, now I understood all too well. Some of the spice levels in Mom's old books surprised even me. "She'd make a cup of herbal tea or hot chocolate and sit in that little nook area in their bedroom."

Bryce scrunched up his face as if trying to picture it, but I knew it was a lost cause. "I remember her reading to us, but I don't think I ever saw her with a book in hand."

Now who was the one with memory problems?

"Are you kidding me? She had stacks of books everywhere. Anthony always complained about them." How was it possible we remembered two different things?

Bryce shrugged like it didn't matter. "You should donate these to the library," he suggested.

"After I read them first, *thank you very much*." Over the years, I'd found some books on our shelves where Mom would leave notes inside. I used to think it was like a scavenger hunt, that she'd left them on purpose, but I soon realized she just used scraps of paper as bookmarks. Some would have shopping lists. Others would have reminders for upcoming appointments. A few were little love notes between her and Anthony, which always weirded me out. Mom was always just . . . Mom.

"If we find the dollhouse, will you donate that? I'm sure the girls would love it," Bryce asked, as he shifted more boxes around.

My gut response was no. That was a part of my childhood I wasn't willing to give to someone else. That was something I should keep for my own children, assuming I'd have some one day.

I came across an old photo album, one I didn't recall ever seeing. I had all the other albums upstairs, sitting on a shelf, and I'd pull them out every so often, especially when I was missing Mom.

"What did you find?" Bryce came over and checked what I held in my lap. I flipped the cover open and gasped at what I saw.

There were four pictures on the page. There were no dates or names, but none were needed. There were Bryce and me, covered in long-sleeved shirts and pants, wearing sun hats, and very young.

"Wow, haven't seen these before." Bryce sat beside me. "You know where these were taken, right?" We flipped through the pages; sure enough, they were all from the Farm.

"See, I told you," he said, pointing to a photo of the two of us fast asleep in our beds. "We grew up there."

I had no words. The missing years in my memories were all there, in that book. Photographs of me as a young child, from babe to toddler to early school age, in settings that had only played out in my dreams . . . scenes that showed I should have been very familiar with life on the farm.

Why would she hide the album? Why did she pretend that part of my life never existed?

By the time we reached the end, tears silently cascaded down my face, and it was Bryce who noticed that an envelope with my name written in Mom's familiar handwriting was taped to the back cover.

Bryce slowly peeled off the tape and then handed me the letter.

"Wonder why there isn't one for you?" I whispered.

"Maybe because I didn't need it. I wasn't the one she took away from the Family. You were."

I swallowed hard. Everything inside me wanted to read the letter right that very minute, but I also didn't want to share the last moment I had with Mom, despite how selfish that made me. I turned the envelope over so I didn't see her handwriting and pasted what I hoped was a carefree smile for my brother, but he wasn't even looking. He was over in a corner, moving boxes around.

"Do you think we could take the stuff to the Farm today? I've got time if you do." I brought the conversation back around to our original topic.

The way he paused and twerked his lips, the answer was no. "I'll make the arrangements, and we can go another day.

Hey, look what I found." He'd made a pathway to the back of the pile, and sure enough, there was my old dollhouse. It looked exactly like I remembered it.

It was a two-story, attic wood house with a front porch and a little porch on the second floor coming off one of the bedrooms. There were ziplock bags full of furniture meant for the house, and my heart swelled a little at the memory of the hours of playtime spent with that house.

"Why can't we go out today?" It was important that he knew I wanted to, that I wouldn't fight him about the Family anymore.

"They don't like people showing up unannounced," he said. "It's a disruption to their routine. I'll text one of the Elders, and maybe we can go this weekend." He pulled out his phone and started typing away.

"Think Lily will be around?"

He briefly glanced up, and I saw the thoughts running through his brain. Was I being too pushy? Was he suspicious of my insistence?

"No, Lily won't be available, but I'm sure one of the other girls will be more than happy to play tour guide."

"Why not Lily?" How did he know if she was available or not?

"She just . . . she's not there anymore, that's all. Listen, I need to go run an errand." He quickly pocketed his phone and left me among all the boxes. "I can come back down and help later if you'd like."

"Where did Lily go?"

He paused at the foot of the stairs. "Why so curious?"

"Why so secretive?" I could do that all day, slinging questions back and forth, if that was what he wanted. My brother loved to evade questions by asking questions, something I found extremely irritating.

He rubbed a hand over his face. "She's just not there, okay? There are things about how the Family works that you won't understand."

173

It was on the tip of my tongue to ask if she was okay, if she was safe, even if she was still alive, thinking back to that late-night phone call when someone at the farm had died, but before I could, he stomped up the stairs, his rush to get away not going unnoticed.

## CHAPTER TWENTY-SEVEN

It felt fitting that I found myself in the garden to read Mom's letter.

Bryce was gone. He'd left more than an hour ago, and even though he said he'd be back to help sort through things, he wouldn't be back till late, if he came back tonight at all.

What deserved so much of his attention out at that farm? It had to be something important, a reason for him to slowly let go of the life here . . . because that was exactly what he was doing, as hard as it was to admit.

All the signs were there, all the indicators that he was moving on.

I sat on the porch swing and gently kicked off. I emptied my mind of everything that raced within, like the concern for Bryce, my ever-growing to-do list for the Parlor, the Family . . . everything. I wanted no distractions, no disrupting thoughts or emotions when I opened Mom's letter to me.

With my nails, I gently pried open the envelope and pulled out a single sheet folded into three. Already, the surge of emotions crept upward, lodging in my throat. A few escaped and settled on the edge of my lashes.

I didn't want to cry. I wanted to take it all in, before the tsunami of emotions crashed together and destroyed me in its wake.

I should have known better. The second I saw Mom's handwriting, I lost it. The words ran together as the pools of tears waterfall from my eyes.

The ache of missing her shredded my heart into pieces with its strength. For so many years, she'd been my everything: my best friend, the person who believed in me more than I believed in myself. I thought I'd always have her in my life, that she would always be around, guiding me with her insights, teaching me her lessons.

I was supposed to have watched her grow old.

I wiped my face with the sleeve of my shirt and stared straight ahead toward Mr. Baxter's house. It took me a moment to see that he was waving. I waved back, and then I realized he was on his way over.

I set the letter on my lap and waited for him to walk down the pathway he and I had set a few years ago.

"It's been a while since I've seen you out," he said. I scooted in my seat to give him room to join me. Jasper sat at my feet and held out a paw for me to shake.

"I always loved that you taught him to do that," I said, scratching the dog behind the ears.

"Manners are always important." His voice was gruffer than usual.

"You feeling okay? You almost sound like you're coming down with a cold," I asked.

He waved away my concern. "Just seasonal allergies. They get worse as you age; just an FYI for the future." He glanced down at the envelope I'd placed over the letter. "That looks familiar."

"Really?"

He nodded. "Yep. If memory serves, your mom was out here on this very swing, too. You were in school and she had a photo album in her lap. I seem to remember seeing photos of you and your brother when you were just that big," he said, holding out his hand a little higher than his knee.

"I brought her over a rose cutting, and she'd been crying, much like you." He gently wiped a tear from my cheek. "Don't be afraid of the sadness; it's good for our souls to remember the things that cause our hearts to hurt."

"I'll never not miss her, you know."

"Of course you won't. She was your momma. She's not gone, though, not really. Death isn't the end of things, it's just a different path someone walks than you. You still hear her voice, don't you? Still remember the things she said to you? The lessons she taught you about life and her plants? If you still remember all that, then she hasn't left. Her presence has always been here." He pointed toward the flowers. "And in here." He then tapped my chest.

I glanced down at the letter in my lap and bit the inside of my cheek. "There's a lot I don't remember, too."

"Harumph. That's just life, sweet girl; that's just life."

I sighed. "You seem to remember a lot of things, whereas I don't recall a single event from that photo album. In all truth, I don't recall much about my life as a young child. Don't you find that . . . odd?"

He didn't answer for the longest time. "Some memories aren't worth protecting. I wouldn't stress on it too much."

Protecting? That was an odd choice of word to use.

"I've always had to lean on Bryce for things from our childhood."

He shrugged. "My own wife never remembered her birth date." He made it sound like memory loss wasn't a big deal.

I got the impression he knew more than he let on.

"What did my mother tell you?"

His head tilted back, and his brows shot up. My question was an obvious surprise.

"Well . . . that's between me and her, I reckon. Your mother needed someone to listen, someone who wasn't part of . . . well, a part of all that nonsense your father was involved in, and she needed someone who wouldn't judge."

Which meant he wasn't going to tell me anything.

"She was involved, too, for a while," I said softly.

"Harumph," Mr. Baxter muttered. "There comes a time when you need to stop judging a person for their past mistakes and focus on who they became because of them." He pointed to the letter in my lap. "Have you read it yet?"

I shook my head.

His knees cracked as he stood. "Then I best be letting you get to it. There'll be answers in there, I'm sure. Come on, Jasper, let's head home."

I watched as he walked home, my heart working through his words. There'd been an apparent closeness between Mr. Baxter and my mother but I never knew just how close. Was that why Anthony had never liked the man? Because he'd met a need in my mother's life that Anthony hadn't or couldn't?

I picked up the letter and unfolded it. Seeing her neat handwriting was overwhelming as my gaze skimmed across the paper. It took me a solid three attempts before I could focus on what she wrote, word by word and line by line. By the time I was done, I wasn't sure how to feel.

*My dearest Brynn,*

*If you found this letter, it means you also found the photo album I'd kept hidden from you for all these years.*

*Parenting is the heaviest responsibility, full of agonizing decisions, countless mistakes, heartbreaks, and regrets. However, it's also the most joyous thing ever, and I cannot imagine what my life would be like without you and your brother in it.*

*You're probably wondering why I didn't leave a letter for Bryce. The simple answer is that what needed to be said has already been said. This letter is to say the things I never could say, the things I should have said, and the things I hope I one day will have the nerve to say. But if I don't or can't, I'm writing it here.*

Being your mother has been the greatest gift I could ever have received, and I'm sorry that I didn't treasure that gift the way I should have. I have made plenty of mistakes over the years, but one weighs on me more than any others.

When you look through this photo album, what do you remember? What emotion fills you when you see the images of you and Bryce?

I expect you'll say the emotion is emptiness and that you don't remember much or anything from those photographs.

The reason for that is me.

Much of your early childhood was spent on a compound, or what you know as the Farm. We were members of the Final Family, and our lives revolved around that group and those beliefs. I'm not going to go into what they believe and why they believe it — I hope to tell you all that in person soon. What I will say is that they believe you (and your brother) are the fulfillment of a prophecy all because of your albinism. It's because of that belief that I did what I did to protect you.

Our memories are so powerful that they guide all our future steps. It was important to me that your steps not be guided by your childhood, at least, not from what you could remember. I didn't want those childish memories to sway you — and I knew they would or could if your father had his way.

So, I used a specific memory suppression technique on you so that those years would be like a fog in your mind.

However you must feel now, I want you to remember that everything I have done is for your protection and safety. The Family wishes to use your life for their own benefit. I want to save your life so you can live a long and happy one.

I love you, my beautiful daughter,
Love, Mom

# CHAPTER TWENTY-EIGHT

*Present Day*

The shadows in the room flicker, and my eyes strain as I struggle to take in my surroundings. This deepens the headache that's already settled in like a boa constrictor wrapped around my skull.

It's hard to move my body, let alone my head, but I refuse to show the fear coursing through me, so, despite the coarseness of the rope scratching the skin around my neck, I turn my head so I can get a better view of my captor: Maximus Rutledge.

He sits there like a king. He doesn't care that I'm in pain. I'm a mere peasant compared to him.

"Why is this necessary?"

"The rope? That's simple," he says, his deep voice echoing in the room. "Like I said, you gave us no choice. You can't be trusted. What's that saying: Give an inch, they'll take a mile? You went against the Family, Sister. You tried to hurt Elder Allison. You betrayed all of us by refusing to go through with the blessing." His face is a mask of hurt I know I put there.

The guilt eating away inside me intensifies. Is this all my fault? I don't know what to believe anymore. I don't know what's real and what's imaginary, what's true and what's a lie. I'm so confused.

"This all ends now. Just say the words. Confess your sins, and all will be forgiven. We can then celebrate you and your blessing like you deserve, and you will save everyone. You want that, don't you? Or do you truly wish to let everyone up there die?"

Will their deaths really be my fault? That's something my soul won't be able to bear. What if what Max is saying is real? What then?

"You need me to be willing."

He strokes his chin as if he's thinking about my statement. "Willing. There's a lot of leeway when it comes to that term, don't you think? You've been willing, haven't you? You told me you were. You told me you understood the prophecy and the power of the rebirth. So, were you lying to me then or now?"

"I wasn't lying. I just didn't understand . . ."

"Tsk tsk, Sister. You understood, and we both know it. You've always been aware of the prophecy, even before your mother tried to shield you from us. Her sin separated you from those who love you the most. I'm sure she eventually would have changed her mind if she were still alive today."

The whirlwind of confusion within me intensifies.

"I don't want to die." That's the only truth I can grasp right now.

Max leans forward, letting his hands dangle between his legs. "Death is only temporary, Sister. There will be no pain, no discomfort. You will close your eyes to this world and reopen them in the next. Just like the rest of us will." The smile on his face grows. "Tomorrow is the rebirth for everyone here. Not just here, but in our other communities, too. You are what we've been waiting for. You and your brother are the prophesied ones. Your father knew it. Your mother knew it. Your brother gets it. The only one suddenly not on board now is you. I blame your mother. I'm sorry you lost her like you did; I'm sorry that she couldn't be the one to walk you through all of this. I've let you down, and that is on me." He looks away, the smile gone, and I realize I'm not the only one in pain — he is, too.

There's a part of me that feels horrible for the pain I'm causing him and everyone else because of my hesitation and misgivings. I want to apologize, ask for forgiveness, change my ways, and accept what is about to come . . . but then I realize how ridiculous all that sounds, and that he's gaslighting me.

The only one to blame is him. The only one who needs forgiveness is him. The only one who has the power to change the future . . . sadly, is also him.

He holds my life and death in the palm of his hands.

"Please release me," I whisper.

"Say the words."

I can't.

"Then I'm sorry, but I won't. Your blessing is too important. The lives of our Family are too important. I'm sorry you're blinded to that now, but it is what it is."

"The prophecy says I must be willing."

I turn as much as possible so I'm no longer looking at him.

"The prophecy only says the willful blessing . . . not that you both have to be willing." He leans back, watching me carefully.

My stomach twists and turns, knotting together as his words sink in.

"What if I promise to cooperate?" I won't. He knows it. I know he knows it, but . . . I have to try.

He laughs. "You broke my trust once; I'm not letting that happen again." He reaches for something on the table and holds it up.

It's a needle.

There's a hole in my chest that gapes open, claws of fear sinking in deep, tearing me apart as I realize there's absolutely nothing I can do.

"Please don't." The words are ripped from me.

Max stands to his feet. "I could have had any of my guards do this, but I wanted to ensure you knew how personal this is to me. All of this is on you. It could have been different, but you chose this. Remember that."

"I didn't . . . I didn't choose this." My body is frozen with fright.

"But you did, when you went after Elder Allison. She's important to me, just as important as your parents and, in turn, you and Brother. You threatened my family, which tells me you are a threat to me."

"I'm not." My words come out as a whisper.

"Ahh, Sister, I feel for you, I really do. Ever since you arrived, I've done everything I could to embrace you, to help you remember the Family you belong to, but all you've done is throw it back in my face with your delusions, and try to turn everyone against me. Here's the thing you don't know about me, something I tend to hide from everyone. In my world, you can be one of two people — the ones who issue the threats or the one who makes those threats disappear. Bet you can figure out which of those two I am, can't you?"

He approaches with a swagger as if this is all a game to him, like my very life is a game to him, and the way he holds the needle confirms that this is a game he knows he's going to win.

# CHAPTER TWENTY-NINE

*Then*

I didn't return to the Farm for another few weeks.

I wasn't sure if I wanted to, truth be told.

On the one hand, Bryce was excited that I had expressed interest, and he wouldn't stop selling the benefits of the Family to me. But on the other hand, I couldn't let go of the idea that something truly horrific must have happened for my memories to be suppressed.

My mother's letter didn't help. The only thing she explained was the reason for my lack of memories — nothing else. That alone sent me into a tailspin, googling "memory suppression" and looking for information on how to reverse it.

The best way to reverse it, or so the internet experts claimed, was to be exposed to what you were supposedly forced to forget.

So, other than looking over the photos until their images were stamped onto my brain, going back to the Farm seemed to be my only answer.

A simmering anger built inside me at the idea. I'd always been angry with Anthony, but now that anger was directed toward my mother, and I had no idea how to deal with that.

She'd never been the enemy before.

"I'll need you to put the blindfold back on," Bryce said as we drove down a country road.

"This is ridiculous." I repeated a phrase I'd said over and over since we left the house, yet he handed me the blindfold. Why did I need to wear it? I wasn't a stranger, a journalist, or someone who would sell them out.

I secured the blindfold over my eyes.

"I'll talk to them, I promise," Bryce said. "Let's roll down the window a bit, maybe that will help."

Surprisingly, feeling the air on my skin did help. I kept one hand wrapped around the door handle, and the other held my travel mug. I worked on my breathing exercises.

"I have a question for you," I said, the need to talk about something, anything, other than the dark, strong. "You knew Mom had suppressed my memories, didn't you?"

"We've already been over this," Bryce said. I heard the sigh in his voice.

Yes, we'd been over it. Ever since reading that letter, that was all I'd wanted to talk about. It annoyed me that Bryce hadn't been surprised by the news.

"And you've never really given me an answer," I told him.

"Yes, Brynn, I have. I told you I knew. I told you that Anthony had explained it to me once when it became clear we didn't share the same memories of the Farm. But I don't know whom Mother took you to, I don't know how she did it, and yes, I will try to help you find someone within the Family who might know anything about it."

The exhaustion within the words was enough for me to keep my lips clenched tight. Fine, I'd brought up the subject more times than was probably necessary, but he couldn't blame me.

Our mother had me hypnotized to forget something from my past, and I seemed to be the only one who was bothered by that fact.

Bryce and Mr. Baxter were the only two people in my life who knew about it, and neither one had any information to share with me, intentional or not.

185

"But if you knew, why didn't you tell me?"

"Anthony told me not to. He said until you found out for yourself, it would only complicate matters. Besides, he'd told me that he hadn't agreed with Mom's decision, so he believed it was up to her to tell you or fix it."

"I wish you'd put yourself in my shoes . . ."

"I can't, Brynn. Listen, I know it must be frustrating, but I promised to do everything I could to help you regain those memories, and I meant it. The best way to do that is at the Farm, don't you think?"

The truck slowed as he made a turn.

"You never did tell me how your golf day with Daniel Sawyer went. He sent me a message the other day saying you were a surprise and that I don't deserve you." I heard both the question and the jealousy in his voice.

"Yes, he told me that was how he felt." My mouth was dry, like I spoke around a cotton ball.

"What exactly do you do for the Family?" I hadn't wanted to ask. In fact, I swore to myself that I wouldn't go down that dark hole, and yet here I was, doing exactly that.

"What did he tell you?" There was a hesitation to his words, a wariness that told me to tread carefully.

But why?

"Some nonsense about how powerful Anthony was and that you got him out of a jam or something." I played it off like I hadn't believed any of it. "He also told me a lot of stories about what life was like in Tinseltown, and to be honest, I wasn't sure how much to believe." I didn't know why I added that part, other than to give my brother an out in case he needed one.

If there was nothing to what Daniel had said, Bryce would pester me for every detail.

If there was something, he would do the opposite. He'd drop the conversation, which would tell me more than I wanted to know.

Bryce was silent for a moment. "He does like to tell stories, that's for sure."

My heart sank. There was a side to my brother I had no idea about and I wasn't sure how to process that.

We drove for a bit, made a few more turns, and then slowed down completely.

"You can remove the blindfold now. We're at the gates."

I reached up and pulled it off. The first thing I noticed wasn't the beautiful scenery or the buildings within the compound, but the two guards who stood at the main gates.

"What's with the guns?" I tried very hard to keep the fear radiating through my body out of my voice. The men looked fierce, with their wide-leg stances and machine guns slung across their chests. They weren't here before, or at least, I didn't recall seeing them.

"They've had some security issues the past few weeks. Don't mind them." Bryce's voice was relaxed and the complete opposite of how I was feeling.

"Please place your phones in this bin. They'll be returned when you leave." A guard held a small container out, and while Bryce readily handed over his phone, I was more hesitant.

"Come on, Brynn," Bryce said. "Don't make a scene, okay? It's just for security reasons." He held out his hand, and even though I didn't want to, I handed him my phone.

"We didn't have to do that last time," I said, watching our cells being zipped into a bag and our names written on a small white square.

"Things have changed since then." Bryce kept his voice low, but I heard the anxiety. Was it directed to me? Was it because of me and my questions? Or was it because of the guards and the new security measures?

I twisted in my seat as they opened the trunk and went through the donation bins we'd brought. Why were we being searched? I had so many questions rushing through me, wanting to be asked, but the quick shake of Bryce's head told me this wasn't the time.

I stayed mum as he parked in front of a very large farmhouse, complete with a wrap-around porch, beautiful garden, and walkway.

"This is the main house," my brother told me, even though I didn't ask. "That one across the driveway is for the Elders, and that small cottage is for the guards." His voice was now strained, and I wasn't sure if it was from my silence or if he was picking up on the weird vibe that filled the air around us.

I joined Bryce at the back of the truck as he pulled out the bins. My arms were crossed tight over my chest as I stared at the guards, who paid me no mind. "I don't like it," I muttered.

"Like what? Honestly, Brynn, you need to relax. You were the one who wanted to come, remember?"

"You could have at least warned me," I told him, giving him a pointed look. "Are the machine guns really necessary? There are children here." I tilted my head back for a good look around and noticed a watch tower in the far corner. I barely made out the man standing at the top.

"Just ignore them, okay? They're here for protection."

I shuddered at his words, not feeling any comfort at all. I didn't feel protected. I felt threatened, worried, fearful.

"What kind of security issues?"

From the slight huff Bryce gave, he was annoyed with my questions. His tightened lips and taut shoulders warned me to be quiet.

Together, we pulled some boxes from the back and handed them over to a group of waiting teenage boys who were there to help.

"Brother Bryce, Sister Brynn, we're so honored to have you here today." A tall man wearing black pants and a plain button-down shirt appeared on the porch and waved.

"Sir is here." Bryce left my side in a rush. I couldn't hear what was said between them, but I saw the man giving Bryce a reassuring nod, one hand on his shoulder before he glanced my way, the intensity in his gaze unsettling.

I had no idea who that man was, but something about him was oddly familiar. I swear I'd never seen him before, yet I smiled as if he were an old friend.

"I can't tell you how long I've waited for this moment," he said as he left Bryce's side and met me at the bottom of the stairs. He took my hands in his, and how he held them, tender and firm, left me feeling oddly warm inside.

"Between your father and Bryce, I feel like I know you," he continued.

"And yet, I have no idea who you are." The words came without hesitation, and you'd think I would have pulled my hands from his grip, but I didn't. I left them within his grasp, unsure why.

"Well then, I think we need to change that, don't you?" He tucked my hand within the arch of his elbow and led me up the porch to the front door.

I glanced back toward Bryce. He had one of those *see-I-told-you* grins on his face that he needed to wipe off and fast. I disentangled myself from the man's hold and stepped to the side, waiting for Bryce to join us.

"How about we start with a name?" I directed the question to the man, but gave Bryce my attention. His grin disappeared, and there was a warning in his gaze — a warning for me to watch myself.

Why?

We weren't alone on the porch. At least six people were in front of the door, all looking at me. The other men were dressed in suits, and one held the door open. A sense of heightened intensity surrounded the suits, which set me on guard once again.

"Of course, how rude of me. I'm Maximus Rutledge, but please, call me Max." He directed an award-winning smile my way, and my insides fluttered like a closet full of moths.

I knew that name. Mona had mentioned it when we were at the wellness center. Didn't he die in an explosion on his mega yacht off his private Caribbean Island.

"I thought you were dead?" The words tumbled from my lips before there was even a chance to stop them.

Bryce shot me a look of death, but Maximus just chuckled.

"So I've been told, and yet, here I am in the flesh." He held out his hands in a 'this is me' gesture. "Don't tell anyone, though; I'd hate to cause more rumors to surface."

There was a look in his gaze that stopped me in my tracks and cemented my feet to the porch floor. His words might come across as friendly, but the chill in his gaze said otherwise.

"Let's go inside, shall we?" He waited for me to walk ahead of him.

I expected to walk into a quaint old farmhouse with rustic furniture and hand-sewn wall hangings. Instead, the house could grace any architectural magazine cover as a featured piece.

The foyer was massive. In the middle of the room, a large white antique water jug holding freshly picked flowers sat on top of a large round cherry table. A winding staircase led upward, while three other doorways offered views into different areas of the house.

Max headed to the left, and we all followed into a large living room, complete with a massive fireplace carrying a large wood beam similar to the beams on the ceiling above.

Max sat on one of the cream-colored couches in the room. Everyone else remained standing until Max indicated with a slight twist of his hand where he wanted us to sit. He had Bryce and me sit on a loveseat beside him while the other three men stood.

"Sir, can I offer you some tea or coffee?" A woman stepped into view, her hands clasped behind her back. She gave me a quick smile before she lowered her gaze to the floor.

"Auntie, yes, that would be wonderful. Thank you for your kind hospitality. Let's go with coffee, shall we? It's been a long day, and there's still a lot of work to be accomplished before the evening meal."

The woman gave a quick nod before she backed away into what I assumed was the kitchen area.

"Sister, Brother, I hope you'll stay for dinner tonight. I know the children have something special planned, and we've saved you two seats at the head table." Max turned his attention our way, and Bryce nodded enthusiastically. I guess that was our answer, then.

"Did you just arrive as well?" Bryce sat on the edge of the seat, elbows resting on his knees, fully enraptured with the man beside us.

"A little while ago. We almost didn't make it, but when I heard you two planned to stop by, I didn't want to lose another opportunity." Max leaned back, one leg crossed over the other. "I hear you brought some donations. That is kind of you." He beamed a smile my way, his gaze intense and penetrating.

I smiled slightly, but said nothing.

"It also gave me a great idea," Max continued, as if my silence didn't bother him. "Our centers have so much, and with the end so near, it's more prideful than anything else to keep it all for ourselves. Brother Bryce, as you know, we have a lot of celebrities who work hand in hand with different charities, which is important to us."

Bryce nodded, then glanced my way. He wanted me to notice what was being said, recognize Maximus Rutledge's greatness, and understand that being there, in his presence, was a huge deal.

I wanted to know why.

"So, because of your generosity," Max continued, "we've decided to donate our belongings to those organizations, but we'd like to start with you first. Tell me, there must be a charity that your funeral home works with regularly, isn't there?"

When Bryce looked at me, I knew he expected me to answer.

"We have several memorial donations set up to local charities within the community. Is that what you mean? Many families prefer to do that instead of receiving floral arrangements."

Max nodded. "Yes, that's perfect." He glanced toward one of the men to his left. "For the next upcoming weekends at the farmers' market, let's focus on that. You'll take care of it?"

The man nodded, making notes on his phone.

"Brother Bryce, maybe that is something you can help with as well?"

Bryce's face turned a shade of pink. "Of course, I'd be more than happy to." He directed his words to the note-taking man, who nodded.

"I'm sorry, I must have missed everyone's name." I kept my hands in my lap but leaned forward slightly, looking toward the men, who had yet to speak.

"Oh, don't mind them," Max said. "Kenneth is my assistant. Douglas and Jacques are here for security."

I leaned back, suddenly feeling slightly more uncomfortable than before. I glanced over at his security detail. They were the types that could be in any action movie, firing shot after shot, killing all the bad men while they never once got hit.

"Just ignore them, Sister Brynn," Max said, trying to disarm me with a smile.

"Do they need to be here? You can't possibly think Bryce or I would hurt you?" I had no idea where my boldness came from, yet the words leaped from my mouth with no effort.

Bryce gave me a sharp jab in the side.

"Of course, you wouldn't," Max leaned forward and lightly touched my knee. "Unfortunately, not everyone is like you. They rarely leave my side, but . . . gentlemen, why don't you grab yourself a drink and enjoy the sun for a little bit?" He kept his gaze on me as he spoke.

The tension in my chest eased as they walked out, taking their shroud of danger with them.

"So," Max drew the word out, appearing relaxed, one arm spread out across the back of the couch, the other resting on the edge. "You know, Sister Brynn, I think asking the guns to leave was the right move. How wise you truly are," he said, with marvel in his voice. "I didn't realize how heavy their presence weighs until now." His gaze and smile were once again disarming and vaguely familiar.

I felt like I knew him. Not just because I looked him up, but because . . . there was something there, something teasing my memory. Yet the more I tried to grab hold of it, the slipperier the memory became.

"Sir, it is an honor that you would go out of your way to be here with us," Bryce said.

My brother was posturing before this man. Why?

"Brother Bryce, don't think twice, please. Now, and especially now, my full attention is on our Family. I have been visiting each community over the past few months, but soon I'll remain here as . . . as things end. Where else would I want to be than here, with you?"

Bryce's face reddened slightly. On most people, it would be barely noticeable. He, though, with our albinism, looked like a tomato.

Who was this man to command so much attention from my brother? From everyone here? Even the women deferred to him as they brought in a tray full of coffee and small-cut sandwiches, personally handing him his cup and creating a small plate.

We were having a tea party, and the three of us were the honored guests.

"The fact you'd grace us with your presence, especially here, out of all the communities you could stay at, means a lot, Sir." Bryce handed me a cup of coffee before taking one himself.

"Where else would I be than with the prophesied ones?"

A ten-pound weight dropped from my brain to my chest. The whole interaction, with Bryce and everyone else calling Max 'Sir,' to how he brought up the prophecy, felt wrong to me.

I wanted to leave. Everything inside me screamed at me to get up, to take the keys from my brother if he wouldn't join me, and drive as fast from here as I could.

And yet, I ignored those warnings within me and remained seated. I was here for a reason. I wanted to regain my lost memories, and since those memories were of this place, the only thing I could do was stay.

Stay and watch. Watch and catalog all the little nuances occurring around us. Like how crowded the kitchen area off to the back was getting, with more people filling the room.

Like how my brother no longer acted like the confident man he was, and instead became a sycophant, a fan of the man beside us, like how Kenneth, the assistant, watched me like a hawk, with something between intrigue and sympathy in his gaze.

I wanted Max to clarify the boat explosion story, but kept my questions to myself. Now was not the time. Besides, why would he tell me the truth?

Everyone acted like this man was their savior, god-like in their presence, and I was itching to know why.

# CHAPTER THIRTY

A woman approached from the entryway. She wore a long tunic over her leggings and carried a basket on her hip.

"Ahh, Aunt Belinda. I hope our arrival hasn't been too much of an inconvenience to you and the others?" Maximus stood and stepped toward the woman.

She dipped her head slightly. "Not at all. Sir, I have your rooms all ready. I assumed your other men would be satisfied with staying in the guard house during their rotations?"

"Once again, you treat me too well." He took her free hand in his. "That will be fine for them," he said. "Sister Brynn reminded me that a little space between them and me while here is a good thing." He half twisted and gave me a wink.

He winked. At me. I didn't know what to make of that.

There was no smile on Belinda's face, but also no disapproval. There was just acceptance in her gaze, acceptance toward me.

"Your rooms are also ready, Sister Brynn." She might have said the words to me, but she was staring at my brother. Blushing, as well.

A magnetic current of attraction connected my brother with that woman. Was he aware? Was it shared? If so, why hadn't he told me about it? Was she why he'd been coming to the Farm and staying overnight?

"Brother Bryce, yours is as well." She dipped slightly, not enough to be a full curtsey, but enough of one to give that impression.

"Why did you just do that?" The words tumbled from my lips. I seemed to have no filter at the moment. "Dip your knees. Why?"

Belinda blinked but didn't respond.

"It's a sign of respect," Maximus said. "You and your brother are very special to us."

"You are the prophesied." The awe and deference in Belinda's voice bothered me.

"So people keep saying." If an eye roll could be heard, mine would have been louder than a cat in heat. I turned my back before heading to the window.

"Surely your father has told you of the prophecies? Brother Bryce?"

Outside, the world continued, while here, it had stopped. Men and women were busy with their lives, working in the gardens, and children playing together in the grass. It seemed all so ethereal and simplistic.

"The prophecies—"

"Our father raised us on the prophecies." Bryce stopped me from saying more.

There was another warning in his voice. Being a twin meant that we could read each other's thoughts and know each other's minds without spoken words.

He was embarrassed by my words, actions, and lack of deference to the man who played host.

"I hope you realize this is your home," Maximus said.

"As nice as this house is, my home is in Bervie Springs." I softened my tone just enough not to come across as rude.

The way the man's brows furrowed told me something was off. But what?

"This is where you belong, however. Your father helped build this home for you." He searched my face for an answer, maybe, then turned to Bryce. "You, of course, have told her?"

Desperation and anxiety crossed my brother's features, while disgust and anger boiled in my blood.

I breathed in and refused to look at my twin. If I did, I'd lose any resemblance of sanity. I wanted to blast Maximus, too, at his audacity and assumptions, but I did what I'd always done and was taught to do, and I turned the other cheek.

For the moment. Bryce wasn't going to get off so easily on our return home.

"As kind as the offer is, I'm not prepared to stay for the night. This was supposed to be a quick trip."

Bryce swallowed hard. "Yes, we, uh, have a few upcoming services we still need to prep for." He stared at his feet while worrying his hands together. Good. I was glad he was nervous.

Maximus's attention was divided between my brother and me. He was trying to read the vibe between us. Good luck with that. Not even our parents could, when they'd been alive.

"Well, we still have time," he finally said.

Time? Time for what? I clamped my lips shut. That was a question I would throw to my brother once we were alone. That and so many more.

"Sister Brynn, would you mind dreadfully if I steal your brother away? I know the children will be excited to see you, and I can see if one of the Aunties is free to take you to them?" Max didn't wait for my reply. A woman appeared, her hands folded in front as if she'd been waiting to be called.

"Of course." I forced my features to relax, to become docile and malleable. The tension in the room suffocated the air from my lungs.

Maximus led my brother away, his arm around Bryce's shoulders, their heads close together. I heard my name, and one of them say, *the end is almost here.*

"Sister Brynn?"

Elder Allison stood before me.

197

"Nice to see you again."

"I heard about your donation," she said. "It was very kind of you."

It took me a moment to switch gears. "I'm not sure if it's that I have a kind heart or just want to clean out my basement." I did my best to add a twinkle in my gaze as she beamed a bright smile my way.

"Decluttering is good for the soul, and it's the perfect time to get started."

I wanted to ask why it was the perfect time, but I had a feeling it had to do with the whole end-times mystique, and I doubted she would give me any answers.

I followed Allison into a large, ultra-modern farmhouse kitchen, complete with a butcher's block cutting board on top of a large island.

"Wow," I said as my steps slowed to take it all in. Copper pots and pans lined a wall, each hung by a wooden peg. With its six burners and two ovens, the gas stove would be in any cook's dreams. "No wonder my brother loves this kitchen," I muttered.

"He was out here so much, watching the progress, being as hands-on as possible. It was supposed to have been completed before your father's passing, but unfortunately was not." Allison said. "But now that it is, we're happy to have your brother in his kitchen, where he belongs. We quite like his food."

"My brother can't go anyplace and not cook, especially in a kitchen like this one. His cooking is to die for, don't you think?"

"That's one way of putting it."

"I'm sorry?" I said, as I followed her, but she seemed not to have heard me.

We continued out a side door into a large garden area. We walked along the pathway toward the main road, where a group of women stood on top of a hill, waiting for us.

"As promised, I set up some time for you to meet our artist. Hopefully, we'll have time to sit and chat about your mother afterward."

A small kernel of hope slid into my heart. Of all the people who might be able to walk me through my mother suppressing my memories, Allison would be the one, especially considering they had been good friends.

"I would like that," I said as someone approached.

"Sister Brynn, I'm Cousin Darinda. I'll be your host today," she said, placing her hands behind her back. "I heard you enjoyed my paintings. I'm honored. Thank you."

That was the artist? In my mind's eye, I had pictured her as an older woman with gray-streaked hair pulled back in a messy bun, wearing green overalls covered in dabs of paint. Instead, she was younger than me, probably in her early twenties. She wore paint-splattered jeans and a pink My Little Pony T-shirt, and her hair was in one long braid. She had the appearance of innocence, and a fresh farm-girl vibe.

"You're very talented."

Her smile was gracious and tender.

"Would you like to see our studio?" She glanced at Allison, who gave a deep nod in approval. "Maybe there's a painting in there that you'd like to hang in the main house?"

"I'm surprised there isn't one in there yet," I said. I adjusted my steps to match hers as we headed off into a field where a circular building, something like a roundhouse, stood.

"Brother wanted you to find some that spoke to you," she told me.

As we walked, she explained that the studio was open to everyone on the Farm and that she would soon teach classes at the FAM Casa Center.

"I heard you will join us for our exclusive three-day week-end session," she said. "I will also be there and hope you'll join me for a class. In fact, I would love to give you some personal lessons, once you move out here full-time. Brother told me you'd always wanted to learn how to paint with watercolor."

"Cousin . . ." One simple word, but Allison's warning tone was all it took for Darinda's face to shade. "I'm so sorry." The words rushed out. "I didn't mean to overstep."

I wanted to roll my eyes. Why did everyone assume I'd be moving out here?

# CHAPTER THIRTY-ONE

The sudden tension between the three of us was obvious. Darinda's face showed her misery, while Allison did her best to mask the frustration she obviously felt.

Me, I pretended like nothing had just happened. "Do you only paint watercolors, or do you dabble in other mediums as well?"

"I dabble, but watercolor is my passion." Her eyes lit up as she clasped her hands tight to her chest.

"As I mentioned at the farmers' market," Allison interjected, "Cousin Darinda's works are available in galleries and hang in many homes worldwide."

"Sir says I have a gift, and it would be wasteful not to share it." Darinda's chin dropped with embarrassment.

"While we may be in this world, we're not of it. The world sees talent and squirrels it away. That's not who we are. We're given gifts to share them." Allison paused, and I was tempted to argue with her logic. The world saw talent and exploited it — how was what they did any different?

"If you'll excuse me, I'll let you enjoy your tour, and hopefully, we can have that coffee afterward. Cousin Darinda, I trust you'll take care of Sister."

I waited until Allison was far enough away that we wouldn't be overheard for what I was about to ask.

"Sister—" Darinda leaned close, with a friendly smile — "please call me Dara, if that's okay?"

"Only if you'll call me Brynn."

"Oh, I couldn't possibly." There was a look of horror in her eyes. "You don't understand . . ."

I understood better than she knew, so even though I thought it was ridiculous, I let it pass.

"Can I ask you a question? I would have asked Allison, but . . ."

"Elder Allison isn't always the most approachable person, I get it."

From the tilt of her lips, she understood. I was intrigued by her story, why she was there, and why she painted there and sold her artwork at farmers' markets instead of exclusively in studios and galleries.

"It's this whole title thing. I don't get it," I said instead. "Sir . . . why not just call him by his given name? That holds more weight, don't you think, considering who he is and all that?" It was a question that had hovered since Bryce first called him that.

"Sir? Oh, that's because he's the head. Well, technically, it's Father, but according to him, he's not old enough for that title."

All these years, I thought Anthony was the 'father' of the group.

"So you call him Sir instead."

She nodded. "Besides, names don't hold weight, not here. We have titles, sure. Cousin," she said, pointing to herself. Then, pointing to me, "Sister. It's all about respect: your position in the family, your contribution to its success, and such. It's not about who you were, because when the end comes, who you were in the past has no bearing on who you will become in the new world."

New world? Position and contribution? I felt like I'd gotten more from her than I had from my own brother.

"Is there a Mother?"

She chastised me with one simple look. "We don't speak of Mother. She gave her blessing, but once a blessing has been given, we move on from what was to what will be."

If I had my checklist, all this cultish mumbo-jumbo nonsense would be added to it.

"We're here," she said, opening the door. "Please, won't you come in?"

I stepped inside the circular building and took it all in. Windows surrounded the whole room, starting and ending at the door. The room was light and airy, which added to the spacious feeling I didn't expect to find.

Above the windows were framed art pieces, which could be in a museum or an art gallery, many similar to the painting I had bought. Below the windows were what reminded me of children's drawings you'd find on the fridge. They were cute and colorful, but not frame-worthy.

Within the center were a plethora of easels, all set up with small tables holding trays, jars, and paintbrushes.

The moment we walked in, Dara held herself differently. She was relaxed and carefree, light and comfortable. She was where she was supposed to be.

"This is your spot, isn't it?"

Her sweet smile said it all. "This is where I come to get away from it all, to find sense in all the craziness. Some of the others love being in the kitchen, working in the garden, or going for walks along the property, but when I walk in here, I feel like I'm home, you know?"

Dara led me to an easel at the back of the room, beside the window. "This is what I'm working on right now."

She was a little hesitant to show me her artwork. I imagined most artists felt the same way, showing something not ready for viewing.

The image was of a girl, one I'd seen before. "Is that Lily?"

Dara nodded. "I paint all the girls who are blessings." She pointed to the framed images, and I took the time to focus on them.

If I was blown away by what I saw at the Sunday market, these stole my very soul away. The level of emotion depicted in each stroke was just as mesmerizing as before.

They were all portraits of women in watercolor. "They are beautiful," I whispered, awe in my voice.

"Thank you." She gently laid her hand on mine. "May I sketch you for your painting?"

"My painting?" She made it sound like it was a foregone conclusion. I couldn't imagine my likeness being hung on the walls with the others, flattering though the idea was.

"Once we receive your blessing, I'll complete your painting. This is my small way of ensuring your blessing is never forgotten. I need a sketch first."

My blessing? Did they expect me to give a speech or something? Couldn't Bryce have warned me?

"It won't take long, I promise. I have a photographic memory, so I only need you to sit the once." Her eyes sparkled with excitement as I agreed, and she positioned me on a stool.

"Most of the time, I like to do a side profile, and the background is their favorite place on the farm, but I'd love to do one with you facing me. If I have your permission?" Her head was buried in her sketchbook; she glanced up at me quickly, then looked back down.

"Whatever you want to do is okay with me. What kind of background will you use?"

"Oh, that's easy. I'll have you sitting on the porch of the main house with a glass of coffee and a book in your lap. Brother Bryce told us how much you love to read, and showing you at your home will be a gift to everyone here."

"That's not my home," I almost whispered, instinctively not wanting to offend the girl, despite the fact that I only spoke the truth.

"Not yet, but it soon will be. We're all so excited to have you come, I don't know if you know that. We'll have a big celebration dinner, too."

She sounded so sure of my impending arrival.

I glanced back toward Lily's painting. "You did an amazing job with Lily's likeness. I was hoping to see her today." I watched Dara's face for a reaction. There wasn't much of one — but I did notice a slight hesitation as she lifted her pencil off the paper.

"Lily is giving her blessing."

"What does that mean?"

"She is giving her blessing." Dara's voice was almost rote, with no inflection of emotion.

"I don't understand what that means, Dara." Despite the growing unease, my voice was soft and not sharp.

"Sir will explain." She looked at me then with a forced smile on her face. "I'm done." She closed her sketchbook and set it on a table. "We should get back. It will be dinner soon." Her movements were almost frantic as she headed to the door and opened it, waiting for me to join her.

I slowly got down from the stool and looked at Lily's portrait more closely.

"Is Lily gone? Dying? Is something wrong with her? Is that what you mean when you say she's giving her blessing?" I didn't know where the words came from, but they were suspended between us.

"Lily . . ." She paused, closing her eyes. My breath stilled as I waited for her to finish. She slightly nodded as her lashes lifted, staring directly into my eyes. "Lily is—"

"Lily is giving her blessing." Allison stood in the doorway, a firm frown filling her face as she crossed her arms over her chest. "Cousin, I think it's time you head to the dining hall. Ask Aunt Sharon where you can be of service."

Dara's chin almost hit her chest as her shoulders bowed forward. "Yes, ma'am." She cast me a glance before shuffling out, barely squeezing past Allison as she left.

In that one look, I witnessed the fear in Dara's eyes, and I found myself stepping forward, wanting to follow her.

Allison had other plans, though, as she blocked me.

"Is there an issue?" I mirrored her body posture, crossing my own arms and lifting my chin.

"I hope not. What happened?" Her gaze swept throughout the room.

"Nothing. Dara was excited to show me her paintings. She's quite talented. I sat on that stool, and she sketched me in her book." I point toward her sketchpad.

Allison headed there immediately and flipped through the pages.

"Maybe you can answer a question for me," I said to fill in the silence. "I did ask Dara, but . . ." I lifted my shoulder in a shrug.

"What question is that?" Allison closed the book and set it back down, her fingers lightly trailing over the cover.

"I want to know what's going on with Lily. Why won't anyone talk about her when I bring up her name? All Dara says is she's giving her blessing. What does that even mean? Has she left the farm? Gone somewhere else?"

Allison turned so I couldn't see her face. She tidied things up in the room that were already neat and in place.

"You asked Cousin Darinda that?" The censure in her tone was forceful enough that I stepped backward. "Why would you ask a young girl such a thing? No wonder she was so upset." With her lips set firm, she headed outside. "Prophesied or not, you have so much to learn . . ." Her voice trailed off as she walked ahead of me, leaving me to feel both shame and frustration.

## CHAPTER THIRTY-TWO

Allison brought me back to the farmhouse. Once we were in the kitchen, she indicated toward the island chairs, which I assumed meant she wanted me to sit.

Neither one of us had said a word on our walk back.

She might have been upset, but I was more interested in taking in the surroundings and comparing them to the mental images I had from the photographs. So much had changed over the years, I wasn't sure how I would recognize anything.

Allison pulled a large jug from the fridge. "My apologies, Sister. I spoke out of turn and in haste, and I should have understood that you only ask questions based on lack of knowledge and curiosity."

She proceeded to fill two large glasses with ice. "Your brother mentioned you're as addicted to cold brew coffee as I am." She set out two small containers, one with sugar and one with cream, then pulled out a small basket of flavored syrups.

"I always have a jug in the fridge." I added a few drops of vanilla into a cup, along with a small teaspoon of sugar, and swirled it together.

I waited till she sat next to me before I barraged her with questions.

"You mentioned you and Mom were close friends."

She nodded.

"Did she ever explain to you why she pulled me from this group? Why she suppressed my memories?" I skipped the small talk, knowing we probably didn't have much time alone.

Allison took her time enjoying her first sip. "Nothing like starting with the hard stuff. I'm not sure who you remind me more of — your mother or your father."

"Anthony and I had very little in common."

"I wouldn't be so sure of that." A hesitant smile appeared. "He often said the two of you butted heads more than anything. That tells me you're more alike than either of you wanted to admit."

"Anthony spoke of me to you?" Why that surprised me, I wasn't sure.

"Of course he did. My friendship wasn't only with your mother. Your father and I . . . we had a special bond."

I reeled back with disgust. "Please do not tell me that you and him—"

"Oh, sweet heavens, no. Please, that's not what I meant." Her hands trembled at the shock of my assumption. "I was happily married for many, many years. My husband and your father were best of friends, just like your mother and myself. Oh no—" her hands covered her chest — "no, no, that would . . . I'm sorry if I let you think . . ."

"When you led with 'we had a special bond,' I just assumed . . ."

She gave a small laugh. "Ahh, yes, poor choice of words on my part. That bond was because we were part of the originals, that's all. Many revered your father, whereas I could get away with speaking to him plainly. Not that he always took it."

"About my mother . . ." I needed the conversation to turn from Anthony and to what I really wanted to know.

"You wanted to know why she took you from here, from the only real home and family you knew, and why she was so desperate to protect you. Yes, of course you do. Did you find the photo album? I'm assuming you must, since you're asking."

"How do you know about that album?"

"I was the one who suggested it."

That surprised me. "Why?"

"Your mother and I were best friends, Brynn. We didn't keep secrets from each other. I knew this day would come. Destiny is always a full circle. You can run from it, hide from it, or do whatever you can to change the path that you are on, but ultimately, you'll end up exactly where you are supposed to be."

"And that's here?"

She nodded. "With your real family. Tell me there isn't a part of you that feels connected to something larger than yourself when you're here?"

I couldn't. So I didn't.

"I thought as much. Your mother did everything possible to erase us from your life, but her mistake was thinking it was possible. You grew up here with us. We all raised you. We all loved you. We are your family, Brynn, and deep down, you know what I'm saying is true."

Did I? My memories were a blur, unattainable and unreachable. There was a sense of familiarity with Allison and with some aspects of the farm, but not enough to say with certainty that being here was where I was destined to be.

"Mom always told me that this group was a bunch of fanatics built on a foundation of greed and hypocrisy. If I ever followed Anthony's path, it would destroy everything about who I am and who I can become." There had to be a reason she was so determined to keep me separated. "It's because of the prophecy, isn't it?"

Allison's eyes were sad. "That prophecy has been twisted into something unrecognizable. Your mother's disillusionment with us hurts me the most. Do we look like a family focused on greed? We live simple lives here."

It was true. Other than this excessive kitchen, I hadn't seen anything that would tell me they lived off the money people donated to them. Or maybe I just hadn't seen it yet.

My every move was watched, and anything I was shown was on purpose . . . so greed might be hidden from prying eyes.

"What about the other centers? Like the one in LA, Texas, South Carolina . . ." From what I'd gathered over the years, there were at least a dozen around the country. I'd overhear Anthony's conversations with his guests about those locations. "You can't tell me those aren't focused on greed. The amount of money people put down to join . . ."

"That is on Sir. He has his reasons for creating those outside spheres. But here, at the core, our focus is true, our hearts are pure. That is why this community is separated from the others, why this community is the real Family, the only one that truly matters. And that includes you."

Sir. Maximus Rutledge. How much did he play into my mother's decision?

"Something had to have happened that was bad enough for my mother to not just pull me from here, but to erase my memories."

She didn't answer.

"Do you know?"

She was more focused on the cold coffee between her hands than on me.

"That's all I can think about, you know? That something horrible must have happened to me for her to go to such extreme measures. But what? Did I witness something I shouldn't have? Did someone harm me? What happened to me that was so irrevocably damaging that there was no choice but for me to forget it happened at all?"

The longer we sat there in silence, the more the pain in my chest grew from mild discomfort to a solid ache. Every breath hurt with each inhale. Every swallow swept across jagged pieces of glass in my throat.

Her hand covered mine, and at her whispered words, "*I'm here*," a warmth infused my body. Every single area of discomfort and unease melted away.

I'd imagined that, right? I stared at her hand, at the way our skin touched.

"Feel better?" she asked.

"I . . . do. What was that? Magic?"

She chuckled. "The power of a healing touch is amazing, isn't it? Our skin is one of the most sensitive organs in our bodies. Physical touch releases oxytocin into the bloodstream, reducing pain, easing emotions, and even decreasing stress."

"But how did you . . . I felt that warmth . . ." I struggled to put into words what I experienced.

"It's called touch therapy. I've trained in it for years and even now teach to others."

"FAM Casa."

She nodded. "I envisioned a place where we could focus on healing, not just for the body but for the mind and soul, in a way God truly intended. You can call it whatever you want, but what we teach and how we live dates back to biblical times, even before the Israelites were enslaved in Egypt."

"So you created FAM Casa? It's your . . . dream? Vision?"

She rinsed her glass in the sink before placing it in the dishwasher. "There is so much death in our society, and I don't mean just the physical death when the air leaves our bodies, and our hearts no longer pump blood. Look at what is happening in Hollywood, for example. All the sin, brokenness, and evil are always in the background, but are just now coming to light. Those in that sphere cried out for help and healing, and Sir recognized the need. Together, we provided a way for them to find that healing. FAM Casa was private for a long time because the people who came to us needed that privacy. But we have other centers now that are open, and FAM Casa can be what it was truly meant to be: a place of healing for everyone who needs it." She paused. "Do you want those memories back?"

"I do." At least, I thought I did. "My mom expected me to want them back if she left me that letter, right?"

She sighed. "I doubt your mother expected you ever to find it, honestly."

"And yet, here I am."

"Here you are."

There was a commotion in another section of the house. I heard Bryce's voice and knew my time for answers was coming to a close.

"You're coming to the retreat weekend, yes?" Allison glanced toward the doorway. "We can discuss this further then. I might even have a way to help you retrieve those memories, if that is what you want."

"Thank you." Something inside me believed her, believed that she could help.

Something inside me also knew that she knew what happened to me all those years ago. That she wasn't just aware, but possibly part of it, too.

# CHAPTER THIRTY-THREE

Everything was arranged for my three-day absence. Merilyn was on the schedule for the weekend, and Bryce promised to stick around and help as needed. I even made him pinkie-swear he wouldn't go out to the Farm while I was away.

To be honest, I was excited about my time away. Maybe because it was my first real vacation in a while. Maybe because I was looking forward to the time Mona and I would spend together. Maybe because Allison promised to help me regain those blocked memories of mine.

I'd decided to come clean with Mona about my family's involvement in the Family. It was getting harder and harder to keep that part of my life a secret, and if Bryce really did move out and join them on a full-time basis, Mona was going to have questions.

I just hoped she wasn't too angry with me for not being honest with her until now.

My first stop before heading out of town was, of course, to Sweet Beans for coffee and a treat to enjoy while on the road. I hoped Sharlene was in. I wanted to make sure things were going smoothly with our new contract in place.

Sharlene now catered all the memorials and viewings, providing hand-held items to nibble on, giving families and friends the freedom to mourn without worrying about cleaning their house afterward. Years ago, Anthony had an area added onto the Parlor, for that very purpose.

The bell rang as I entered the store, and the first person I saw was Lexi Kaarns.

"Well, hello, stranger," she greeted me, kicking out one of the chairs at her table. "Do you have time to join me after you've ordered?"

I always had time for Lexi.

"Would love to." I hugged her before heading to the counter.

Sharlene saw me from the back and waved. She came out carrying a tray of chocolate mousse tarts with a dollop of whipped cream on top. "Interested in one?"

"Like that's even a question." I doubted there would be very many sweets or unhealthy desserts available during the weekend, so I would enjoy what I could while I could.

"They seem to be a popular item at your place," she told me. "I've been trying different items, but whatever is popular here seems popular there."

"Maybe because word is spreading that you are our new provider."

She shrugged. "You service more than just the Bervie Springs area, though, so I expected a difference. Guess I was wrong."

It was true. We were the only funeral home and crematorium in the area, and serviced several neighboring towns and villages.

"Things going smoothly?" I asked, after placing an order for a flat white and the tart. "I haven't heard of any issues, but if something comes up, please let me know."

She waved my concern away. "Merilyn is on top of things, so everything is running smoothly."

That was exactly what I wanted to hear. Moving Merilyn into an upper management role was one of the best decisions we'd made all year for the business. I knew she could handle the extra responsibility.

I brought an extra tart for Lexi and smiled at her groan when I set the plate in front of her.

"You know I don't need that," she said. "My partner has the worst sweet tooth. All Spikes does is bring in treats his wife bakes."

"Need, want, who cares? Life is short; enjoy the dessert."

"So says the woman who doesn't have to run after criminals all day."

I laughed. "When was the last time you had to run after a criminal?"

"More than you would expect." She leaned forward. "Some sneaky teenagers in this town think tagging buildings gets them an after-school credit."

"I've noticed an uptick in graffiti lately."

"Bane of my existence. Although, give me that over dead bodies any day."

I knew she referenced Donald Dixon and the bodies he'd hidden in the gardens within Bervie Springs. That was a tragedy no one would ever forget.

"Any plans for the weekend?" she asked after we'd both taken our first bites of the tart.

"Actually, I do. I'm headed out of town this weekend." I noted the surprise on her face. "I know, right? Me, take a mini vacation? Imagine that."

"And you didn't invite me?" The tease was in her voice, but I also caught the longing.

"Join me next time. I received an invitation for a three-day retreat at that wellness center out of town."

Lexi leaned back in her seat. "FAM Casa? Don't tell me you're going there?" Her smile disappeared.

"That's the place. Why?"

"How determined are you to go? I mean, I'm owed some vacation time. We could find a cute hotel on the beach and relax, or go take in some Broadway shows . . ."

While her idea was appealing, spending time with Allison was at the top of my priority list for the weekend.

"Someone there knew my mom," I told her.

"You know they're associated with that group of Anthony's."

"I know."

"And you're still willing to go?" Her brows furrowed. "I don't get it. I thought you wanted nothing to do with them?"

It took me a moment to answer. I wasn't sure how much I wanted to tell her. Sometimes, it was hard to separate the cop from the friend, and right now, I wasn't sure who I'd be speaking to.

"Brynn, what's going on?"

Apparently, I'd hesitated too long. "I found an old photo album of my mom's when I was cleaning the basement a while ago."

She nodded and waited for me to continue.

"It was of me, Bryce, my parents . . . at the Farm."

I knew the moment she put two and two together.

"The Final Family compound, the one that has security walls and gates and guards now? That farm?"

I was surprised at how much she knew. From what I understood, the security measures were a fairly newish addition.

"That one. Turns out, we were raised there."

Her nod was slow. "Thus the connection for Anthony and now Bryce . . . huh, interesting."

"Interesting? That's all you have to say?"

She held up one hand in defense. "Hey, give me a minute, okay? I mean . . . I knew the men were involved, but I figured, with your insistence that you wanted nothing to do with them . . ."

"I don't, and I'm not lying to you, Lexi, if that's what you're getting at. All my life, all my mother did was warn me to stay away from that group."

"So why join now?"

"Who says I'm joining?" My hackles were raised, but I wasn't sure why — at her, for assuming I was involved with the group, or at me, for leaning that way.

She lightly touched my hand. "This is me, your friend, wondering why you're getting so defensive." She then leaned back in her seat, her arms crossed. "And this is me, as a cop, warning you to be wary of that group, regardless of your childhood ties, because they're more dangerous than you think."

"My mom . . ." I bit my lip as I thought about my next words. "Mom left me a letter in that photo album," I told her. "She said she had suppressed my memories from my time with that group." I rubbed the back of my neck, uncomfortable. "It makes me wonder why, you know?"

"She what?" Blinking a few times, surprise laced across her face, Lexi hadn't expected me to say that. "Holy sh— That's messed up, Brynn."

"I know."

She tapped her chin a few times, a clear sign she was thinking. "You said someone there knew your mother . . . is that why you're going there? To get some answers? Is there something you can do to get those memories back?"

In front of me was the friend I needed — the friend who could look at all the angles and ask the right questions without me explaining everything.

"Her name is Allison, and she said she can help with that."

Lexi's lips tightened the moment I said the name. "Do you know her last name?"

I shook my head. "All I know is she's an Elder and has been there since the beginning. She was friends with my mom and Anthony and, from my understanding, basically runs the wellness center."

Lexi glanced out toward the store windows, and she had a faraway look in her eyes. I let her be, understanding she knew more than I did and was no doubt figuring out her next words and actions.

"I really wish you weren't going there this weekend, but I get why you are. Can you promise me you'll be careful, please?"

"Is there something I should be aware of?"

She tapped her index finger on the table for a second. "Nothing I can tell you, but we've got our eyes on the place. Their ramped-up security is a concern, and we've heard some things . . . I want you to be super careful, please. Check in with me every night, too, if you don't mind."

I shook my head. "It's a device-free place, so once I'm there, I won't have access to my phone."

"What? That's crazy, and not something you should agree to."

"I don't mind; not really. Bryce is on call all weekend, since he knows he can't reach me, so he has to be around instead of heading to the Farm like usual."

I watched Lexi exhale, and a worm of worry burrowed into my stomach. "Lexi, what's going on?"

She took one long sip of her coffee and gathered her purse over her shoulder. "Listen, I need to run. Please, please, please, keep your phone on you, okay? I mean it. Hide it if you have to, lie, and tell them you left it at home, I don't care, but I need to know you are okay every night. This is non-negotiable, Brynn. I'm serious." She stared me down, and the seriousness on her face worried me.

"Okay," I said. "I won't be alone, though. Mona received an invitation, too, so she'll be with me the whole time."

Lexi's body deflated with noticeable relief. "Good, thank God. Still, keep that phone and stay safe, okay?"

Once she left, I pulled out my phone and sent Mona a text message.

*About to leave, just grabbing a coffee to go. See you there!*

I waited as the three jumping dots that represented her writing a message appeared, disappeared, and reappeared.

*Great! See you soon. I'm bringing extra wine. Drive safe. I'll let you know when I am leaving.*

Lexi's words wouldn't leave me, not while I grabbed a large vanilla cream cold brew, not while I left town with the music blaring, and not even as I drove down the road. There was a niggling fear that I was driving toward my doom, and while I knew that had everything to do with Lexi's words and nothing to do with what was going to happen, I couldn't shake the feeling that maybe, just maybe, I should have turned my car around and headed home, where I would be safer.

# CHAPTER THIRTY-FOUR

FAM Casa was just as quiet as I arrived as it had been when I came with Mona. There were a few vehicles in the parking area, but other than the staff all dressed in white, I didn't see anyone else.

Perhaps I'd arrived too early.

Allison walked out of the main office as I pulled up. Her full and genuine smile made almost all the doubts that had crept up from my conversation with Lexi disappear.

I reached for my weekend bag and stuffed my phone and charger deep inside. I knew if Lexi didn't hear from me tonight, she'd be out here first thing to make sure I was okay. I didn't feel right about lying to Allison, but truthfully, I feared Lexi's reaction more than Allison's at that point.

"I'm so glad you took my suggestion and came early," Allison said, this time reaching out to hold my hand. A familiar tingle of warmth radiated from her hand into my body.

"You can leave your bags here; I'll have someone take them to your cabin for you." A woman appeared from the side.

I wanted to object, but before I could, the woman took my bag and headed off.

"I hope you don't mind, but I scheduled you for a nice Swedish massage session and one of our special facials. If I recall, Mona seemed particularly interested in our skin care products."

"She called it magic," I said. "Something about your lack of wrinkles."

Allison lightly patted her face. "It's a mixture of good genes, red light therapy, and my products, but thank you for the compliment."

She led me toward the spa, and I appreciated that the pathway we took was shaded with tall trees and covered archways. "Once you've completed your spa time, I thought we could meet in one of the shaded garden areas to discuss more about your missing memories."

"I'll be honest," I said, "I'm both excited and nervous, if you can believe it. All my life, I've recognized that a part of me was missing, and I just accepted it. Until now."

"Are you prepared for whatever comes?" She didn't say the actual words, but I knew she didn't think it was a good idea.

"You tell me," I said. "You know better than I do why my mother had my memory suppressed . . ." I ended the sentence there and waited to see if she would pick it up.

She didn't.

There was more to the story than she let on, and I wished she'd come clean and be honest with me.

"Then I guess I'll deal with whatever comes when it comes."

She left me at the spa building, promising to have someone waiting to bring me to our meeting spot when I was done.

They had spared no expense when it came to the spa, and I couldn't help but wonder what celebrities had been in the room, relaxing in the chairs, spending time healing their soul . . . and then I realized it didn't matter who had been here. That was more Mona's thing than mine.

When I finished the massage and facial, I was ready to nap in one of the heated chairs with a warm cup of herbal tea. Unfortunately, as promised, someone waited to lead me toward a garden oasis where Allison sat on a mat, her legs crossed, her body relaxed. A tea service had been placed to the side.

"I don't need to ask how that was. You radiate relaxation," Allison said as I sat across from her on the waiting mat.

"It was wonderful. Thank you for scheduling that for me." I eyed the tray beside her. The china looked beautiful in its simplicity. The cups were pearly in color, with a soft floral print along the rim and bottom of both the cups and teapot. It reminded me of a small tea set I'd had as a child.

"Of course."

She said it as if it had been no big deal, and for her, it probably hadn't been, but I couldn't remember the last time I'd had a massage and facial, let alone spent any time at a spa.

"Let's start with this, shall we?" Allison poured me a cup of tea. "This special blend is created to help unblock your mental pathways, open up those locked gates, and generally produce a calming, meditative state. It's one of my favorites," she said. She poured herself a cup and held the delicate china in her hands.

A sense of unease circled me, taking root in my soul. A vice tightened around my chest, and a part of me wanted to tell her I'd changed my mind, that maybe it wasn't worth it, but then she reached out and placed her hand on my knee, and all that panic and that fear lifted.

I sighed with relief.

"There is freedom in knowledge," Allison said. "What you're about to do won't be easy, but it will fill those missing pieces you feel within yourself."

"Do you know what happened to me?"

A soft smile settled on her lips. "Brynn, nothing happened to you."

"Nothing?" I wasn't sure I believed her. If nothing happened, why would my mother suppress my memories?

"It's more like you saw something, and with your childish mind, you could not comprehend what was happening. It affected you in a way that worried many of us. You became mute."

"Mute? As in non-verbal?"

Allison nodded.

"For how long?" What could I have seen that affected me so I wouldn't speak? "How old was I?"

Allison held her cup to her lips and gazed at me over the rim.

"You weren't very old, maybe around six years of age. We tried everything. At first, it was like you'd retreated within yourself . . . your body was present, but your mind was elsewhere. You wouldn't let anyone touch you, or even be near you, other than your brother. Your parents despaired over what to do. In fact, we all did. We all loved you as if you were our own, so when you hurt, we all hurt."

I had so many questions, but she held up her hand, stopping me.

"After a few months, your mother was willing to try anything and everything to help you. You have to understand the change — you went from a vibrant six-year-old, full of life and laughter, one who wasn't afraid of anything . . . you'd climb anything and everything, especially if someone told you not to," Allison said with a chuckle. "You were bright and inquisitive, always asking questions, never taking no for an answer. You were exhausting at times, don't get me wrong, but you were special too. We all saw it. We all knew it. So when you became mute, when you stopped interacting with your family, with life around you . . . it scared us all. You became a different child, and when your mother took things into her own hands and decided to leave our community, most of us understood."

I bit my lips to keep from asking more questions. That child she described didn't seem like me at all. That child was a stranger, and yet . . . as she described who I'd been, I could see that little girl in my mind's eye climbing trees, sitting on the roof outside my opened bedroom window in the early morning hours, and marveling at the beautiful sky as the sun rose.

"You went back to Bervie Springs. At first, it was just you and your mother, like a test to see how you'd react to being away from all of us. You got better. You still weren't talking, but you weren't as absent as you'd been either. I recall coming for a visit, and the first thing I noticed was the life within your gaze. The window of your soul had opened, and I knew you were there, peering out, checking to make sure it was safe."

My tea was almost gone. Allison noticed and refilled my cup.

Hers had barely been touched.

"I was the one who suggested the memory suppression. If I'd known it would take you from us, I would have kept quiet."

Her words jolted me in my seat, and I fumbled with the cup and saucer in my hand.

"I knew someone within our community with the skill," she said, lifting her shoulders slightly with a shrug. "Your mother was desperate and willing to try anything. Turns out, with all the things she'd tried, this was the only thing that worked. It was night and day. The method was used right before bed, and when you woke up, it was like a cloud had been lifted. You woke up with a smile, your first words being *I love you* to your mom."

Tears swelled, searing hot in the corners of my eyes as I pictured in my mind's eye what that must have been like for my mother. To have her mute child finally speak and to say *I love you*, of all things.

"I don't remember any of that," I whispered, distraught because, of all the memories I should have, I wanted that one most of all.

A wave of tiredness swept over me, and I closed my eyes for a few seconds. Was it the tea, or the massage from earlier?

"Drink more of the tea, please," Allison suggested, nodding at my cup.

The water was lukewarm, so I drank a few mouthfuls, almost emptying the cup. She refilled it one more time. I didn't hold it this time; my arms felt a little heavy, and I didn't want to drop the cup accidentally.

"If you're feeling tired, don't worry," Allison said, reading my thoughts. "The key to reversing the suppression lies in five words, but after I say those words, you need to lie down and sleep. Your brain needs to be relaxed for your subconscious to work."

"I'll wake up with the memories of what I saw?"

She shrugged. "Possibly. Or, perhaps your brain has hidden those things so far down that it might take some time. Once I utter those words, the rest is up to your body. The key will be in permitting it to let those memories come or not. You can't force it, Sister. I need you to understand that."

I thought I understood, so I nodded. But truthfully, much of what she said was starting to sound garbled, like words spoken underwater.

While I struggled to focus on her, I noticed her looking off to the side. She nodded, and suddenly, her hands gripped my arms and pulled upward. Two men stood on each side of me.

"Our cousins are going to help make sure you make it back to your cabin safely," Allison said. "I fear I waited too long."

I had no idea what path we took, but I was thankful for the strength in their arms; they held my body upright as we walked.

Once inside the cabin, Allison helped to settle me into my bed, pulling a blanket over me and even setting a glass of water on the side table.

"Where is Mona?" She was supposed to be here by now.

"Mona had to cancel, unfortunately." Allison sat beside me on the bed. "Something to do with work. But she will come on Sunday and join you for sunrise yoga," she said. "I told her I'd book her in for a facial, and then you both could end the day with a pedicure."

I was disappointed to know Mona wouldn't come until later, even though I was looking forward to spending time with her. Even as my eyes drooped low and it became harder and harder to keep them open, I made a mental note to text her later.

"Things always seem to work out for the best, though, don't they? Once you wake up, your energy will be focused on your mental and emotional journey, and having Mona here might have been a distraction." She placed her hand on my leg, and even through the blanket, I felt the warmth of her touch.

"How do you do that?"

"I told you, it's just the power of touch. Now, I want you to concentrate on these next words I say. Mentally hold on to them, reach for them as I speak them, and pull them tight to your chest. Repeat them, over and over, until even your internal voice says them as you fall asleep, okay?"

I nodded and opened up my palms, ready to catch the words.

"Light."

"Light," I muttered, watching the word fall from Allison's lips into my waiting palm. I pulled it to my chest and pushed the word inside me.

"Shadow. Flicker. Protect. Renew." The soft cadence of her voice lulled me further to sleep.

With each word, I repeated her instructions, copying her, grabbing on to the word itself, and holding it tight to my body. I imagined the words fusing within my soul as darkness blanketed my being.

Light. Shadow. Flicker. Protect. Renew.

Light. Shadow. Flicker . . .

CHAPTER THIRTY-FIVE

Light. Shadow. Flicker. Protect. Renew.

I woke up speaking the words. I didn't know what they meant or why I said them, not at first, then I remembered Allison's instructions.

As I lay there, the stillness in the room enveloped me like a warm blanket, and I poked at my memory to see if anything had changed.

There was nothing.

No new memories. No fog that lifted. No sudden recollection of what I'd lost.

I felt defeated.

Allison said it would take time, that it was up to my brain when to release the memories. Except my brain and I were one, were we not? Frustration mounted at the idea I wasn't in charge, nor had I ever been; at the same time, my heart broke for the little girl who witnessed something so horrifying that she lost her ability to speak.

Connecting the fact that I was that little girl was difficult.

The first real thing I remember from my childhood was sitting in the garden with Mom. While she weeded, I held a book in my lap and read her a story. I remember sounding out each word, the way the letters formed together rolled on my tongue, and even as I struggled, Mom never corrected me or offered the word — I just remembered her praising me.

I wished I could recall the memory of saying *I love you* after being mute for so long.

I wished I could retrieve the look on her face, the tears in her eyes, the feel of her arms around me as she held me close.

I wished I could remember the girl I'd been before we'd left the farm, the bright girl, full of laughter, always on the move, always wanting to know more.

She didn't sound like me at all.

Or the me I became after whatever it was I'd seen.

What had I seen that was so horrendous?

The dull throb of a headache formed, so rather than forcing the memory, I searched for my bags to unpack and text Lexi and Mona.

When I opened the closet, my bags were already unpacked.

All my clothes were either hung on hangers or folded into drawers. My shoes were on the floor, and sure enough, when I checked the bathroom, my toiletries had been put away as well.

My bag was tucked on the upper shelf of the closet, and the only thing inside it was my phone cord. Everything else had been put away for me. Even my purse was tucked away in an open shelf inside the closet.

The only thing I didn't find was my phone.

Lexi was not going to be happy. Would she believe me when I told her that I'd tried, that I'd hidden my phone away in my bag as she'd instructed, but that they offered butler service and unpacked everything for me?

She'd probably claim it was their way of controlling my experience there and that it should have been a red flag.

For her, maybe. I decided to try to take it in the vein it was probably meant — another level of service.

However, having someone take my phone without telling me was invasive; it didn't sit well.

A tray of food awaited me on the kitchen table with Allison's note.

*Rest, relax, and enjoy your evening. Take a look at our programming for tonight, and feel free to join any session that interests you — or if you're not up to it, enjoy a guilt-free evening, and I will see you tomorrow morning.*

I studied the sessions that ran from dinner until nine o'clock, and while I knew I should attend at least one of them, the idea of having a quiet night was more enticing.

Dinner was a healthy option of salmon over a bed of rice and a salad, along with a little note card requesting the tray be left outside for pick up.

The idea of exploring the grounds, of being out in the fresh air, called to me. The sun was setting, and there was a quiet vibe as soon as I closed the front door behind me.

As I followed the trail paths, the lanterns along the walkways turned on, illuminating the stone.

As I walked, the words Allison repeated played over in my mind.

Light. Shadow. Flicker. Protect. Renew.

Why were these words so important? Why had these words been chosen as the keys to my memories?

Light. Shadow. Flicker. Protect. Renew.

With each step I took, the words matched my footsteps. My gaze was drawn toward the lights, the shadows they cast, and the flicker . . . and just like that, a memory swallowed me whole, the images pulsating within, and I stumbled, my foot catching on the stone. I would have fallen to my knees if someone hadn't appeared, grabbing my elbow and steadying me as I found my footing.

"Thank you."

Maximus Rutledge stood at my side.

"These stone pathways can be tricky at night," he said, his smooth voice sending me into a shocked state. He was the last person I expected to see here.

He circled me like he was the predator and I was the prey. "I wanted to check in and see how you are doing." He placed his hand on my back and led me toward a bench.

My mind was in overload right now, between the new memory and seeing him . . . my brain couldn't comprehend what was happening, let alone answer his question.

"Is everything okay, Sister? Do I need to get someone?"

His touch on my hand woke me out of my stupor. "I just . . . sorry, I feel a little off . . . I just . . ." I cleared my throat, wishing I'd brought my water bottle.

"Sister—" he angled so he faced me on the bench and took both my hands in his — "you don't look well. Maybe I should walk you back to your cabin?"

I didn't feel well. When I looked at him, I saw his younger self by almost thirty years. Was he there, at the farm, all those years ago?

I had images of him standing in candlelight, wearing a white robe, with a knife held tight in his hand . . . my head splintered in pain, so powerful it was like a hand pushed me from behind, forcing me over my knees. One hand covered my mouth, and it was all I could do not to vomit all over my shoes.

"Elder Allison mentioned your desire to retrieve some hidden memories, but I don't think you quite expected how hard it would be on your body. Take some deep breaths," he said, one hand on my back. "Let nature soothe your soul as you inhale."

"How do you—"

"I know everything that happens within my family, Sister. Everything. There are no secrets between Elder Allison and me." He stood with a look of fatherly patience on his face while he held out a hand. "Are you strong enough to continue our walk? There's something I would like to show you?"

The headache formed at the base of my neck bubbled in size, spreading upward and walking with him was the last thing I wanted to do, but I took his hand with a pasted-on smile and let him lead the way.

The gentle evening breeze lightly kissed the skin at the back of my neck as we slowly descended the path, winding our way through the garden maze until I was no longer sure where we were. The only thing I did know was that we'd followed a trail of flicker lights.

"Feeling better?" He patted the hand that I'd wound around his arm. My breathing had returned to normal, and the subdued pain in my head no longer pounded with every step I took.

The path ahead was shrouded in shadows with what appeared to be tea lights to guide the way. "Where are we?"

"My own little sanctuary, I guess you could say." He held out one hand, indicating I should take the lead.

Ahead of us was a building that reminded me of a large shed found in a backyard or farmers' market. It was covered in darkness except for the candle-lit pathway that led through two large doors, showing a gathering of people inside.

I took a few timid steps before the noise inside stopped me.

It was a low hum of voices chanting words I couldn't fully hear or understand. I glanced back to Maximus.

"It's the time for preparation," he said. "A very special night where we, as a community, prepare for the upcoming blessing." He watched me with interest. "Does any of it look familiar to you?"

All of it looked familiar, much like what was on that video in my brother's room.

"It's a ceremony," I whispered.

"Yes."

"For what?" I couldn't tear my gaze from the building, the flickering lights, the shadows that moved with the wind, and the hum from the crowd inside.

"For the time of preparation," he repeated. "Will you join us?"

He walked ahead, not giving me time to answer. Wearing a gray robe, someone else appeared at my side and directed me to follow Maximus.

Chills chased one another over my skin, and everything inside me screamed not to go into that building, and yet, like a lamb being led to the slaughter, I followed, pulled by an invisible tether.

Flashes of memories from another time appeared dizzyingly as I walked along the flickering pathway and then inside the building.

My mind flashed back to a room like the one I stood in now, where a group of people had stood in a circle, all in robes, chanting phrases I couldn't understand.

Was this an actual memory, or from that video?

"Sister, this way, please." The haze of that memory broke as a man appeared at my side and led me to a bench along a wall. While I sat, I noticed two things: despite being alone at the back of the building, I was flanked by two men, and Max went to stand on a small platform where a black lamb had been chained.

What was happening?

Max stood in front of the crowd, now wearing a white robe. In his hand, he held a knife.

"In Genesis, God told Abraham to take his son and to offer him as a sacrifice. Why? He wanted to know how obedient Abraham would be in the midst of turmoil. It wasn't that God questioned Abraham's obedience, but He needed Abraham to take that step of faith and prove to himself how important his God was to him." Max looked out over the group and pointed the knife. "It is no different today. We are in a time of preparation for the imminent rebirth. Not everyone has been selected, nor will everyone be invited to receive the gift. But we have and will, and during this time of preparation, we are showing God and ourselves just how far we will go in our obedience to Him."

The room was quiet, his words loud and bold.

"Our children have raised this lamb, a black lamb who carries our sin upon its flesh, and during this time of preparation, we will offer its life as a blessing to renew our families' commitment and to protect those who will offer their blessing on our behalf."

My stomach twisted into a nest of knots as I realized what would happen.

What kind of religious group sacrificed animals? What kind of cult was my family tied to? I searched the room, praying that my brother wasn't there, but everyone looked the same in their gray robes from the back.

I wanted to leave. I didn't want to have any part of what was about to happen, but the moment I stood, the men at my side closed in with the obvious intention of stopping me from leaving my spot.

I sat back down.

The low hum in the room intensified as Max approached the lamb. I couldn't see what was happening, but I heard the bleating of the scared animal before it abruptly stopped, and I knew that it was dead.

Bile rose up my throat, scorching it on its way, and I twisted to the side and threw up, uncaring who saw.

I sensed the presence of someone in front of me, and the moment they laid their warm hand on the top of my head, I knew it was Allison.

Unlike other times when she touched me, I didn't feel the healing heat of her touch. Instead, I felt the fire burn its way through me, in me, the invisible wall separating my hidden memories turning into ashes as everything slammed into me.

The flickering lights within the room all went out at once, and darkness rushed through my body, settling into each limb, one at a time, pulling its way up to my throat until I couldn't breathe or even utter a sound. My vision swam in and out of focus, into darkness, then into shadows as memories over memories pulled at me like a riptide until I'd lost all control.

I knew why it was all so familiar to me. Not because of that video, but because I'd witnessed this once before, as a child.

A sense of horror filled me. "Who is about to die?" I barely managed to get the words out.

"You still don't understand, do you?" The gentle shake of her head showed her disappointment, then she reached for my hand to help me stand. "There is no death within the Family," Allison whispered as she led me out of the building and back down the lit pathway. "There are only blessings and honor. What you are remembering, you see with a child's eye and understanding. Look past that; focus on the message and not the fear."

Focus on the message? What message? They twisted the biblical story of Abraham for what gain?

Fear was the only thing I felt as Allison led me back to my cabin, our protective detail walking behind us.

She led me inside, and on the counter was a tray with a decanter and a teacup.

"Did you know that someone unpacked for me?"

She nodded. "Yes, of course. If you are looking for your phone, we will return it when you leave."

"I'd prefer to keep it with me, if you don't mind." I shivered, feeling a chill in the room.

"Of course, if that is what you prefer. But please, keep it out of sight of our other guests."

Other guests?

"You mean those who were just at that secret ceremony?"

"No, of course not. Those were family members."

"If they were family members, why not hold that ceremony at the Farm?"

When I asked the question, Allison had been pouring tea into the cup. Now she paused. "Sir wanted you to be a part of it."

That didn't make sense to me at all.

"My memories are coming back," I told her. "They're jumbled still, and I only see fleeting images, but I was just a child, and I was forced to watch an animal I loved be killed. I'm not surprised I was traumatized."

"You were the last," she said softly.

"The last?"

"The last child. It was obvious you were too young to understand what was happening at the symbolism of the ceremony. They now need to be sixteen before they are allowed to participate in the preparation."

There was a knock on the door, and Maximus walked in.

He had to have noticed the tension in the room.

"Is she willing?" He asked Allison the question but kept his focus on me.

Willing? Willing for what?

"I don't believe so," Allison said. She walked around the kitchen island to stand beside me. "There hasn't been enough time."

He sighed.

"Then we've no other option. It is time," he said, with a nod.

Time for what? I half turned to ask Allison what was going on when I felt a prick in the side of my neck, and everything faded to black.

# CHAPTER THIRTY-SIX

Everywhere I looked, it was green: green gardens, green grass, green edge tableware beside me, and a china teacup with green, pink, and yellow flowers painted on the edges.

Nothing looked familiar, and yet I knew I'd seen it all before. My mind was a field covered in haze, aware and functioning, but on a level slightly above stupor.

I closed my eyes, but somewhere in the distant fog, I heard my mother's voice scream at me to wake up. *WAKE UP!*

The voice was loud enough that I jolted, my hand swiping the teacup toward the floor with a crash.

"Oh, thank God. Are you okay?" My brother appeared from inside the house. It took my eyes a moment to settle firmly on him.

"I feel . . ." Finding the words was a struggle, just like keeping my eyes open, or even keeping him in focus.

"Here, lean your head back." He grabbed a pillow off a chair opposite me and propped it behind me. "There, is that better?"

"Where are we?"

"At the Farm," he said, leaning forward and taking my hands in his. "Elder Allison brought you here from the wellness center a few days ago. You weren't . . . well."

A few days ago?

"What day is it?" I squeezed his hand as hard as I could. I didn't like how I felt, how my body was not my own, how every movement was slow and brought about waves of dizziness.

"Tuesday." Something in his voice sounded off, but I couldn't pinpoint what.

"Tuesday?" How could that be? I was just . . . my memory was cloudy, and I couldn't pinpoint anything.

"Bryce, I don't feel right."

He pulled his chair closer to mine so that our knees almost touched. "I know, Brynn, I know." He swallowed hard. "Elder Allison worried that retrieving your memories would be too harmful for your body, and she was right."

The worry and fear in my brother's voice scared me.

"What happened?"

Bryce sighed. "It's a good thing Sir was there. They found you in your cabin, lying on the kitchen floor. They had no idea how long you'd been like that either. When you wouldn't wake up, they called me."

"Why not take me home?"

"This was closer."

I closed my eyes and waited for the jumble of sounds and feelings to settle.

Off in the distance, a bell sounded. Wind chimes sang, crickets chirped, the low baying of sheep and the deep hum of a tractor in the distance, filled the air. I also heard the screech of a door opening and the thud as it closed.

"How is she?" Allison's voice was faint, quiet. There was a squeak from Bryce's chair as he pushed it back, and then there was the soft thud-thud-thud of his footsteps as he walked away.

"She's awake but disoriented, like you said she would be," he told her, his voice almost too low to hear. "Should we give her another dosage?"

"No. She's been given so much of it, and we need it to be out of her system before . . ."

"So what do I say?"

"Stick to the plan. This will all be over soon. It will get easier, I promise. It's time. Do you think you can get her to join us?"

"Yeah, I'll need a bit of time, but we'll be there soon."

The screen door opened and closed again, and my brother returned.

"Hey, sleepyhead, you awake?"

I slowly opened my eyes. Thankfully, the world had stopped spinning.

"Everything okay?" I asked. Not much of what I had overheard made sense.

"How is your head?"

"Heavy with a slight headache, if that makes sense."

He held out a hand to me. "Dinner is almost ready. Do you think you're up for a little walk?" He plopped a hat on me and then adjusted the one he wore.

Honestly, I didn't know if I could even get to my feet, let alone go for a walk.

Somehow, we made it across the porch and down the stairs.

"Where are we eating?"

"It's a special day," he said, "so we're eating out on the patio as a group. It's beautiful; I think you'll like it."

"Why is it a special day?" I leaned against his shoulder as we slowly approached the yard.

"It's Blessing Day, and I was in charge of the kitchen." There was a measure of pride in his voice.

"So . . . you made dinner?" I tried to understand what was so important about Blessing Day, but I drew a blank.

"I was in charge of the blessing dish, which is a true honor." A flash of anxiety danced across his face as he tucked my arm in tighter to his body.

"What's wrong?"

"I'm just a little . . . nervous, I guess," he said.

"Whatever you made, they are going to love it. You know that as well as I do," I told him. I was surprised at how nervous he was. Tiny beads of sweat dotted his forehead.

"Bryce, have I really been here for four days?" I wished I could remember those days. I wished I could remember what happened to me at the retreat center . . . but I couldn't even recall arriving there in the first place.

"You have," he said, patting my hand. "Don't worry — I've been in touch with Mona, Merilyn, and even Lexi. They're all worried about you, but they also want you to get better."

"Where was Mona when all this happened?" We'd intended to enjoy a spa weekend together.

"You really don't remember?"

I carefully shook my head.

"She canceled at the last minute. Something about work. She feels horrible, Brynn. No doubt, once you're home, she'll spoil you like crazy to make up for it."

He wouldn't look at me, which warned me he wasn't being entirely truthful.

"What else?"

"Nothing. I swear. I'm just nervous about tonight."

"Because it's Blessing Day."

He nodded.

I stood still, forcing him to stay with me. "Would they be upset if I asked you to take me back, so I could lie down? I don't feel up to being around so many people right now."

His gaze narrowed. "Is it your head? I thought you only had a slight headache?"

I glanced back toward the farmhouse with almost envy. "Bryce, I feel weird, like my body isn't my own; I don't remember half a week of my life, and it sounds like tonight is really important to you, and I don't want to mess that up."

A myriad of things swept across his face, but he wore that mask I couldn't see behind, the mask he usually kept for strangers, not for me.

"It's important to me that you are there. I want to celebrate this with you, please?"

There were so many things I wanted to say, like I did not feel well or that I didn't trust anyone here, but instead, I asked the one question that was on the tip of my tongue: "What did they give me?"

How I felt, it wasn't natural. It had to come from whatever they had given me, whether in the form of medication or in my tea. That was the only explanation I could come up with.

"What? Nothing," he said. "I mean . . . you were unconscious for so long, and then when you came around, you were panicking, and honestly, it scared me."

"So you were here?"

He nodded. "As soon as they called me, I drove here, and Brynn, I can't even describe what you were like. They gave you a mild sedative to help calm you, that was all."

The fear in his eyes, the flutter in his voice — he wasn't lying to me.

"Can we go home, please?" I didn't want to be here anymore. I just wanted to leave; there was no sense of safety here.

Bryce looked around us, almost desperate, like he didn't know how to answer me.

"Do we need permission?" I asked, with a hint of sarcasm in my voice.

That seemed to make an impact.

"No, no, it's just that . . . of course, we can go home. We'll leave right after the ceremony, I promise."

A wave of exhaustion hit me. I was tired of fighting. "After dinner, then, swear it."

He wrapped his arms around me in a hug, holding me tight. "I love you, you know that, right?"

I leaned into the embrace. "I love you too." We stayed that way for a solid minute before we continued our slow walk. "So it's a dinner party, then," I said, trying to make small talk.

"It is. It reminds me of a wedding reception; you remember, my college friend's? Wait till you see it. Everyone is there, waiting on us."

As we slowly crested the small hill leading to the dinner patio, I was half expecting to hear a kaleidoscope of noise, from a murmur of voices to a clattering of plates and utensils and the ruckus of children getting in the way.

Instead, we were greeted with silence.

# CHAPTER THIRTY-SEVEN

Bryce was right.

I took it all in, the scenery, the backdrop, the ambiance, and it really did remind me of that wedding reception we'd been invited to. It was that beautiful.

Beneath large maple trees sat a long table covered with a white cloth. Above the table, dancing twinkling lights moved with the breeze and gave off a fairytale romance vibe.

Almost every seat at the table was full, and everyone was dressed like they were attending a summer party. They all sat there, subdued smiles on their faces, even the little ones, as they watched us approach.

Having all these eyes on us was unnerving.

"Ahh, our guests of honor, please come join us." Maximus stood at the head of the table and beckoned us with open arms.

He pulled out a seat for me. I was to his left, with Bryce beside me. I knew Bryce was a little put out by the seating arrangement right away.

I glanced down at the table and smiled at the people who met my gaze. No one said hello; they simply nodded or smiled back at us.

Someone appeared at our side with drinks. I hesitated and waited for Bryce to drink as well. It was a sweet sangria.

"Now that we're all here, let's begin," Max said.

The chairs scraped back one by one as the children left their seats. Elder Allison joined them, and they headed to a small garden plot off to the side, where a table with a basket waited for them.

Allison took the basket and held it, pointing away from her. Each child after another took a small scoop, filling it with whatever was in the basket, and headed to the garden patch, where they sprinkled it over the dirt.

When all the children were done, Allison poured the remainder of the basket into the dirt, and one of the teenagers, who was waiting with a rake, worked it through the dirt.

I took mental notes. I had questions that needed to be answered afterward.

The children headed to a small sink area and washed their hands before returning to their seats, remaining silent as they did so.

The reverence for the moment wasn't lost on me. Whatever they did must have been considered sacred.

Max stood, hands held out in front of him and said what sounded like a prayer: "Whether in life or death, God has blessed us with abundance. How we treat that blessing determines the next steps in our journey toward enrichment and everlasting life." He bowed his head, and I noticed everyone else copied him.

"May the blessing we receive today be one of your favor; may we not partake with unholy thoughts, desires, or actions in any way that would rebuke what has been given today. We accept this blessing and tribute with grace, as intended."

When he was done, he gave a slight nod, and just like that, everyone reached for a serving dish in front of them and took a small portion of food.

Max dished out spoonfuls for himself and me, then handed the dish to Bryce.

Max raised his voice before he took a bite: "We accept this blessing as it is intended."

"We accept this blessing as it is intended," rang down the table, each person uttering it before they ate.

My fork remained in my hand; I was too intrigued to eat. I'd never been served a meal where you had to utter a prayer before every bite, yet that was what was happening. Bryce was focused on the food in front of him, and a look of awe and happiness settled on him with each mouthful.

Bryce finally glanced my way with a raised brow. He wanted to know what I thought of the dish.

"Sister Brynn, Brother Bryce, I can't tell you what an honor it is to have you both here finally," Max said, setting his fork down.

I heard a clatter of silverware on plates and realized everyone at the table had followed Max. Not just that, but they were all staring our way. I squirmed in my seat, feeling uncomfortable with the attention.

"It truly is a sign to have you here at this table," he continued, his booming voice heard by all. "We have been waiting for this moment, haven't we, Family? *For in the last days, before the rebirth, the twins of white flame will arise and join in. The preparation of the willful blessing will, in one accord, bring about the end of a fallen world, and the anointed ones will be birthed into new life.*"

The prophecy. Hearing him utter it sent shivers of dread up my spine. I'd never understood it, and I never wanted to, either. Twins of the white flame . . . who were they kidding?

Someone had got their meanings mixed. Growing up, Anthony always made sure we understood what a white flame and a twin flame were; he drilled this into us over and over. It wasn't until I was older and looked into it myself that I realized he'd twisted the meanings.

A white flame symbolizes divinity, enlightenment, and ascension. A twin flame is about the relationship between soulmates or someone you connect with on a spiritual level that transcends everything else. Those within the twin flame complemented each other, something Bryce and I did. But we were no symbol of divinity, and I wished everyone understood that.

Bryce and I were twins. Period. We shared a genetic defect as well as a closeness only twins could experience, but that didn't mean we were the fulfillment of a prophecy for someone with a god-like personality.

"Today is the beginning of the end of everything we've worked so hard for. Of all our homesteads, this is the one I'm most proud of. The unity among our Family is the epitome of everything we stand for. As we continue our preparations, I want you all to know how thankful I am for you, how loved you are, and how excited I am that together, we will experience the rebirth in a way no one else will, mainly because of the gift the prophesied ones have bestowed on us." Max reached for his glass and raised it high. "To our Brother and Sister and the blessing their presence is for us."

"To Brother and Sister." The words were whispered down the table, glasses all raised, and a rush of embarrassment flowed through me.

There were no words as I looked at all the faces turned our way. Were we expected to say anything? Should we have smiled and nodded? Bryce basked in the admiration. What was I missing about all this, that he'd dived in head first?

"Please, enjoy the blessing before us. Let's celebrate and honor our Cousin Lily."

Hearing Lily's name was rather startling. "What happened to Lily?" I whispered to Bryce the second everyone picked up their forks and resumed eating.

"She died."

My stomach curdled as grief for someone I'd only barely known struck me. She was dead? When? How? The last time I was here, everyone told me Lily was giving her blessing, like that should have explained it all, but it explained nothing. Not to me.

"How?"

"Leave it be, please." Bryce's words came as a warning at the exact moment he squeezed my leg — our way of telling the other to be quiet.

Biting back all my words, I raised my fork and took another bite of the meal on my plate.

Wow. If I hadn't known my brother made that dish, I would have with that first bite. The braised meat was so tender that it fell apart in my mouth. The gravy was a tender kiss, and the chopped carrots and potatoes were melt-in-my-mouth good.

"You've outdone yourself," I said, my voice soft, meant only for his ears.

He smiled in response. "I wanted to make Dad proud. I finally understood what all this meant to him, in making this meal. Everything from how they honor one another to the ceremonial aspects of their beliefs, I get why all of this was so important to him. It was an honor to be asked to prepare this blessing." Bryce's gaze turned toward Max.

Hearing Bryce mention Anthony caught me off guard, but before I could respond, Max interrupted the moment.

"Of all of us, your father understood what this community means and how integral death is to us as a Family. Losing him was difficult, for me especially. Anthony knew me better than most, accepted me despite my faults, and encouraged me to continue where others would have given up. Anthony knew how special our Family is, and do you know why?" He paused, but I knew he didn't expect a reply. "We are the only homestead to be privileged with honoring the blessings the way we do. Without us, without this core and this location, what will happen at the end wouldn't be possible. Anthony, more than anyone else, understood that."

Max leaned back in his chair and looked out over the garden area.

That's when it clicked: what the children had spread earlier was ashes. Human remains. Lily.

Why? Cremation ashes were high in salt and contained high pH levels, which were toxic for many plants. They were killing their vegetables before they had time to grow.

"I see the questions building in your mind, Sister," Max said. "Yes, you're right. Those were Lily's ashes, which we placed in the soil. After dinner, those remains, along with some activated charcoal and compost, will be worked into the soil and spread throughout the area so the toxicity levels are nil. We'll also water down the area heavily. Brother Herb—" he pointed down the table — "is our local horticulturist, and knows what he's doing."

"You're going to use that as a garden bed? To grow what exactly?" I tried to wrap my head around it all. I'd heard of ashes being used in flower gardens, but for vegetable growing?

"That's up to Brother Herb," Max answered. "We firmly believe that all aspects of a person's being should be honored. When a member of our Family passes away, we believe in creating a permanent connection with them, so that when the end comes, they will be part of that rebirth journey. We are all one, and one is in all of us."

His fork pierced a carrot, and he raised it to his lips. "With every bite we take of this meal, we consume that person's essence. Whether it's the vegetables that grew in the soil of their body or in the meat that we ingest through their organs." He took a bite and slowly chewed, never breaking eye contact with me.

He then repeated the process with the meat on his plate; all the while, my stomach churned, knotted, and cramped with the realization of what I had just eaten.

I pushed my dish away in horror. I jumped from my seat and rushed as far as I could before I threw up in the grass. My stomach twisted and cramped, the nausea folding into one spasm after another until every single bite I ate was gone.

Someone was at my side, their hand on my back. Coils of disgust sent shivers over my skin.

"Brynn . . ."

It was my brother. My brother, the person who cooked Lily's organs. He knowingly . . . my brain froze as things pieced together. My brother would have harvested her organs himself when he did the autopsy.

Was that why he'd been so secretive about the whole thing?

Just like Anthony had in the past.

I needed him to tell me I was wrong.

"Tell me this isn't what I think it is! Tell me you didn't do what I know you did!" I slowly straightened, pushing his hand off of me. I balled my fists at my sides, the need to hit him strong.

My brother, the one man I thought I could always depend on, the one I thought I knew inside and out, was unrecognizable now.

"Tell me, Bryce, please, tell me you weren't part of this." I begged for an answer I knew I wouldn't get, one that I knew wouldn't be true.

"It's not what you think," he said, his voice void of apology or shame.

Something inside me broke into a million little pieces as I looked back toward the people sitting at the table, eating pieces of Lily, one bite at a time.

It wasn't what I thought? He had no idea of the thoughts running through my head at the moment: my brother was a monster, these people were sick, this cult was dangerous, and all of Lexi's warnings were very, very valid.

I needed to call her right away.

# CHAPTER THIRTY-EIGHT

*Three Days Ago*

A distracting hum pounded from one side of my brain to the other, and it turned into a heavy thud the moment I sat up.

I blinked several times, working through the headache that filled my head with a pounding pain. Bryce said they'd given me something before to help me relax, but this felt different . . . was I drugged?

I groaned as the memories of last night — the ceremony, the ashes in the garden, and the food we ate — came rushing back.

The urge to vomit took over, and bile rushed up my throat. I raced toward an open doorway that led into a bathroom and dry heaved until my whole back ached with the effort it took for my body to expel what was not in there.

I crumpled on the floor, the memory of everything sinking in as I felt my soul being ripped from me, one piece at a time.

I ate vegetables grown in human remains. I ate meat that was retrieved from a deceased body that my brother had cooked.

How could Bryce do that? How could he buy into the ridiculous lies this cult sold, and go against everything he knew was right and true?

I climbed to my feet and splashed my face with cold water as I tried to make sense of how all this could be happening.

The first thing I did was take stock of the room. Soft white walls, cornflower blue bedspread, heather-colored throw draped across the edge of the bed, prints of famous cozy libraries and bookstores from around the world on the wall across from the bed.

My room, but not mine. All my things were here, right down to the perfume I used and the books on the bookshelf. There was even my small stuffed black sheep sitting on a wall shelf, a toy my mom bought for my first birthday. She got me the sheep, and Bryce, a little monkey he lost long ago.

I had asked Bryce to take me home last night. He'd promised he would, so why break his word? Why was I still at the farm?

A thought niggled at the back of my brain as I looked around the bedroom. In the bathroom, I searched through the cupboard and the medicine cabinet, hoping not to find what I did indeed find: my face cream, medications, vitamins, eye serum, and the sunscreen I needed.

*Bryce, what did you do?*

Thinking back, my last memory was Bryce trying to hug me, whispering in my ear that it was not what I thought, and Max behind him, a concerned look on his face.

After that . . . there was nothing.

I racked my brain and tried to remember something, anything . . . but other than a sense of disorientation and a feeling of being jostled, I came up blank.

I pulled back the curtain covering the window and stared out at the people below, the girls in the garden, the men working on the farm equipment.

I also saw Maximus, and panic sank in.

I rushed to the door and pulled it open, but it wouldn't budge. Not only that, the handle wouldn't even twist. It was locked.

Why was I locked in this room? Was I being held prisoner?

This couldn't be happening. I banged on the door, once, twice, three times.

I yelled for help, screamed for attention, and demanded that someone, anyone, let me out of that room.

Footsteps pounded up the stairs, and I screamed louder.

"That's enough," I heard Allison's voice, firm and authoritative. "Move away from the door, Sister, so that I can come in."

I did as requested and heard a key slide into the lock and twist.

Allison opened the door, holding a tray of covered plates and a carafe. Behind her were two guards.

Fear set in, and set in hard.

"Your brother made you breakfast," she said, her face stern. "He said to tell you the coffee is extra strong."

"Why isn't Bryce the one bringing it to me? Better yet, why don't I eat it downstairs and ask him myself?"

Allison's look told me that she was not to be played, nor was she stupid.

"Enjoy that coffee. Bryce spent extra time making your favorite breakfast. I'll be back in an hour to retrieve the tray."

An hour?

"Am I a prisoner?" There was no sense beating around the bush.

Allison's smile was condescending at best. "You are where you belong. This is your home, not a prison. The sooner you accept that, the easier everything will be."

Allison left, the door closing behind her, and before I could even take a step, I heard the door lock being engaged. I also overheard her tell one of the guards to stay close.

I knew she knew I heard her.

If I was scared before, that feeling only intensified.

The only thing from the tray I grabbed was the coffee.

Why was I here? Why was the door locked? Why did the room look like a replica of my own at home? What did Bryce think he was doing?

Why was I being held prisoner?

I refilled my cup and took another sip of the surprisingly strong brew, when everything in the room spun, forcing me to grab the desk for support.

What the hell?

I set the cup down and staggered toward the bed. Tears formed as the realization my brother had betrayed me took root as I laid down on the pillow and closed my eyes, knowing once again I'd been drugged.

## CHAPTER THIRTY-NINE

I'd lost track of the days I'd been living in that small room, of Allison, plus the guards being the only people I saw, and never having my questions answered.

I hadn't been drugged again. After refusing any food or liquid following that coffee, Allison brought up a box of coffee pods along with an individual coffee machine, along with an apology.

It turned out she'd been the one who drugged me, not Bryce.

That made me feel a little better, but not much.

It had been days, and my brother had yet to visit me. Sure, he cooked the food I refused to eat, but he never actually came up to see me to explain anything about what had happened and why I was being held prisoner.

Because that's exactly what I was. Except, no one would tell me why.

Although I had yet to have a visit from Bryce, that didn't mean I hadn't seen him. I had, multiple times, but through the bedroom window that had been nailed shut. Every time I saw him below, I'd bang on the windowpane, but the only reaction I received was the guards warning me to knock it off or else.

Their *or else* scared me.

I sat by that window for hours, looking out, watching the world below, questioning why no one paid me any attention.

I still had no idea why I was here. Allison said that Max would explain, except that man seemed to have forgotten my very existence.

I was trying not to freak out, but it was hard.

So, so hard.

I held on to a small hope that Lexi would rescue me. Except I knew that wouldn't happen, because my brother had probably fed her some lie to explain my absence and non-responsiveness to her phone calls or texts.

Would she believe him? Part of me hoped she wouldn't, but still I knew the likelihood of being rescued was slim.

One of my highlights was watching the children playing in the distance. Those little ones were so small and fragile. They played, ate, and even napped outside. The only times I didn't see them were when the weather turned, and rain fell or at night when they were tucked in their beds.

Allison said the children grew up feeling connected to the earth, that it was crucial to their growth and development. It reminded me of an article I read online once about how, in Nordic countries like Sweden, Finland, Norway, and others, babies were bundled up in their carriages and napped outside, even in the winter months.

I'd never met the young ones the few times I'd been here. Allison let it slip that it was important they remained pure from outside influences.

My gaze wandered over the farm, and I noticed my brother stepping out of his truck. My heart paused, my breath caught, and I prayed that he would look up.

When he did, it was all I could do not to shout out a cry. I leaned my head against the window and held up my palm, needing my twin's acknowledgment.

We gazed at one another for a count of five, and then Max appeared beside him. The look on Maximus' face as he glanced up at me made me drop my hand and instinctively step away from the glass.

The heartbeat that paused before now ran in full force. I felt every single beat in my chest as it climbed its way up my esophagus, choking me with panic.

Fear became my constant companion.

In what felt like hours, the heavy tread of footsteps came up the stairs.

I slipped my hands beneath my crossed legs to hide the slight tremors. I didn't understand the fear cascading through me. I was confused, sure. I was also frustrated and furious for being held captive in my room. But why the fear?

Tension settled in my chest, binding me tighter and tighter until it felt like my rib cage was collapsing. My breath was haptic, with slight intakes that lasted mere seconds — in-in-in, barely filling my lungs, barely calming me down.

The knock at my door, the jingle of keys, the murmur of voices . . . anxiety flowed through my veins. I jumped off the bed and stood, hiding my shaky hands behind my back just in time as the door opened.

"Sister." Maximus walked in, carrying a basket of fruit. "I'm sorry it's taken me so long to come see you. I only just arrived after having to ensure our community is prepared for what's about to happen."

Shivers spread up my arms at his tone. "What's about to happen?"

"Why, the end. The end is here, dear Sister, and it's all because of you." He made his way to the middle of the room, arms behind his back, but not for the reasons mine were. "How do you like things? It was important to your brother that your room be similar to what you're comfortable with." He glanced around, then headed to the dresser. "I really don't believe you understand just how important you are, do you?" He grabbed a framed photograph from the collection and held it up. "Twins, with your genetic disposition. You are very rare, my dear. Very, very, rare." He replaced the frame and made his way to the lone chair in the room, forcing me to step backward until my calves hit the edge of the nightstand by the bed.

"Sit, please." He indicated to the bed. I complied, my hands clasped tight in my lap. "I'm sure you have so many questions," he said, his tone placating, making me feel smaller than I should.

"Why I'm being held against my will." My bravado surprised him. Did he expect me to fall at his feet and worship him like the others did? Or quake in fear and become a mouse?

I was quaking. But I was also no mouse.

"Yes, this is unfortunate, but hopefully, after our chat, you'll understand. Truthfully, I didn't want you stressing your brother with demands to return to your old life. Anthony always promised when the time came, you would both be on board, but . . ." He lifted a hand in a shrug-like motion.

"If you think holding me hostage will force me to change my mind, you're mistaken. And Anthony never would have told you we'd both be on board. He has always known how I felt about all this."

Maximus crossed one leg over the other and examined his fingernails. "Yes, yes, you've been skeptical. I blame that on your father. He never treated you the way you deserved, did he?"

The last thing I wanted to do was discuss Anthony and the complicated relationship we had when he was alive.

"Why am I here?"

"Why, to fulfill the prophecy. I thought that was obvious." He replaced his hands in his lap and smiled. "*For in the last days, before the rebirth, the twins of white flame will arise and join in. The preparation of the willful blessing will, in one accord, bring about the end of a fallen world, and the anointed ones will be birthed into new life.*"

I hated that prophecy. Hated everything it stood for in my life. Hated the impact and force it carried. Whether I believed it or not, it shaped my life.

"Why now? Why do you assume Bryce and I have anything to do with this prophecy?"

The tilt of his head and the disappointment in his eyes was a clear rebuke.

"I know your father raised you better, Sister. You know, as well as I do, that you and Brother are the harbingers for the rebirth."

My stomach coiled, and the footprints of fear found their way up my throat.

"Aren't you forcing the issue, though? I mean . . . don't you need a willing blessing and tribute?"

"Willing is preferable, but I think we're past that." He glanced at the door, then back to me. "Willing would mean that door didn't need to be locked." He held up a hand, stopping me as my mouth opened to argue. "Do me a favor and don't lie. We're both adults. We can consider this a free zone for truths."

That ignited a spark inside and filled me with a boldness I knew I would later regret.

"You want truths? The truth is, I'm being held hostage, and you will be charged with kidnapping once I leave here."

A sardonic smirk played with the edges of his lips.

"What makes you think you're leaving here?"

It was like a slap to the face with enough force to push me backward.

"You can't keep me here forever."

"No, that's true. But we don't need forever, do we? I just need you here to bring about the end days."

A chill swept through me as the words behind what he didn't say filled me with unease. "If this is such a free zone for truths, why do you keep skirting the edges?"

He stood and headed to the window, tapping on the glass. "Polycarbonate. So strong, that nothing will break it. Not your fist, not a bullet. When we built this house, we used only the best materials, just in case anything were ever to happen. One can't be too careful, especially in my world. People have been trying to kill me for years, did you know that?"

My brows knit. "Aren't you supposed to be dead anyway? Killed in an explosion while out at sea? You and all your followers . . ." Something snagged in my memory. "Those followers, they're all here, aren't they?"

The way he smiled, I knew I was right.

"Why would you fake your own death? Why would you fake all these deaths?"

"Why? Well, that's easy. I was too much of a target and needed the world to believe I was gone. The truth of our message was muddied with my past, and that couldn't continue. Did you know that was actually your father's idea?" He laughed at the shock on my face, the startled gasp. "You really have no idea who your father was, do you?" He turned his attention from me to something outside.

"You know, it's too bad so many people around you have to hide their truths and live a lie all so you can live with a sense of comfort. They didn't want to rock the boat too much, which I understood. The ends always justify the means, at least in this case."

"What are you talking about?" He spoke in circles, hinting at things that didn't make sense.

"Your father and I were childhood friends and created all this together. He was the brains, and I was the face. He used his connections and know-how to establish our community, and I used my influence and status to bring in the funds and make us legitimate. You might think this is a cult and a scam, but it's not. Your father received a blessing as a teenager, a word from God that changed both his life and mine. That's how the prophecy was birthed, years before you were born. Your mother was also a believer, until the realization that your birth brought about fulfillment. She couldn't handle that, which meant she was a danger to everything we'd built."

"You knew my mother?"

"Knew your mother? I loved your mother. She was my sister." His truth bomb detonated with a deadliness that stole all the air from the room.

"Your . . ."

255

"That's right. We are family. The blood running through your veins is the same in mine."

I shook my head, not wanting to hear anymore. We were not family. We couldn't be.

"Your mother embraced our beliefs and helped to mentor so many of the women. She's the foundation on which all of this is built. The truths taught, the beliefs we live by . . . your mother embodied them all. Losing her nearly destroyed me, but I understood why she had to die. She became a danger."

His words played in my head, circling round and round until I made sense of what he was saying. She had to die?

"You killed her?"

He looked at me with disgust. "No. I would never. Family means everything to me. I would have hidden her away, somewhere off-grid, where her destructive touch couldn't be felt. I've become very good at hiding people, so it would have been no problem, but your father disagreed. We argued, then he took action — without my consent, let me add. I almost hated him for it, almost."

He couldn't be implying that Anthony killed my mother, could he? My parents had been so in love, and her death destroyed him . . . unless the destruction was his own fault?

"Your mother was the first blessing. Your father prepared her himself. He said God had spoken to him, giving him a road map to the beginning of the end, and that your mother's blessing was instrumental to it all."

The weight of his words, of the truth of my mother's death, my father's actions, that I was related to Max . . . it was too much.

"I'm sorry, did you say *Anthony* prepared . . ."

He nodded. "She was the first blessing. Up until then, a lamb was sacrificed; we'd eat its organs as a symbolic gesture of cleansing. Then God spoke to your father, reminding him of what the act of communion really entailed."

"What do you mean?" I couldn't believe I was asking.

"God himself told us to eat of his flesh and drink of his blood, did he not? You don't seriously think he meant juice and crackers?"

My stomach heaved.

"How is your head, by the way?" Max continued, sounding concerned. "I know you've been having some blackouts and memory loss. Feeling better? You were warned what attempting to regain your memory might do to you . . ."

"I just wanted the truth," I whispered.

"And the truth shall set you free," he whispered. "Was it worth it?"

His question stretched between us. I knew the answer, but I wouldn't give him the satisfaction of giving it to him.

Ignorance was never bliss. I understood why my mother hid my past from me, but now, as an adult, I needed to have all the answers so I could make the right decisions for myself. I wished she'd told me everything before her death . . . maybe then I wouldn't be here now.

Max alternated from staring outside to staring at me, giving me space to take in all he'd just said, until that space became suffocating.

"All I ever wanted was for you and your brother to be here with me." He finally broke the silence. "Then our family would be complete. At least I have Bryce. He's very competent at what he does. A chip off the old block, you could say. Your father taught him well. Plus, he loves it here. There's a peace about him, have you noticed that? This is his home. This is his family. He wants to be here, but he's also torn . . . torn between his old life and his new." When he turned toward me, I noticed a nerve in his jaw tensing. "You're the reason why he hasn't allowed himself to fully immerse himself in this life, the life he's chosen for himself. Of all people, I thought you would have understood."

His reprimand caught me off guard.

"Understood? What exactly? That he wants to belong to a cult, a cult apparently our parents helped create, that involves cannibalism? I don't believe that. My mother wouldn't have been a part of this, and I know she wouldn't have wanted Bryce or me to be here. And of all people," I parroted his words, "I understand what a bad idea all of this is. He has a life. A life with me. A life within our own community. And he has a family, a real family, a family that doesn't include you or anyone here."

In the middle of my emotional vomit, he turned his back and once again focused on whatever was outside. When I took a breath, he beckoned me over with a cupping of his hands and pointed outside.

"I don't know," he said. "That to me looks like he's found his family, don't you think?"

I inhaled a breath full of knives. My brother held out his arms as a woman placed a small child into them. He held that child close and kissed its skin before kissing the woman in front of him.

I gasped, taking in the scene. I didn't want to accept what I was seeing.

"That's Belinda, and the child he's holding is baby Anthony, his son." Maximus's eyes danced with sarcastic joy. "Your nephew."

I shook my head. "No, that's not true." He was lying. He had to be. Bryce wouldn't keep something like that from me.

"Why would I lie to you? Think about it, Sister. Little by little, his time has been here, his heart has been here, and he's tried, so many times, to get you to embrace this life . . . but you won't, will you?"

I stared down at my brother, at the woman at his side, at the child in his arms, and the truth was so clear, so bright, so unwanted that it hurt. My heart and soul were being sliced with thrown daggers, their aim so true, so deep, that I knew what I was seeing wasn't a lie.

My brother had a family. A family he'd kept from me.

My brother had a whole life I didn't know about, a life he hadn't shared with me . . . and why? Was it my fault? Maximus certainly assumed it was.

I barely noticed as he stepped away from me, my focus only on my brother and the life that didn't include me.

"It didn't have to be this way," Maximus said.

I turned as tears silently escaped, falling down my face, my throat swollen from sobs I refused to share with him.

"This pain you're feeling will be over soon. In a few days, we'll receive your blessing. Your brother will prepare his tribute, and our family will finally experience a rebirth, something I have been waiting for a very long time. It's all thanks to you." The smile on his face was true, giving his words credence.

All my words, questions, threats, insults, and emotions were stuck inside me, unable to grow and be given life. I understood what he was saying with more clarity than I wanted.

I was about to die.

I was about to die, and instead of trying to save myself, I stood silent and hated myself for it.

# CHAPTER FORTY

One more day passed.

A day of stewing in the words Max spoke, in the truths he laid bare.

A day of losing my mind, with tears and screams and exhausting frustration.

Following his visit, I overheard Max instruct Allison and the guards that I should be left alone until the following day, and that he'd left me with enough fruit so I wouldn't go hungry.

I didn't take a single bite of anything he brought. I searched the fruit for needle pinpricks, but even though I didn't find any, I still refused to eat them.

His words haunted me. Not just the idea that we were related, but of Anthony's actions, the fact my mother tried to save me, save us, and lost her life for it.

I couldn't ignore the truth that my death rushed toward me, and there was nothing I could do about it.

Sometimes, the very idea made me laugh. As if he was going to kill me. As if that was actually the life I now lived. As if any of what Maximus had said could actually happen.

And then, sometimes, the truth set in, and all I could do was cry. He was going to kill me. He was actually going to kill me.

I didn't even know how many days I'd been missing. The last thing I knew, it had been a Friday. Then I woke up here, and it was Tuesday, and today was . . . I had no idea. Did anyone miss me? Merilyn must be wondering where I was. If we didn't see each other at work, we texted questions, memes, and links to cute videos.

And what about Mona and Lexi?

What had Bryce told them all? I imagined a multitude of things . . . that I was still at the retreat center, that I'd decided to go on a long-awaited vacation, that some distant relative in our family had fallen sick, and I went to take care of them . . . would they have believed any of his lies?

Bryce still hadn't come to see me. So many things about him bothered me; I didn't know how to process any of it. Like the idea he knew all along that I was going to die. Or that he'd been keeping a secret family from me. I didn't even want to dwell on the fact he was okay with my death and eating my organs.

Vomit rose, scorching my esophagus.

The image of him kissing the forehead of his son, of the look of love in that woman's gaze, of him with a family, a family I knew nothing about, it wouldn't leave me alone.

Why hide that from me? Didn't he think I'd under-stand? Didn't he trust me enough to know that I'd accept it? Accept them? If I'd known, I'd never have kept him from his family. Never.

All that time, I'd worried that I was losing him, when it turned out I'd lost him a long time ago.

Deep inside, I'd been hoping that Bryce would find a way to help me escape, but he wasn't going to do that, especially since he was the one who bought into the lie.

He was now one of them.

Which meant it was all on me.

If I was going to escape, I had to get myself out of here. How, I had no idea. I didn't even know where *here* was, so once I escaped, where would I go? How would I leave? Every entrance was guarded, so my likelihood of escaping was close to nil.

Max kept talking about the rebirth. What did that even mean? Was everyone going to die? What would happen to all the young ones? The babies and children and teenagers who had no choice but to be raised in all the craziness?

When I researched doomsday cults, I was horrified by what I'd read, by the measures the leaders took to maintain their control over the people and how they handled their failures.

Failure equaled death unless they could accept their mistakes, but Maximus admitting defeat . . . I didn't see it.

If it was true that he created all of this with my parents, then they'd bought into their own lies, and that in itself was extremely sad.

I heard the clap-clap-clap of footsteps on the stairs, and I knew it was Allison. She was the only one with such a light step. All the others were thuds or thumps.

I hid behind the door as it unlocked and slowly opened.

"Sister, I brought you some food." Allison's voice was light, friendly, almost apologetic.

She didn't see me.

I waited until she set the tray down on the table before I rushed her, wrapping one arm around her body and my other hand around her mouth.

"I need to get out of here; he's going to kill me," I whispered into her ear.

She didn't struggle against me, didn't try to get out of my hold; she only stood there, stock still, silent, and waited.

I finally dropped my hand. "Please, I just need help."

Her face was void of any emotion. "I can't help you," she said, keeping her voice low. Her gaze went toward the opened door, then back to me. "There are two of them outside your door, one at the bottom of the stairs and then two more out on the porch. They'll never let you leave. He will never allow it."

If there was any hope inside me, it was gone now. Five against one. What was I thinking? Of course, I couldn't escape.

"Your blessing is too important to Sir," Allison continued. "It's too important to the Family. You are too important. You will be honored, and your blessing won't be in vain," she said, as if that actually meant anything to me.

A bubble of chaotic laughter expanded through my body, overtaking all sense, and I dropped onto my bed, burying my head in my hands as my body shook with the crazy emotion flooding me.

"I'm going to die. You know it. I know it. Everyone here knows it, and all you can say is my blessing won't be in vain. Do you understand how ridiculous that sounds?" All the laughter died as she sat beside me on the bed and placed her hand on my back, rubbing it in a gentle, motherly fashion.

"Your mother believed in the blessing."

Six simple words that shattered me.

I didn't want to believe it. How could she have bought into the lie — a lie that she helped create? What benefit could there have been?

"That changed when she finally had twins and realized we would be sacrificed."

"Not both of you. Your brother isn't the chosen one. You are. You provide the blessing. Your brother's only role is to prepare it, so we may all receive it and be reborn."

Circles and more circles that didn't make sense.

"I'm going to die and my brother . . ." I waited for her to finish my sentence, but she didn't. "Why won't you help me?"

"My mother and sister gave their blessings, and I was skipped over. Sir said my gifts are too valuable, that God needs my hands, and that my work will bring me favor and see me brought into the new life."

"You hear how that sounds, right? God doesn't need anything from us but our belief, and if He's bringing a new life, don't you think He's powerful enough to bring it about on His own, without needing our help?"

My words didn't register. I knew from the way her eyes glazed over.

"I can't help you. I'm sorry." She laid one hand on top of my head. "Your blessing will be honored," she whispered. "Thank you for bringing forth the new life."

When she left my room, I heard her whispering to the guards.

I closed my eyes with defeat. What was I going to do?

There was a slight squeak from the door, and I looked up to find two guards standing before me, with Allison between them.

"Sister, I'm sorry this has to happen," she said.

The next thing I knew, I was being chained to the bed with leather straps, two on my wrists and two on my ankles. There was enough leeway that I was able to half sit up against my pillow, but not enough for me to get off the bed.

"Why?" My voice cracked under the pressure of what was happening.

"This is for your own safety." I saw the regret in her gaze. Words were nothing without actions, and while she could regret this if she wanted to, she also caused it to happen.

I should be fighting them, screaming, demanding my release. I didn't know if it was just that I'd given up or accepted what was happening, but I did nothing. Said nothing.

"I'm sorry," she said as she left, the door locked behind her again.

I had no idea how much time had passed when I heard another set of footprints come up the stairs.

Steps I hadn't heard since being locked in this room, but steps familiar to me.

I swallowed the hope that swelled inside, not wanting to be disappointed, as my door unlocked and my brother finally walked into the room.

"Bryce," I whispered, my voice laced with both hope and hurt.

I used to be able to read him like an open book, where the words were in large print, but no more. Now, he was closed off, and the distance between us was like a wide chasm, no longer crossable.

"Please help me," I begged, my tear-laced words filling the room.

Someone followed him in, carrying a tray with a container. I barely gave it a glance, not wanting any more of their food. All I wanted was freedom, and for my brother to be the one who saved me.

But the shuttered look in his eyes, the tightness of his jaw, and the way he remained silent and distant told me that wasn't going to happen.

The minute we were alone, he sat in the chair beside the bed and rested his elbows on his knees.

"How did we get to this?" He looked toward my restraints.

Was that a glimmer of regret in his eyes?

There were so many things I wanted to say, but for reasons I didn't understand, no words were waiting on my tongue, so I remained silent.

I gave him room to speak.

"When Dad explained it all to me, I thought I understood what he meant, you know? But now that it's happening . . ."

"It doesn't have to." I wasn't ashamed to beg for my life.

He looked up in surprise. "Of course it does. Everything has led to this moment, Brynn, don't you understand that? This is all we were meant for. You with the blessing. Me being the one to sacrifice it all."

*Him* sacrifice it all?

"Are they killing you, too? Or is that only reserved for me?" I swallowed past the ball of tangled emotions in my throat and struggled not to let my simmering anger explode.

"You have the easy part. I'm the one who has to live with it. I'm the one who has to carry the heavy burden. Don't you get that?"

I couldn't believe the delusional words that dropped from his lips, but if I said what I wanted to say, I was only going to push him away further.

"I wanted you to be a part of all this," he said, his hands sweeping outward. "I've tried to bring you in, to share this part of me with you, but you were never interested. I think out of everything, that will be my main regret, that I couldn't get you to understand just how important this is to me."

"This is your family." Tears that had clung to my lashes now fell with abandonment down my cheeks, and I gave a shuddering breath as I wiped them away.

He nodded. "It is. I know . . ." He swallowed. "Sir, he told me you now know everything. Our parents, who Sir is to us, Belinda, and our baby. I've always wanted you to meet him, baby Tony. We named him after Dad. Belinda won't let me bring him up here, though. She doesn't want this to affect him with the stressful energy, and I get that. If things were different . . ."

A sob I'd been holding at bay ripped through me. If things were different, I would be holding my nephew, I'd be meeting the woman my brother fell in love with, I would . . .

"They'd still be killing me, regardless of whether I embraced this life or not, right?" The defeat in my voice covered us both.

He wouldn't look at me as he nodded. "But at least you wouldn't be alone. The others, when they gave their blessing, it wasn't like this."

"What is it like?" I didn't want to ask the question, but they were now there, spoken, and hung between us.

"They are celebrated. Honored. It's like having the wake with them there. We share stories, we remember the good times, we laugh at the memories, and then, when it's time, we make a toast in their honor and circle them as they fall asleep. That's how it was supposed to be for you. Not . . . this." He motioned to my restraints.

"You didn't expect me to embrace this, did you?"

The look on his face said *yes*, even if he couldn't say it out loud.

"How can you do this, Bryce? How can you sit here, knowing I'm about to die, and act like this is normal?"

"This is what has to happen. It's the only way."

I fought against the restraints, but there was no give. "According to whom? To Maximus? To our father? You

266

know they made all of this up, right? Dad, Anthony, and even Mom. All of it. It's all lies, a fabricated truth based on some drugs they took as teenagers."

He shook his head.

"Do you understand what is about to happen? You are going to kill me, carve up my organs, and then eat me . . . you're going to *eat* me, Bryce!" The hysteria took over, filling me, flooding me, drowning me in a truth I didn't want to accept.

Bryce reached over and lightly touched my hand. He tapped his finger twice, paused, and then tapped it again three times. It took me a second to understand what he was saying.

Two taps: *I'm here.*

Three taps: *I've got you.*

He's here, and he's got me? Like hell he did. In what universe did he think anything he was about to do was remotely okay?

Bryce breathed in deep, and I knew nothing I could have said would have made a difference.

"I brought you something to eat. I'm told you aren't eating much, so I made you some stew." He pulled the dish off the tray and set it on his knee. The steam from the soup bowl wafted toward me, and I picked up hints of beef and gravy.

He moved his chair even closer and spoon-fed me. I wanted to say no, wanted to clamp my lips together and lock the words inside me, but I didn't.

Maybe it was the way he looked at me. Maybe it was the mixture of hope and sadness, of love and a small hint of forgiveness. Maybe it was just the smell and the way my stomach grumbled. Maybe . . . the answer didn't matter because I ate a few spoonfuls, savoring the thick gravy as it coated my tongue, biting into the tender morsels of beef and the soft potato cubes.

He'd made my favorite dish, and with each bite, I could taste the love.

My face rinsed with tears as he told me about his son. I heard the deep, overwhelming sense of pride, the depth of his love in his voice, and I ached with a sadness I never thought I'd feel.

I was alone now. Where there used to be a bond between us that only twins could feel, now it was gone. We used to be two spirits in a boat anchored in the middle of a lake, where no one and nothing could harm us. Now, I was alone in that boat, and the water around me was choppy, sharks circled me, and that safety I always felt with him had disappeared.

I knew he'd drugged me. I knew it the moment he fed me that first bite, and yet I still ate it.

I closed my eyes as a heavy weariness flowed within me, starting at my head and moving sloth-like toward my feet. I heard the clatter of the spoon in the bowl and the light thud of the bowl on the table, and then there was a slight dip in the mattress as he laid down beside me, his arms encircling me.

"I'm sorry," he whispered over and over as he smoothed my hair. "It wasn't supposed to be like this, but you gave us no choice."

"Why?" It was hard to get the word out; my tongue was wrapped around itself.

"Your blessing is almost here, and I didn't want you to stress over it. I talked Sir into letting me drug you, so that you'll be unaware of the preparations and then asleep when it happens. I also promised Father that you would partake of his blessing so that his spirit would always be with you," he whispered. "That was the last of him. Little by little, I'd been adding portions of him to the meals I made for you at the other house."

The realization of what he was saying threw my stomach in a lurch resembling a rollercoaster ride, but at the same time, darkness swelled around me.

There was something I needed to say, I wanted to say, I had to say . . . but a black shadow swept over me, and it was too late.

# CHAPTER FORTY-ONE

*Now*

Death. I refuse to welcome it with open arms.

Everything hurts. My whole body screams in pain from the tip of my head to the bottom of my feet, but I embrace the pain, welcome it, and crave it because it means one simple thing: I am alive.

I don't know how.

Maximus intends to kill me. Until he does, I think it's a game to him. He's a sick, sadistic monster who has gotten away with murder. He's a schoolyard bully whose father happens to be the school principal. He can get away with anything, and he knows it.

The rope around my neck and wrists is gone.

There's an exhaustion that fills me, but I don't know if it's from the sedation of drugs I've been fed for who knows how long, or if it's from the coursing fear that hasn't yet let go of its hold. Battling the constant fight-or-flight is overwhelming and energy-draining, but if ever I needed those endorphins, it's now.

The heaviness of my head has me worried. Head wounds can be dangerous. My fingertips gently probe my scalp, and

I feel the clotted lumps of dried blood everywhere I touch, along with areas of fresh wetness.

What happened to me? How did I go from being tied up and drugged to feeling like I'd barely survived a beating?

I hear a click. It rings out like clanging bells, breaking the silence. That click is followed by the sound of wood scraping along the ground, like a door being pushed open, and someone clears their throat.

I flinch.

A sliver of light repels the darkness, highlighting a set of rickety wooden stairs.

I know instantly I will never make it up them.

"Oh good, you're awake." Allison holds up a light and aims it my way. She makes her way down the stairs and toward me, a bag slung over her shoulder that she sets down on the ground once she reaches my side.

"It was never supposed to come to this," she says, her voice shaking as she takes in my appearance. "Your mother will never forgive me for letting it go this far."

She pulls out bandages, wipes, ointment, and rolls of compression wrap. "I know you're in pain, but this will help until you can get to a hospital," she says, as she starts to clean the wounds on my wrists, ankles, neck, and rib cage.

"I can't believe he let those thugs of his touch you." That was the first time I'd actively heard anger in Allison's voice. "Oh, sweetheart, what did they do to you?" She gently lifts up the hem of my shirt, and I know from her expression that it's bad. "I'm sorry," she whispers.

I feel every single light touch from her fingers, and I welcome the warmth that saturates my skin.

"Do you think you can stand?" She keeps glancing over her shoulder toward the stairs.

"I can't make it up those." The words sound warped, and the effort shreds through my throat. She pulls out a water bottle and helps me to sip through a straw slowly.

"You won't need to," she says. "There's another way out."

What game is being played with me now?

"If you're going to kill me, just get it over with, please." I hate that I'm begging for my death.

"Oh honey, I'm trying to save your life. And I'm not the only one. I had some help."

I don't want to trust her, yet if there's a small chance I can escape, I have no other choice.

"How?"

"Max went too far when he had you beaten. It was never supposed to come to this." Her lips thin as she tilts my face. "Your eyes are so swollen, I hope you'll be able to see the way," she mutters.

"Tell me what happened." Her cryptic replies irritate me.

"Max had his goons bring you here to beat you and leave you for dead. They were instructed to shoot you with enough morphine to kill you and then have your body cremated, to erase all evidence of what happened to you. Your brother found out and got here to stop them in time. He bandaged your eyes and gave you some pain meds, then came to find me. I was only just able to get away."

I want to laugh, but it will hurt too much. I don't believe a single word she said. My brother was ready to serve me in a stew. He wouldn't save me.

"So where is he now?"

"Trying to get Belinda and his son out in time. They're going to disappear until it's safe, but he'll be in touch as soon as possible."

Hope blooms in my soul, but I squash it. I don't want to hope, I don't want to believe. Not after all of this.

"I know you don't believe me, and trust me, I get that. The house is bugged, Brynn. Every single space on this farm is bugged, so we all had to be careful with what we said. I think your home is bugged, too. You'll want to get your friend to check it once you get home, okay?" She stares into my eyes as if trying to gauge whether I believe her or not.

I don't.

"You have no idea who Maximus is, or you would understand his absolute need for control. He knows everything because he's aware of everything. There is no safe space when he is involved. Well . . . except for this basement. Too much has happened down here," a haunted shadow passes through Allison's gaze, "and he wouldn't want any recorded evidence. It's about the only place where we can speak freely. Your mother and I used to meet down here if we needed a space to talk." She sighs as she sits beside me on the cot. "If Maximus suspected that we weren't going to go through with your blessing, he would have taken matters into his own hands and killed you himself. It wouldn't be the first time." She swallows hard. "He killed my husband when we told him we were done and wanted out. No one leaves alive. Not even your mother, his own sister . . ." Her voice breaks into a sob that she tries to squash.

"He said Anthony killed her."

"That's been the lie he's told for years. I think even he believes it now." She hands me the water bottle and urges me to drink more.

"I know there's no reason for you to believe me," she repeats, "but we would never have let you die. I promised your mother I wouldn't let that happen. It's too late for the rest of us, but it's not too late for you. You can still get out of here, and maybe, just maybe, you can expose Maximus, before he's even aware you're gone."

"But you said Bryce is trying to leave?"

"Trying. I hope he makes it. I convinced him to focus on his family, on keeping his child safe while I help you."

His son. Tears gathered, but I blinked them away.

"Here, let's get you to your feet," she says, as she helps me stand. She pulls out a pair of running shoes from her bag and helps me to step into them.

She leads me to a side door and unlocks it. Walking ahead of me, she holds my hand as we slowly make our way through a dark tunnel that opens to a dirt path covered by a large bush.

Every step is painful. Every movement is excruciating.

"Follow this," she says after we wedge ourselves past the bush. "It will lead out to the main road. It's a bit of a walk, but don't give up. Once you reach the road, I need you to hit redial on this phone. Your friend should be waiting. I've called her enough times now that she should assume it's you reaching out for help." She hands me an old flip phone. "When she gets here, give her this." She wraps my fingers around a folded piece of paper. "It's a list of the drugs that you've been given, as well as some other key information to help the authorities."

"Why don't you come with me, tell them yourself?"

She shakes her head. "That will alert Maximus that something is up, and he'll disappear. There are photos on that phone of him and other details that your friend will want to see."

My friend? Who is she talking about? The only person I plan on calling is Lexi . . . except I don't know her number; it's programmed into my phone.

"Where is my phone?"

"Max destroyed it. You'll need to get a new one. I'm sorry." She pulls me into a quick hug, and I can't help but wince at how much it hurts.

"Remember, press redial once you get to the road, and stay hidden until you know you're safe."

"Come with me," I beg. "I don't know if I can do this." Everything hurts so much.

"You can do this. It's this or death," she warns me. "There's a full moon, so you should be able to see the path clearly, but it'll be rough, so don't rush. Watch your step and stay quiet," she warns. "There are patrols out. I don't think they'll come this way, but I'm not sure."

She leaves me there, walking through the bush into the cellar where I'd been kept.

My mind races with everything she's said and all her instructions as I make my way down the rough and over-grown path.

Every step I take echoes like a gunshot in an open space. Every twig I snap, every rock that scuttles beneath my shoes, every leaf that crunches will alert my presence to the patrols, and my time to escape will be gone. As I inch closer to the road ahead, my heart pounds against my ribs like a caged lion.

I can see it in the distance. It takes forever to reach, but once I'm close enough, I open the phone Allison gave me and press redial.

One ring. Two rings.

"Brynn, please say this is you." It's Lexi's voice on the other end, and I let out a sob of relief.

"Oh, thank heavens, it is you," she says, her voice catching, and I hear all the feels, which has me tearing up. "Finally. You have no idea how worried I've been. You keep calling but never say anything, so I know you're in danger. It's okay if you can't talk . . . I'm almost there, okay? For the love of all things holy and sane, please stay put. I lost you for a bit and panicked. I'm a few minutes out . . ."

I hear a rustling behind me, and a jolt of panic pushes through me, propelling me toward the long grass where I press my cheeks into the dirt. All the fear, the anger, the heartbreak I've experienced over the past few days fills every space within me until the thump-thump-thump of my heart stuttering in fear fills my ears. I shelter my head beneath my arms, the muscles through my shoulders screaming in pain, as the rustling behind me, to the side of me, all around me, continues.

Is this the end? Will fear be the last emotion I experience before there's nothing else?

The rustling stops, and in the silence, I freeze. Each passing second is an eternity, where the whispering shadows offer warnings of dangerous sounds, and I need to become invisible.

My breaths are shallow and haptic, the sound a trumpet in my ears. I struggle for a sense of calmness, straining to hear through the night sounds. The dark is broken by a sliver of light as headlights approach in the distance. Gravel crunches beneath tires, but Allison's warning rings loud and clear in my mind: stay hidden until you know you're safe, so I wait, frozen, barely breathing.

A car door slams. Someone walks in front of the lights, casting a long shadow.

"Brynn?" That's when I hear it. "It's me, Lexi. Where are you?"

The voice of my angel.

# EPILOGUE

*Three Months Later*

My garden lies in a dormant state, much like myself.

Mom used to say this was a magical time for the garden, and as a child, I believed her. I sat out here, bundled up in my snowsuit and mitts, and I'd imagine little magical fairies taking care of the seeds buried deep beneath the snow and dirt.

I know this season is necessary for the growth of my garden, and without it, I wouldn't have the beauty that emerges, but just because I can appreciate the necessity of what's occurring, it doesn't mean I like it or even enjoy it. Much like what's happening with me.

This season I'm in has been hard.

The chill wind threads itself through my bones, replacing my sinews, my veins. The term *Winter is Here* feels more appropriate than I let on to anyone within my inner circle.

I curl up tighter within myself as I sit on the swing. Mr. Baxter is at my side, his dog at my feet, but we've been silent for the past thirty minutes, and neither one of us seems to mind.

What else can be said? What else can be discussed?

With a sigh, I lay my head down on his shoulder and he lightly pats my hand. Jasper lifts his head and sniffs, slowly curling up to his feet and stretching out before he takes a few steps forward, then looks over his shoulder to see why his owner isn't following.

"Guess it's time for dinner. You coming?" Mr. Baxter's gruff voice breaks the silence between us and I force my lips into a semi-smile.

Eating dinner with Mr. Baxter at his place has become a habit, one neither of us minds keeping. I haven't gotten used to eating alone in mine yet.

He moves so he's standing off to the side and glances over my shoulder. "Looks like you've got other plans," he says.

I twist and see Mona stepping out of her vehicle. She waves.

"Tomorrow, I guess. I've got a few more casseroles in the freezer. Any preference? I think there's a lasagna still left."

"As long as it's not that veggie nonsense like last time. Eggplant noodles do not freeze well," he grumbles, before he leans forward and places a soft kiss on my forehead. "See you tomorrow, kiddo."

A lump the size of a small planet lodges in my throat. Every day for the last three months, Mr. Baxter has checked in on me, making sure I'm not just okay, but that I get out of the house and face life.

*No good withdrawing from life after you've been saved*, he says. And he's right. I know he's right. He knows he's right, and yet, withdraw I do; I can't help it.

My whole life was caught up in the twister of the now infamous Family Doomsday Cult, and the destruction in its wake has been devastating.

Mona waits for me at my kitchen door, a bag of groceries in hand.

"I'm in the mood for some authentic fettuccine with cream sauce," she says. "I watched this really cute Italian chef online, and it's ridiculous how easy it is to make. No more premade sauces or packets for me." She beams me a ridiculously wide smile as she hefts the brown bag into my arms.

"You grate the cheese, and I'll do the rest. I even brought wine."

Mona is another person who hasn't left my side since that fateful night when Lexi came to my rescue. It's like everyone has a babysitting schedule for me, and while I've never appreciated being so coddled in my life, I'm ready to step up and face things as an adult would.

"You know I love you, right?" I tell her as I set the bag down and pull out everything she brought, huffing a laugh when I see the huge chunk of parmigiana she brought.

"We'll need to grate that," she tells me.

"All of it?"

She eyes the cheese and then shrugs. "The video said we need it to be the size of a baby's head. I wasn't sure if he meant a five-pound baby or a seven-pounder, so I hope I bought enough."

We both stare at the cheese, and then I rummage in a cupboard for the shredder. "It's times like this I really miss Bryce," I mutter.

"How is he?"

I hesitate before answering, glancing toward a planter sitting in the corner of the kitchen. Since the kidnapping, Lexi has found a handful of listening devices and cameras around the house, the last one being two months ago when she found a listening device on the back of the pot.

The idea that someone came into my house without me knowing, despite changing all the locks, has been more than unnerving.

I'm still thinking about burning the house down, just in case. Lexi says that's not practical, but at this point, I don't care. When will I feel safe in my own home? It's been three months and I'm still worried someone is listening in.

When will I ever be free from that cult?

"Is this clear?" Mona mouths the words while pointing around the room with her finger.

"Lexi came by last night and found nothing, so we're good."

Mona fills up a pot of water and then turns on the burner. "I can't believe that even after everything, they were still watching you. That's crazy to me. The whole thing is just crazy."

While I know Mona has forgiven me for keeping her in the dark about my family's involvement with that cult, I think the sting is still there. She said I obviously didn't trust her enough to share the truth, and even though I've insisted that isn't the case at all, the bottom line is that no matter how I spun keeping the secrets, I kept them.

"I think my brother is okay," I tell her, going back to her original question. "I received a new postcard earlier this week from him, stamped from a small town in Oregon."

"Oregon? That's new. Wasn't he in Utah last time?"

I pull out a stool from the other side of the island and start grating the cheese. "And South Dakota before that. Lexi says he's smart to keep moving around."

"I still can't believe he has to."

I can't either, but the more I learn about Maximus Rutledge, the more I realize Bryce needs to do anything and everything to protect himself, Belinda, and their son.

My nephew. Whom I've never met, and don't even know if I ever will.

"As Lexi says, until we see Rutledge's cold and very dead body lying in a coffin, my brother will never be safe. Rutledge is the master at disappearing acts, without relinquishing any control over the people in his sphere, so who knows." My voice is resigned; it's something I've come to accept — my life will forever be entwined with Maximus Rutledge and his actions in one way or another, whether I like it or not.

"You know who I saw the other day? Allison, can you believe it?" Mona pours the wine she brought into two glasses and hands me one. "I stopped at a little market stand on the side of the road on the way home from a meeting, and there she was, selling homemade muffins, bread, and vegetables."

"Did you buy anything?" I know the stand she's talking about. Lexi has been keeping an eye on it.

"What? Are you crazy? How do I know it's not poisoned with some stupid medicinal herb that will play with my mind? No thanks."

"She's not going to poison you." I force a grin that definitely doesn't meet my eyes.

"You don't know that. If she was okay with letting everyone on that farm be poisoned and did nothing to stop it, who knows what she's willing to do now."

Only a few lives were lost that night. Lives that I know will always stain Allison's soul. Bryce's, as well. At least, I hope he feels the weight of their deaths.

Surprisingly, after being released from the hospital, almost all the people who lived on the farm returned there. They had nowhere else to go — their only choice was to rebuild their lives into something that made sense for them, without the influence of Maximus Rutledge. From what I understand, it's just a group of people living together now as a co-functioning unit. No religious crazy beliefs. Simple yoga, wellness, and general farm life. Allison wants to undo what was done, but I doubt even she can tear apart anything Maximum Rutledge built.

Lexi is also keeping an eye on them.

Mona has made it very clear her strong disdain for Allison, not that I blame her.

It was Allison who texted Mona, telling her that the yoga weekend, the same weekend I'd been kidnapped, had been canceled. Mona was at first disappointed, but she thought nothing of it until she sent me text after text, and I never responded.

Mona had been the one to go to Lexi with her concerns. They'd come to the retreat center in the middle of the night, only to find it completely empty — all the doors had been locked, the people all gone, myself included.

When Mona called Bryce in a panic, he fed her some lie about surprising me with a weekend in the city and taking me to a Broadway show. As much as Mona didn't want to buy it, she'd never known Bryce to lie to her, so she just told him to tell me to call her . . . which I obviously never did.

When Lexi finally found me, she warned me Mona was going crazy with worry.

The first thing Mona did when she saw me was give me a hug, then stare me down with her fiercest lawyer look and tell me she would never forgive me for not telling her the truth.

Now she says she has forgiven me, but I know she hasn't forgotten.

"She says hi, by the way," Mona continues. "I told her to go . . . well, you know. Basically, I told her you never wanted to see her face again, and let me tell you, the misery on her face did my heart good. I hold her responsible, you do realize that, right? Her, your brother, that stupid billionaire . . . I hope they all rot in hell." The venom in her voice dripped, scalding my soul with her truth.

"I know." The whispered words ache within me.

Forgiveness is good for the soul, but whose soul? Theirs or mine? Bryce begs for forgiveness in every postcard, but is it because he's truly sorry for putting my life in danger? For being willing to kill me, and then do the unimaginable and actually eat me?

I haven't let a single slice of meat slip through my lips since then. I will never be able to look at any meat dish and not remember the stew Bryce fed me, claiming he'd cooked portions of Anthony's organs and fed them to me without my knowing.

Can I ever forgive him? I don't know.

What I *do* know is I've lost whatever family I thought I had. I used to think without Bryce, I wouldn't exist. Now I know differently. I'm not the same person without him in my life, but he became someone I no longer recognized, and truth be told, I'm not sure the person he is now is someone I want around me.

While she cooks the pasta and slowly melts the butter in a pan, I look around the kitchen and slowly make a decision.

"I think I'm ready," I say softly, unsure if Mona hears me.

She turns with a smile on her face. "Shut the front door. Are you sure?"

She's been bugging me to go away with her for over a month. She keeps sending me links to all-inclusive resorts in the Caribbean or tour ideas in Europe . . . she says I need to get away and that staying holed up in what's comfortable isn't helping the healing process.

She's probably right.

It's been three months, and it's time to be the adult I know I am and focus on the future instead of living in the fear of the past. Easier said than done, but I have to start somewhere, right? Why not bask in the sun or walk down cobbled stone paths overlooking the Mediterranean while I do it?

"It's about time," Mona says. She reaches for her purse and pulls out a folded sheet of paper. "This is where we're going. For two weeks, you, me, gelato, pizza, pasta, and limoncello . . . and Lexi is even going to join us. She's finally going to take some vacation days. Plus, I know you'll feel safer having her around, right?"

I reach for the sheet and see that she's already planned our trip and even booked our hotel. We're staying at the gorgeous Hotel Onda Verde in Praiano, Italy, with views overlooking the Mediterranean.

"You remembered," I say, thinking back to a conversation that feels like it was another lifetime.

She taps her head. "With this brain? Of course, I remember. Your exact words were: 'Mona, if I ever get lost within myself, I need you to save me. Whisk me away to the Amalfi Coast where we can sip limoncello spritz while gossiping about all the celebrities on their super yachts,' and I, of course, told you to call me your fairy godmother. Well, here I am, making all your wishes come true."

She pulls out a single piece of pasta from the pot and nibbles on it. "Perfect al dente," she says. While she drains and swirls the pasta into the creamy butter sauce she's made, she glances over her shoulder at me. "Text Lexi and tell her it's on, will you? Knowing her, while you and I daydream on the terrace, Lexi will probably be checking out the owners of all those yachts, making sure that billionaire jerk isn't one of them. Although—" she glances around the kitchen — "if anyone in that group is listening in," she says with her voice raised.

"They're not," I remind her.

"In case they are, you can go eff yourself if you think you're going to ruin our vacation, got it?" To me, she adds, "I promised you I'd never let them hurt you again, and I'm going to keep that promise, even if it means Lexi has to come on all our girlfriend trips just so you feel safe." She's staring intently into my eyes.

I push my stool back and jump off, rounding the corner of the island to give Mona a hug I know we both need.

"What would I do without you?" I whisper into her hair.

She holds out her pinkie finger, and I latch mine around it.

"Sisters in life . . ." she starts.

"And death can go eff itself," I finish. I may have lost my family, but I've also created another one to surround me, and I wouldn't have it any other way.

## THE END

# THE JOFFE BOOKS STORY

We began in 2014 when Jasper agreed to publish his mum's much-rejected romance novel and it became a bestseller.

Since then we've grown into the largest independent publisher in the UK. We're extremely proud to publish some of the very best writers in the world, including Joy Ellis, Faith Martin, Caro Ramsay, Helen Forrester, Simon Brett and Robert Goddard. Everyone at Joffe Books loves reading and we never forget that it all begins with the magic of an author telling a story.

We are proud to publish talented first-time authors, as well as established writers whose books we love introducing to a new generation of readers.

We won Trade Publisher of the Year at the Independent Publishing Awards in 2023. We have been shortlisted for Independent Publisher of the Year at the British Book Awards for the last four years, and were shortlisted for the Diversity and Inclusivity Award at the 2022 Independent Publishing Awards. In 2023 we were shortlisted for Publisher of the Year at the RNA Industry Awards.

We built this company with your help, and we love to hear from you, so please email us about absolutely anything bookish at feedback@joffebooks.com

If you want to receive free books every Friday and hear about all our new releases, join our mailing list: www.joffebooks.com/contact

And when you tell your friends about us, just remember: it's pronounced Joffe as in coffee or toffee!

Milton Keynes UK
Ingram Content Group UK Ltd.
UKHW030654130824
446895UK00004B/163

9 781835 266847